Vengeance

K. A. ZAiNE

ISBN: 0615551882
ISBN-13: 978-0615551883

DEDICATION

For my mother. Somebody please tell her she doesn't die in this book.

CONTENTS

ACKNOWLEDGMENT

I must thank cover artist Kaleb Zeringue at Z4designs.com. His cover design and depiction of Tara Boudreaux is spot on. I asked for vengeance, and he delivered.

REVIEWS

"Interesting reading! Lots of suspense. Definitely keeps my attention while I try to figure out what happens next." – Donna A. Semens Davenport, The Wall Street Journal/Dow Jones & Co., Inc.

"Extremely well-written and most interesting, Vengeance captures an interest and a want to read on." – Helen H. Roff, The Wall Street Journal/Dow Jones & Co., Inc.

"Wonderfully intriguing!" – Margie Robeson, The Indianapolis Star

"Grabs the reader right away!" – Art Cassella, Philadelphia Inquirer

"I sharpen my flashing sword and my hand grasps it in judgment, I will take vengeance on my adversaries and repay those who hate me." Deuteronomy 32:41

Prologue

Anxiously awaiting the invitation hymn, the twelve-year-old strained to hear each utterance from the fiery young preacher, along with the echoing chorus of "Amen" chiming from the surrounding packed pews.

This was the day she had waited for. Today she would respond and begin her life anew. She glanced around at the faithful church members. She wanted to remember each face present for her new birth. Sitting on her family's usual pew, second from the front, she studied everything about tonight's service.

She wanted to hold this memory forever.

Sister Williams, Preacher Williams' wife, sat on the front row, smiling and nodding at her husband's every word. She was young, like Preacher Williams, probably in her mid-thirties; however, it was hard to tell for sure since she didn't wear make-up and she kept her long brown hair yanked into a tight bun at the nape of her neck.

The young girl tried to remember if she had ever seen Sister Williams in anything other than an ankle-length dress. No, she hadn't. Even when she and her mother dropped by to pay a visit to Sister Williams, the lady was always clothed as if she were going directly to church.

Or a funeral.

Twisting on the wooden bench, the girl noticed the many elderly men of the congregation clothed in full suits and ties, their silver-crowned wives sitting faithfully alongside.

Most of their laps held giant print Bibles, which they studied to verify everything out of the mouth of Preacher Williams. Everything. Pages flipped violently through the entire service as Preacher Williams' flock made a concerted effort to keep up with his spouted scripture.

Nearly all of the elderly women wore crocheted coverings on their heads during the worship. The young girl knew they did this based on a verse in First Corinthians. She tried in vain to remember the verse then resolved to ask her father about it later. He'd know. He knew them all. Maybe even better than Preacher Williams.

Matthew James Blessing had fervently raised his daughter to be strong in her faith. From the time she was born, he'd read the Bible to her each evening. Thoroughly convinced that you could never start too early, he had actually read the Good News to his unborn daughter while she was still in the womb, and he honestly believed that her strong knowledge of the scripture was due to this initial introduction to the Gospel. Of course, the nightly drill sessions of Bible trivia before she went to bed didn't hurt either.

Betty Jo-Ann Blessing wasn't a Christian when she first met Matthew James, but she was open-minded and studied hard. That was the way the young girl's father had described his first impression of her mother. He continually reminded his young daughter that should she ever fall in love with a non-believer, she should make sure he is open-minded and willing to study, because thorough studying of the Word will show the way and leave no doubt.

That was exactly what he'd said when he baptized her mother into Christ. She could still remember her mother's baptism. It was only seven years ago. And today was her turn. It was her time to be buried with Christ and have her sins washed away.

Bibles closed and songbook pages rattled as Brother Williams began to close his lesson. The young girl's stomach suddenly felt as though she had ridden eight times straight on the Tilt-A-Whirl at the county fair. She knew because that was exactly how many times she'd ridden it last year. Before she'd thrown up.

Her throat was sandpaper dry and her heart raced madly. She wrapped and unwrapped the mahogany ribbon attached to the hymnal around her thumb and forefinger. Wrap. Unwrap. Curl. Unfurl.

The crimson hue of the silken strand contrasted starkly to her lily white finger. The blood-hued fabric seemed to take control, overpower and constrict around it. Like a determined red...snake.

She blinked, shook the image.

"...and if anyone accepts this invitation to be buried in baptism with Christ and begin their life anew, please come as we stand together and sing," Preacher Williams beckoned.

Now. She stood with the congregation, then made her way to the end of the pew. Luckily, it was a short walk to the front, since she was sure her legs were going to collapse at any moment. Preacher

Williams smiled and took her hand as she walked toward him. They sat on the front pew while she whispered her request. "I want to be baptized."

"I am very proud of you," Preacher Williams said as the invitation song ended. He draped a protective arm around her and gently squeezed her back. Then he walked to the podium and smiled broadly to his faithful congregation. "We rejoice today as Tara Blessing has decided to enter the watery grave of baptism. As we know, Brother and Sister Blessing have trained Tara in God's way and prepared her for this important step in her Christian walk. She has studied fervently and knows what she must do to be saved. Now, being a new Christian isn't easy, as we all know. I implore each of you to strive to encourage this young lady through her Christian walk. I implore you, Tara, to continue to live a faithful life and complete your essential steps to salvation. Tara, please stand."

Slowly, Tara stood and turned to face the congregation. Her mother and several of the elderly women smiled reassuringly. Tears fell from numerous eyes, but she knew they were happy. And she wasn't nervous now, only joyful. The image of the red serpent wasn't real. This was right. She could feel it.

She smiled at Brother Williams, then slid her mouth quickly back to a flat line. She didn't know if you were allowed to smile before entering the watery grave.

"Tara, by responding to the invitation, you have acknowledged that you are a sinner and desire to be baptized, to wash those sins away and begin your life anew. Now, I must ask you one question. Tara, do you believe that Jesus Christ is the Son of God?"

She blinked, stared into the crowd. Sister Rosemary's flaming hair had been tucked beneath her crocheted covering, but a single fiery strand slithered free. Tara gawked at the lone serpentine curl.

"Do you believe, Tara?" Preacher Williams repeated.

"I do," she said, focusing on his gray eyes instead of the second red snake.

"God bless you, my child." He hugged her and directed her to the baptistery.

She knew Sister Williams and her mother attended her and dressed her in the baptismal garments. She knew the congregation sang Trust and Obey. She knew her father's heart was about to burst with pride for her decision to do what was right. And she knew she needed to be immersed in that water.

To wash away that snake.

Hastily, she emerged from the dressing area to the left of the baptistery as the last verse of the hymn completed. She could see Preacher Williams standing outside of the men's dressing area. He wore hip-waders similar to the ones her grandfather had for fly-fishing. She would make sure to remember that image as part of today's precious memories.

Tara thought of her grandfather fishing, but her reflection wasn't the usual memory. He wasn't grinning and yelling for her to join him in the river. No, this time his face was serious and intent, so intent on catching a fish that he didn't see the black-purple moccasin, almost crimson in the sunlight, slithering atop the water. And he had no warning at all when the giant cottonmouth swooped into the waders.

Hurriedly, Tara walked down the two steps into the baptistery. The congregation gasped and sighed. Obviously, the heater for the baptistery wasn't working again; she felt as though she stepped into a block of solid ice. But that didn't matter. That would just help her remember—remember the last day she'd ever have to deal with the evil, with the awful creature.

She could tell by the look on Preacher Williams' face that he felt the iciness, even through the thick waders.

He took her hands and helped her walk to the center of the baptistery.

Hurry, Tara silently pleaded. *Hurry*.

Pews creaked as the entire congregation leaned forward for a better look at their soon-to-be new sister in Christ. She cupped her hand and prepared to hold her nose.

"I now baptize you in the name of the Father, and of the Son, and of the Holy Spirit!" Preacher Williams yelled as he pushed her under the glacial water.

Chapter One

Twenty Years Later – Peachtree City, Georgia

Jade Roberts gasped as she watched her best friend meticulously fold four pairs of lacy thong panties and place them in the leather suitcase perched on the edge of her bed.

"What?" Tara gleefully responded to her friend's astonishment.

"I can't believe this is the same woman who wouldn't even walk past Victoria's Secret with me just four years ago. What has he done to you? And are you absolutely positive he doesn't have any brothers?"

"I'm married now, Jade. And, as I've told you before, God totally intended for married couples to—"

"—blissfully enjoy the wonders of sex within the God-given boundaries of marriage. Tara, you should do commercials. Better yet, I bet parents would line up to have you talk to their teens. Maybe I'll call some local schools. Lord knows that one down the street could use somebody telling the boys to keep their pants zipped and the girls to keep their legs shut."

"Do you have to be so pessimistic? I'm sure plenty of kids out there have determined that abstinence makes the heart grow fonder—at least until they're married."

"The fact that you were still a virgin at twenty-eight when you finally met Prince Charming is one for the record books." She picked up one of Tara's tiny thongs, black satin with red roses, shook her head, then placed it back in the suitcase. "Where is your handsome Cajun anyway?"

"He went to pick up some last minute things for our trip. He should be back soon. Oh dear, I forgot to buy water. Would you mind getting me a few bottles from the garage? I just need a few to hold me over until I get there. Then I'll go to a local store and get some more."

"What? You don't trust the water in New Orleans? Goodness gracious, you—Tara Boudreaux—in New Orleans on Mardi Gras. I mean, you've definitely got the Cajun name to go along with you, but talk about a fish out of water. They'll eat you alive, and the things you're going to see are liable to put you right in the grave with heart failure. I sure hope Johnny Boudreaux knows what he's doing." Jade headed down the hall toward the garage.

Tara sat on the bed and double-checked the items in her suitcase. It was no wonder Jade was surprised at her agreement to attend Mardi Gras with Johnny. Until she met him, she wouldn't have dreamed of going near the sinful city, but things were different now. She knew just because she was around people who were committing sin didn't mean she had to become a part of it. Why, she might even influence some of the partying folks to stop their wicked ways.

Breathless, Jade returned with six bottles of water balanced haphazardly on her crossed arms. She dropped them on top of the folded garments in Tara's suitcase. "How long are you planning to keep that stash in your garage? Good grief, I thought I'd never get over all those canned foods to find the eternal cases of bottled water. Exactly how long are you planning to survive—and how many people are you planning on having with you? Y2K is a thing of the past. We're still here, still breathing, banks still functioning, computers still operating, everything. So, eat the food already."

Tara's eyes involuntarily shifted from the suitcase to the picture of her parents on the bedside table.

"I'm sorry, Tara. I wasn't thinking. Is that why you keep all of that stuff? Because it reminds you of them? You've got more cans than aisle seven at Ingles."

"I'm still not positive we won't need it someday, and it's complete and ready if we do. Johnny thinks it's terrific, by the way."

Tara tossed a black silk nightgown into the suitcase.

"Johnny obviously thinks everything you do is terrific, Tara. Who could blame him? With that auburn hair, green eyes and your figure. I can't believe you're my best friend. What girl in her right mind wants to be hanging out with someone who looks like you? And then you married God's gift to women. Just think of the kids you guys will have—they'll be absolutely gorgeous."

Tara looked at her best friend, nearly deciding to tell her that the first of those beautiful children may already be living inside of her, but she didn't know for certain. She hadn't seen a doctor or even taken a home pregnancy test. However, she could tell something was different.

No, she wouldn't tell Jade. Johnny should be the first one told, and only after she was certain. Tara listened as Jade continued her endless list of reasons why she was crazy to have ever befriended Tara.

"You hang around with me because I think you're incredible," Tara said. "Just wait, Jade, you'll meet the perfect man one day. One who makes you feel the way Johnny makes me feel. And I'll be sitting on the front row at the wedding."

"I guess for now I'll have to take your word for it. For the time being, I'll make do with Brutus."

"How is your favorite canine?" Tara asked, casually tossing her toothbrush, toothpaste and deodorant in her bathroom bag. She knew how much Jade loved to talk about Brutus. Working with the Atlanta Police Department's as a dog trainer for their APD Canine Patrol, Jade primarily covered Hartsfield International with Brutus. The excitement of helping the police apprehend criminals, particularly with the help of her beloved German Shepherd, thrilled Jade.

"Tara, he's just amazing." She plopped down on the bed. "Did I tell you what he did at work this week?"

"Not yet, but I have a feeling I'm about to hear it."

"Well, we were on duty at the International Concourse, nothing unusual about that. Brutus was standing beside me when I received my daily concourse routes from Sergeant Billingsly. This la-de-dah European woman began walking past us and Brutus went absolutely ballistic. He barked and pulled on the leash so hard, he nearly yanked me to the ground chasing the lady. Sergeant Billingsly helped me stop the woman and he searched her."

"What did you find?"

"Absolutely nothing. That's what was so weird. Brutus never barks unless he smells something wrong, so we kept her a while for the police to question her," Jade continued.

"Did they let her go?"

"No way. She was detained, and then they brought Brutus in the room. He started going crazy again, sniffing her like she was a big slab of ribs."

"Then what?"

"Then he went to her face, sniffed her cheek. He just kept barking and sniffing her right cheek. The woman was really freaking with this huge dog going after her face and all. And you're never gonna believe what she'd done."

"What?"

"She used a magician's pouch inside her mouth. You know, the kind that they put in the palm of their hand to hide those foam balls, scarves and that kind of thing. It looks like skin, and it's quite adherent. She had filled the pouch with drugs. Pills."

"What kind of pills?"

"Well, if it was illegal, it was in there. Honestly, I don't know how she kept her mouth closed with that stash. She was even talking plainly. Really quite clever. She would've made it through customs too, had it not been for my hairy partner," Jade said, smiling with pride.

"What would have happened if she would have swallowed them?" Tara asked, amazed at the cunning of modern day criminals.

"Oh, she wouldn't have survived. You wouldn't believe how many she squeezed into that thing. From the mix she had, it would have probably looked like a heart attack. I'm not sure. I'm definitely going to check into it though."

"Do you ever want to get in on the investigating? You seem to really enjoy it when something exciting happens."

"It's fun watching them do their job, but I'm quite content taking care of their canine buddies and surfing the net at home with Brutus. By the way, I now know the exact age of that husband of yours. I was so tired of him teasing me about trying to figure it out. He really does look younger than he is, doesn't he?"

"You're terrible." Tara playfully shoved Jade's shoulder. "Now what will he tease you about?"

"Don't worry, I'll think of something. And just how old am I, Jade?" Johnny asked, entering the bedroom.

Jade felt the heat of embarrassment on her cheeks. The man leaning against the door facing looked as sexy as he had the first time she'd seen him. Tara had been dating Johnny only two weeks when she brought him to meet Jade, and she'd known instantly that they were meant for each other. Tara had always insisted that God would somehow let her know when the "right one" would come along. Jade had never taken that much stock in the Big Guy helping out, but when she saw the gleam in Tara's eyes as she introduced Johnny, she'd wondered if He hadn't done just that.

Additionally, Johnny Boudreaux was the ideal compliment to Tara's perfect physique. He was every inch of six-foot-three, maybe even six-four, with wavy jet-black hair and eyes as blue as a spring sky. A flawless six-pack of abs, clearly visible even through the navy pullover tucked in his jeans, completed the mouth-watering appeal. A poster of Johnny with the caption *Ragin Cajun* would probably make a mint. She should mention that idea to Tara, when he wasn't listening, of course. No wonder Tara turned to mush anytime he was around. Who could blame her?

"How long have you been eavesdropping, Johnny?" Jade threw a pillow at his finely chiseled face.

Dodging the throw with a mere shift of his weight, Johnny grinned at the two girls sitting pajama party style on the bed. He was pleased Tara had a friend like Jade. She'd been so withdrawn after the death of her parents, he had feared she would never come out of that depression.

Then she'd met Jade. What a fireball. Determined to teach Tara how to enjoy life again, Jade wouldn't take no for an answer. Tara admired her friend's lust for life and had even started trying a few of the more adventuresome sports that Johnny loved. And what enthusiasm she had—scuba diving, snow skiing, even repelling. She'd tried it all and had been a challenging partner too. Yes, Jade had brought back the spark in his wife's eyes, and he would forever be indebted to her for that.

"Okay, wise guy. You're thirty-eight, although you could easily pass for thirty. You were born in Baton Rouge. Your parents are Robert and Clair Boudreaux. They live on—"

Johnny grinned toothily at Jade as she spat out more information than he even knew. "Can you tell me what their telephone number is, Jade? It's been a while since I talked to my mom."

"It's area code five-zero-four—"

"I was joking, Jade."

Jade shrugged, leaned over, hugged her best friend and whispered, "I can't help but like him, Tara." She climbed from the bed and began searching the clothing-strewn dresser for her car keys. "I'm going to leave you two lovebirds to get ready for your trip to sin city," she stated as she kept searching.

Glancing at Johnny, she added, "You better take care of her there. She hasn't got a clue what she's in for. When they yell, 'Show me something,' she'll probably pull out her Bible and start showing them scripture."

"Don't worry, Jade," Johnny replied. "Tara's shirt will stay on. At least at the parades," he added with a wink to his blushing wife. "Besides, we're not going to the wild parades near the French Quarter. I'm afraid I'd lose her to pure shock at the things going on there. No, I'm going to start her out simple. We'll take in a small town parade near LaPlace on Saturday. We'll be going to church, of course, on Sunday. Isn't that right, my dear?"

"You know the way to my heart," Tara answered with a besotted smile.

"Since there aren't any large parades during the day on Monday, we'll use that day to take in the sights around the French Quarter. I think she'll love the French Market. The way she loves the flea markets and trade days around here, the French Market with its Cajun flare should be a real treat."

"And what about Tuesday, Johnny? What about Fat Tuesday? How are you going to keep her from the untamed heart of Mardi Gras then?"

"We're going to take in the smaller parades in Metairie. The floats are just as outrageous and elaborate as the floats in the New

Orleans parades, but the people—well, it's different there. Children can actually go to the parades without seeing too much—"

"—skin?" Jade finished.

"Exactly," Johnny said. He picked up the discarded pillow from the floor and tossed it at the back of Jade's blond locks while she retrieved her keys from a pile of laundry.

Rubbing the back of her head, she stuck her tongue out at the sizable man who now leaned against the bedroom wall with his large hands shoved in his pockets and an I-want-you-now grin at his wife.

"Okay, I can see there is nothing I can say or do to deter you two from embarking on your wild romp to party land. Please take care of yourself, Tara. And you," she wagged a finger at Johnny, "try to remember that you're on your stomping ground, not hers. They aren't quite used to scripture-quoting, Bible-toting, auburn-haired knockouts. They're more accustomed to the bombshells that willingly reveal all God-given assets to the world. Tara, I'm going to pray for you everyday."

"I'm so glad your prayer life has moved to a daily basis," Tara said then she and Johnny laughed at Jade's overly annoyed just-swallowed-a-prune face. She'd perfected the look over the years.

"You're both a riot. I can honestly say you deserve each other." Jade hugged her friend again. "Seriously, be careful."

"He'll take good care of me, Jade. I haven't a doubt about that," Tara reassured.

"You can count on it," Johnny said. He also gave Jade a squeeze before she left the bedroom.

Jade made her way outside, listening to Tara's giggles. From all indications, Johnny was obviously in full agreement with her choice of lingerie for the trip.

Chapter Two

Mardi Gras, "Fat Tuesday" – New Orleans, Louisiana

Johnny Boudreaux stared admiringly at the exquisite woman beside him in the passenger's seat. Once again, his wife of three years had surprised him with her zest for life and willingness to try anything. He thought back to the shocked look on her face when he had first mentioned Mardi Gras in the fall. He'd told her how his parents had brought him to the parades when he was just a boy and how much he had enjoyed the excitement. He could still remember the homemade ladder-chair that his father had made where he could sit, hovering merely inches from the elaborate floats, ornate costumes and beads. Beads, beads, beads. Amazing how much those things matter to kids...and to adults.

The carnival atmosphere this year had been no exception to the one in his memory. Children at the Diana parade had lined soldier-style to fill Veterans Boulevard as the massive floats passed. Even the toddlers screamed, "Throw me something, mister!"

His thoughts drifted to their family Christmas card when he was merely three years old. There he was, wearing nothing but his underwear and about twenty pounds of Mardi Gras beads. He smiled at his mother's sense of humor. He would have to put in another objection to that picture the next time he saw her. Or maybe he could thank her for giving him the idea for a Christmas picture with his own son, or daughter.

The thought of having a child with Tara sent a frisson of delight through his veins. He knew she wanted him to commit to religion before they had children. She really wanted their children to be raised with two Christian parents.

Tara had told him when they were engaged, "I want to be there every time the church doors are opened. I want to prepare the Thanksgiving boxes each year with our children beside us. I want to help a foster child, maybe even be a foster parent. And I want to participate in more mission work in Mexico, and perhaps in Africa."

Now Johnny knew he wanted that too, with Tara by his side. Perhaps this weekend would be the time to tell her.

Tara thumbed through the countless strands of glittering beads hanging from her neck. She thought of the last four days in New Orleans. Even the nine-hour drive from Peachtree City on Friday had been enjoyable because she was with Johnny.

They had talked about everything—weather, politics, religion, love and children. She knew how anxious he was for them to have a child. She'd wanted to wait until he had decided to make the commitment to follow Christ, but somehow she knew that it wouldn't be long until he made that decision.

Like her father had encouraged, she'd married a wonderful man who was willing to study and had an open mind. And, like her father had told her, a person can't study God's Word and fail to see the truth. She knew Johnny was seeing that truth for the first time in his life.

She glanced at her husband and smiled. Maybe she would tell him this weekend that he could be a father sooner than he realized. A few more days and she would know for sure. But she just knew that a precious new creation from God was already growing inside of her.

She just knew.

"Too cool for you," Johnny said.

"What?" Tara asked as her thoughts quickly shifted to her husband.

"That car tag." He pointed to one of the motionless cars stuck in Mardi Gras traffic.

Tara glanced at the source of Johnny's comment, a canary yellow Corvette. The Texas tag was personalized with *2CL4U*.

"Clever, but from the way I've seen cars treated down here over the last four days, I'm not so sure it was too wise of someone to bring a Vette in for the festivities. I mean, I've seen at least three people rear-end each other in this traffic, and usually the guys who are driving the vehicles involved are too drunk to care that their cars have been cremated," she said, shaking her head.

"You know, when you put it that way, I'm not so sure we should have brought my baby," he said, patting the dash.

Tara scooted across the bench seat, straddling the gearshift of the Dodge Ram while she tried to get as close to Johnny as possible. She softly kissed his cheek and ran her hand up his thigh. "Which baby are you referring to, dear?"

He cleared his throat. "My lovely wife, of course." Then he playfully nipped her ear.

"That's what I thought."

"I love Tara, three, seven, one."

"Excuse me?" she asked.

"That car tag." Johnny motioned. "ILT 371. I love Tara, three, seven, one."

"You're too cute," Tara said, eyeing the Louisiana tag.

"Well, we might as well do something to pass the time while we're stuck in this jam. We may be sitting here tomorrow morning at this rate." He inched closer to the car in front of them.

"It's after midnight, Johnny. This is tomorrow morning. You know, we could pass the time by counting all of these beautiful beads." She glanced down at her endless collection of green, purple and gold metallic beads. "I really did get some nice ones, didn't I? And the Mardi-Bra and panties! Do you like them?" She held up the next-to-nothing underwear. "I think they're quite transparent, don't you?"

"You're making it difficult for me to concentrate on driving. And I'm sure that the beefy fellow who tossed you that ensemble very nearly crossed his eyes at the thought of you wearing it. And if you're wondering why you're loaded down with beads and undergarments, I think it's got something to do with the way you shimmy. Even with your shirt on, you beat every other female without even trying. From now on, you save that move for me. You were probably the only woman here who left with that much loot *and* her dignity," Johnny chuckled. "Now that you've mentioned it, I think I've got an idea for the hotel room tonight. I want to see a slow-motion repeat of that shimmy with the Mardi-Bra and panties. Or better yet, forget the bra and panties. Let's just go for the beads," he added with a sleek smile.

"You're wicked!"

"You love it."

"I do."

"You know, at this turtle pace, we may not make it to the hotel before check-out time tomorrow. What do you say we veer off the parade route and try one of the side streets? If I remember correctly, we could follow the canal down Esplanade. It runs parallel to Veterans Boulevard and could get us to the hotel, and that shimmy, quicker."

"Sounds good to me," Tara said.

He inched the Ram to the next side street and turned toward the Esplanade canal.

"I guess we weren't the only ones with this idea," Johnny remarked as they slowly moved down the side street with the steady flow of traffic. "But at least we're moving."

Tara leaned her head out the window to peer down the road. Several cars pulled into vacant driveways in order to turn around and head back toward Veterans Boulevard and the parade route.

"Looks as though they're giving up." She watched the steady stream of cars now heading back.

"Yeah, I see it now. I forgot how they block off the side streets during Mardi Gras. There's the silver police barricade. I should have remembered that." His frustration palpable, he leaned toward the door and pressed his palm to his forehead while his other arm draped over the steering wheel. "We'll be out here all night. Our last night in New Orleans, and we're spending it staring at taillights."

"It's okay. Surely that traffic will have to let up eventually," Tara soothed. "I've got another problem besides the traffic anyway."

"What's that?"

"I think that last thirty-two ounce virgin strawberry daiquiri is ready to make an exit. Actually, I don't think I've been to the bathroom since lunch, and I had a peach one during the two o'clock parade also. No wonder I feel like I'm going to bust."

"Yeah, I think that daiquiri shop owner got a kick out of you ordering all of his non-alcoholic drinks. Bet he probably didn't plan on selling more than one of those today," Johnny said with a grin, his mood lifting at the thought of his saintly wife putting her own spin on the celebration.

They neared the shiny silver barricade with blue and white NOPD signs hanging from both ends.

"Time to turn around and join the crowd. I just hope I can finally find a bathroom without thirty people in line to use it. Even those rusty port-a-johns are sounding pretty good right now." She squirmed in the seat.

"I don't want you having to use another one of those things." He opened the truck door and got out.

"What do you plan on doing?" she asked, watching him move in front of the headlights toward the barricade.

Johnny lifted the silver metal and moved it to the side.

"They'll ticket you for that, boy," yelled a white-haired man as he turned his candy-apple red BMW around in a nearby driveway.

"Must be dealing with a major mid-life crisis." Johnny shrugged and climbed back into the truck.

Tara laughed while he moved the truck beyond the barricade and then placed the silver rails back in position. Several additional yells followed, informing him that the five-hundred-dollar fine would hurt.

"I really do have to go, Johnny," she moaned, keeping her legs crossed. "Honestly, I've never had to go this bad." Tara looked down the pitch-black streets. "Do you think there's a gas station nearby?"

"I'm sure there's one around here somewhere," he said, searching the gloomy streets. "Look, I think there's one on the corner up ahead. Yeah, that's Esplanade. Surely there's a gas station there." He sped the truck down the deserted, darkened street. "Well, I'm not believing—"

"What?" she asked.

"Closed. Everything is closed. They must totally shut down the blocks surrounding the parade route. Let me check my phone and see if I can find anything open." He withdrew his phone from his pocket. "Great. It's dead."

"I left mine back at the hotel," she said. "Go ahead and pull into the station, Johnny. Maybe the bathroom doors are open."

"Yeah, maybe." He parked the truck and got out to check the restroom door. "Locked." He climbed back in the truck and squinted down the street.

"Johnny, we've got to find something soon. Oh, why did I drink that last virgin daiquiri," she whimpered, still scanning the blackened streets around the canal. "Why is it so dark here? Don't they believe in street lights?"

"I'm sure some of the partying included busting out street lights. Looks as though they were pretty successful. Don't worry. I'll find something fast," he said, quickly pulling the car down the next street.

"What about one of the houses?" Tara asked. "Do you think they would let me use theirs?"

"These folks leave during Mardi Gras, Tara. Besides, it's 2:00 a.m.," Johnny reasoned. "Wait a minute. That house has a pool."

"I'm not following you, honey. I'm looking for a bathroom, and I'm trying not to think of any type of water. Swimming pools, fountains, waterfalls..." Tara said, shifting uncontrollably in the seat. Her bladder had to be near busting.

"There's a pool house beside it, dear. And if there's a pool house, there's probably—"

"A bathroom," she said. "Pull over!" She jumped from the truck then turned. "Circle the block," she said, "I'll be done by the time you get back." She fought the urge to hold her crotch as she darted across the lawn.

"All right," he called, a low chuckle in his voice. "I'll pick you up right here, okay?"

"Deal!" she squealed, and she ran around the vacated house.

Johnny continued down the darkened street, grinning at the thought of his wife trying to make it to that pool house in time.

Chapter Three

Tara exited the pool house and sprinted back to the ghostly street. She wiped her brow to remove the small beads of sweat that had accumulated in her quest to get to the bathroom in record time. She remembered Johnny talking about the humidity in New Orleans, but she hadn't imagined this kind of heat at two o'clock in the morning, especially in February.

As she approached the road, Tara saw the Dodge Ram headlights creeping toward her on the deserted street. She stood, arms folded, in the center of the empty driveway. "You sure are taking your time, Johnny," she mumbled. "Must not be too anxious for that shimmy."

She smiled as the truck sped up then continued past the driveway.

"Hey, stop playing around!" She laughed as she followed the truck down the street. "I'll get you for this, Johnny."

Ahead of her, tires squealed when the truck came to a sudden stop about fifty feet ahead. A puff of gray smoke produced a faint shadow from the rear of the vehicle and the scent of burnt rubber bit into the night.

Breathless, she ran to the rear of the truck, laid her head against the tailgate and closed her eyes. "You're too much, Johnny," she panted. She opened an eye and viewed a silver chrome bumper christened with a rebel flag sticker. Shocked, she backed away from the truck.

"I'm s-so sorry," she stuttered while the truck doors opened and two men began climbing out. She stared at the tag on the rear of the truck—HHM 783. "Heaven help me, seven, eight, three," she whispered.

"Looks like we've got ourselves a live one, Chet," the driver sneered as he walked toward the back of the truck. "What's the matter, pretty baby, haven't found anyone to give you what you need lately?"

Tara continued backing while a third man climbed out of the passenger's side. He was very large, almost as large as Johnny. She shot a desperate look down the street behind her.

"Yeah, this must be your lucky day," he started, "You've just flagged down three men who are more than willing, and able, to take care of you, darling," he said, gesturing toward his crotch.

A shiny handle protruded from the top of his faded jeans.

What do I do? Think, Tara. God, please help me.

"I've made a m-mistake," Tara muttered, still edging back. "I've made a terrible mistake. S-sorry to have bothered you men."

"You don't really know if we're real men or not, now do you? Why don't we show you about real men? What do you say, Dave? We could teach this little knockout quite a bit about real men, don't you think?" Chet said, then laughed.

Tara's skin crawled at the sound. Repulsive. Sinister. *Evil.* His gloating eyes bore into her, reminding her of an image she thought she'd put behind her. Her finger twitched, remembering the mahogany ribbon, the contrast of white with red.

"I think Billy and I could help her get rid of those shiny beads and show us what she had to flaunt to get them. She must look pretty good to have warranted a bounty like that, don't you think? Yeah, I bet she looks real good," Dave purred.

"I didn't show anything," Tara stammered. "I didn't! I don't want anything." She quickened her retreat and stumbled on the sidewalk.

All three men laughed in unison at the helpless woman. They walked easily toward her as Billy moved his fingers toward the handle of the pistol.

Tara rapidly removed the mounds of beads and flung them at her attackers.

Caught off-guard, the men paused momentarily, but then they merely laughed again while she ran frantically down the street toward the canal.

"No need to make this difficult, missy," Chet called.

Tara darted behind one of the houses and ran through a wooded path to reach the canal. She could hear them talking. They weren't even running. And they were right. Where could she go?

Looking behind her, she saw their shady figures moving closer. Before she could change her mind, she leapt from the levee and rolled vigorously down the embankment, her face, arms, and legs banging against the hard concrete until she finally landed in marshy water that smelled of dead fish and urine.

Help me, God. Please!

Her head reeling, she scrambled along the water's edge, clawing her way through mud-drenched vines and stench-filled marsh to reach a paved overpass.

"She went through here, Billy," one of the men called out.

They're almost here. Where's Johnny? Where should I go? What do I do? Dear God, please help me!

Tara crawled up the concrete slope, shredding her hands and knees on broken glass that had been tossed from the bridge overhead. She hovered in the topmost corner, in the darkest confines of the overpass, and continued praying for her safety—and Johnny's.

Salty tears stung brutally as they dripped across the cuts and scrapes on her face. Sticky blood oozed from her head, hands, arms and legs, but the pain was nothing compared to what she would feel if those three men found her.

God, don't let them find me.

Tara listened intently to the footsteps that continued pressing their way through the grassy levee until she heard them abruptly stop at the overpass.

Straining her ears to hear everything they said, she squeezed herself into a fetal position and pressed her back firmly against the farthest corner of the overpass. The ground was wet around her, and she didn't want to think about what she was sitting in. Blood? Alcohol? Urine? The smell was horrid, and she pressed her hand over her nose only to realize that her shredded palm poured blood too.

"Where to now, Dave?" Chet asked. "We giving up?"

"No way. It's three in the morning and the place is deserted. She's here. We'll hear her soon, and if we don't, we'll just keep looking till we find her," Dave said.

"Well, I don't care what the two of you decide to do. I didn't even get a good look at the face, but the rest of her definitely warrants a swamp search—how about the first one to find her gets to do her first?" Billy sneered viciously as he started down the embankment.

Don't let him find me. God, please, no!

"Wait, Billy. Listen."

Tara heard it too. An engine hummed as a vehicle made its way down the abandoned street.

Johnny. No, Johnny, No!

"What do we do, Billy?" Chet asked nervously.

"Stay calm. It's a pickup, obviously not a cop. Besides, I've got all the protection we need right here," Billy answered.

"Yeah, Billy will take care of this one," Dave added.

Tara listened while the engine purred to a halt. Then her heart stopped when she heard the truck door slam and then—Johnny's voice.

"Hey, fellows! I'm looking for my wife. She was supposed to be waiting at one of the driveways down the street, but I can't find her. She's about five-foot-three, auburn haired and wearing a load of Mardi Gras beads. Should be easy to spot, huh?" Johnny said with a laugh. "Seriously, have you seen a woman around here?"

Tara heard the low, rumbling laugh of one of the men standing directly above her. He whispered, "Looks like this 'fellow' here is the only thing between us and that little vixen, what do you think, Billy?"

"Couldn't agree with you more, Dave. Call him over here, Chet," Billy ordered.

"We saw her a few minutes ago. She was over here. Come on, I'll show you!" Chet yelled at Johnny.

"Where was she?" Johnny asked.

"Now, Billy!" Chet yelled.

"What the—" Johnny started.

"Johnny! No!" With every ounce of energy her bruised body could muster, Tara crawled madly from the safety of the overpass.

"There she is, Dave! Get her!" Billy screamed.

"Tara!" Johnny yelled.

Battered and bleeding, Tara climbing frantically up the levee. Then she watched in horror as three shots rang out and Johnny's big strong body crumpled to the ground. Even in the darkness, she could see the pool of darkened wetness slowly covering the pavement around him.

Dear God—No!

"Now. Get her, Dave. He's not going to bother us anymore. Help him, Chet," Billy ordered.

Tara's body collapsed and she fell backwards down the sloped embankment. She repeatedly slammed against the concrete then landed with a thud at the swampy water's edge.

Dave and Chet toppled down the cement ramp aggressively pursuing their fallen prey with Billy following closely behind.

Tara scrambled to her feet and tore through the marsh, frantically attempting to escape the horrific men who had murdered her husband.

Johnny. God, why? Why? Her mind reeled while her body fought to get away, fought to survive.

"Chet! Dave! Grab her! Get her now!" Billy roared.

Tara made her way to the other side of the overpass then clawed through muddy reeds and grass in a wild attempt to reach the top of the levee. Blood burst from her ripped palms at the effort.

"I'm almost there," Dave called, stretching a hand toward Tara's ankle. He grabbed it hard and pulled sharply, knocking her off balance.

One hand slipped and her forehead banged against the hard slope. Dark blood seeped into her eyes, blinding her. She hastily let go of the levee's edge and plummeted down the embankment once more, taking Chet and Dave along with her as she rolled aimlessly to the water's edge and crashed into a massive concrete pipe.

Billy rushed to the three of them, quickly pulling Chet and Dave to their feet. Groaning, they looked at the beaten woman whose defeated body lay crumpled at their feet. Blood trickled from numerous gashes, cuts and slits that now fully covered her petite frame.

Chet leaned close to the girl to listen for a heartbeat, or breathing. He felt nothing, heard nothing.

"Dead?" Dave asked as Chet continued to listen.

"No way," Billy said. "She's alive. She's gotta be. And she's about to be mine," he continued, picking up Tara's lifeless body and hoisting her up the embankment as though she were a child's doll, rather than a grown woman.

Sirens blared in the distance. The men froze on the levee's edge.

"What do you think? Are they close?" Chet whimpered.

"Closer than we think. Look." Dave motioned toward blue and red streams of light that flashed rhythmically through the trees on the opposite side of the canal.

"What do we do, Billy?" Dave asked.

"I'm not believing this," Billy hissed, as irritated that his two sidekicks were panicking as he was the cops were ruining a good thing. "All right you two, get back to the guy. Put him in the bed of his truck and drive it down the back streets to the lake. I'll be right behind you to help. We'll see what a big body like that does when it's dropped in Lake Pontchartrain."

"What are you gonna do with her?" Chet asked wildly.

"Not what I had planned on doing for sure. I'll stash her in the muck. They won't find her for days. If she's not dead yet, she will be soon. What a waste," Billy grumbled, dropping the sagging figure in the thickest marsh and covering her with swamp reeds.

Chapter Four

Four Days Later

Tara peered through the blue-violet haze surrounding Johnny. He radiated with pride, smiling intensely at the precious infant daughter in his arms. He gazed at Tara and stretched out the angelic little girl for her mother to behold. Tara edged closer to their little angel while tears streamed from her eyes, trickled down her cheeks and entered her lips. She tasted the hot, salty drops and struggled to keep her daughter and Johnny in view.

Without warning, her vision blurred; she could no longer see the picturesque image of Johnny and their little girl. Those hot, salty tears were distracting her focus, taking her away.

"Joh-nny," she mumbled, her mouth stinging from those tormenting hot tears.

"There, there, now, *ma cherie*," a frail voice said.

"Johnny," Tara said more clearly. Her eyes winced.

The dimly lit surroundings virtually obscured the feeble woman who spooned another taste of the hot, salty liquid into Tara's cracked lips. Tara coughed down the fluid and flinched at the hard concrete that brutally pressed against her tattered back. Echoing sounds of rumbling engines and distant sirens dominated the air surrounding Tara and the elderly lady.

"Johnny? Our baby," Tara whispered, moving her hand quickly to her stomach.

"My po' lil' *cher*," the aged voice started, "So sorry, so sorry, the babe tis gone," she said, gesturing toward blood-soaked cloths on the ground.

Tara screamed feverishly as memories of Mardi Gras night flooded her soul. "Johnny. Our baby. No. Why, God, why?" Her throat closed in, burning in defeated agony. "Just let me die. Let me die."

Tara sank into unconsciousness once again while the older woman wrapped her thin arms around her and rocked her soothingly.

"I know, child. I know. You's told me 'bout him. Po' *ma cherie*, po' *ma cherie*," the lady soothed, gently swaying with Tara. "Me and old Jeremiah fount ya in da' canal. I canst lift ya, so's Jeremiah brung ya here. Jeremiah—he's fechin' ya soup from the free kitchen ever' day. Jeremiah—he's good man," the lady said with a toothless smile. "He take care o' me. He take care o' you," she continued as she stared at the battered woman whose lifeless body appeared to be giving up all hope of survival. "Lord, let her live. Dem p'lice— p'lice don' know. She canst do it. She canst kilt her Johnny. Let her live. Let me and Jeremiah help her live. Canst let p'lice find her. Give her a way to let 'em know who kilt her Johnny," the aged woman prayed.

Tara's mind wandered futilely from illusion to reality as her fever continued to rise and subside. She strained to hold each vision of Johnny and their beloved daughter on the foremost of her thoughts. Johnny's adoring face praised the little girl they had created together. He held her so gently. She was precious, a child to treasure, a child the two of them could cherish...forever.

"She looks like you, Tara," Johnny's voice echoed through her memory. "Come closer, Tara. Isn't she perfect?"

Tara tried to mover closer to the two of them. The purple haze surrounding them grew thin, cloud-like. Just a few more steps...

"Help me, Jeremiah! I's losin' her!" the elderly woman squealed in panic.

Tara turned when she heard the undeniable sound of her father's voice.

"Daddy," she whispered.

"Tara, will you hand me another stack of the Styrofoam bowls. Hand me the lids as well, sweetie," her father instructed.

The young girl glanced around the shelter's soup kitchen and quickly identified the items her father needed. She grabbed a stack of bowls and lids and brought them to her father.

"Good girl," Matthew Blessing affirmed. "Makes you feel good to help others, doesn't it, darling?"

"Yes, Daddy."

"Just think of all the stars in your crown already."

"Yes, Daddy."

"You remember Hebrews 13:2, don't you, dear?"

"Be not forgetful to entertain strangers: for thereby some have entertained angels unawares," Tara faithfully quoted.

"That's right, my dear. You know, one day some of these angels may take care of you."

"Yes, Daddy."

"Mo' cold water! Jeremiah, hurry!" the woman yelled.

Jeremiah scurried down the concrete slope under the overpass to dip the ragged cloths in the cool canal water. He and Sarah had worked too hard to help this young woman pull through to lose her now. From the moment they'd found her in the marsh on Ash Wednesday, they had restlessly attempted to care for the girl without aid from anyone. Jeremiah had continually made the six-block hike to the inner-city soup kitchen to bring the nourishment she needed, as well as the scratchy, thin blankets that the shelter provided. Although New Orleans wasn't as cold in February as northern cities, blankets were still a luxury—and a necessity with the girl's fever sporadically rising and falling.

Sarah had stayed awake during the day to watch for the young woman's impending fever; he had taken watch at night. Although they hadn't acknowledged the fact to each other, Jeremiah and Sarah knew that this woman's survival was totally dependent upon them. He hurriedly handed the dripping cloths to Sarah and she laid them across the woman's sweltering face and limbs.

"Lord, please help her," Jeremiah prayed fervently. "Please, Lord, be with your child. Help us keep her alive, Lord. In Your Precious Son's name, Amen."

Sarah handed more cloths to Jeremiah. For the past four days, since he had helped her lift the lady's fragile body from the canal, he had faithfully joined Sarah in her quest to help her survive. Together, they had seen the police as they patrolled the surrounding area in search of the young woman. From the conversations Jeremiah had overheard at the soup kitchen, he had learned that the police suspected that she had murdered her husband. Sarah and Jeremiah felt compelled to protect the woman, at least until she was strong enough to tell the police the truth, whatever the truth may be.

Jeremiah frantically handed the second batch of wet cloths to Sarah and grabbed the first set of cloths, now warm from the woman's heated body, then he carried them to the canal once again. He continued this pace until Sarah finally motioned for him to stop, indicating that the girl's fever had subsided.

"You's good man. You's helped me. You's helped her," Sarah hoarsely cried. Tears dripped freely down the woman's wrinkled, dirt-smudged face.

Jeremiah panted, "That girl's trying to give up on life. She may even be trying to give up on God." Jeremiah wiped his face and added tearfully, "I can't let her do that."

Chapter Five

Sunday Morning, 3:00 a.m.

Sarah slept soundly, knowing that Jeremiah was faithfully attending their young patient. Exhausted nonetheless, Jeremiah steadied himself occasionally as he dozed against a metal pillar and attempted to block out the sounds of bleating sirens and distant gunshots.

Tara squinted as her eyes adjusted to the darkness of the dreary overpass. Trying to decipher where she was, she sat up slowly, nudging her head slightly against the bridge overhead. While her muddled thoughts cleared, she remembered her last night with Johnny. Silent tears streamed from her eyes and she pulled her knees tightly to her chest, rocking, whimpering inaudibly.

Jeremiah stirred in his sleep. Tara steadily recalled the two homeless people who had been caring for her. She wasn't sure how many days had passed since that horrible night, but she knew that they had been there each time she had drifted into reality. She stared down the concrete slope at the murky canal and wondered if this homeless pair had seen what happened to her on Mardi Gras night. She wondered if they had heard her shouting or if they heard Johnny's last scream of her name.

Tara glanced again at the sleeping pair and began to speculate why they hadn't called the police, or at least found someone to help. She didn't know. However, she knew that she was alive because of their kindness, and even though she wasn't sure whether she even wanted to live any longer, their compassion toward her, toward a complete stranger, touched her heart immensely.

She sat in the darkness, tears flowing progressively as she remembered each detail of Tuesday evening. Gradually, she edged her way toward the sleeping man. He wore a threadbare coat, his ebony hands holding the sides together for warmth. The dark man hummed in his sleep. Barely audible, but the tune sparked instant awareness. "Amazing Grace." Tara started to wake him, to ask him what they had seen, why they had helped her, and primarily, why they hadn't called the police. She sat beside him, still listening to the old familiar church tune, and decided that she couldn't wake him. He and the woman were exhausted, tired from caring for her, and Tara wasn't going to deprive them of the precious sleep that their bodies obviously needed.

She moved back to where she had been sleeping and surveyed the mound of thin blankets that had sheltered her from the cool night air. She looked back at the sleeping pair, noticing that neither of them had a single blanket for protection; they had given them all to her. With blanket-laden arms, Tara slowly crept across the concrete slope then gingerly covered each of the angels who had saved her. She still wondered why. Why had they worked so diligently to keep her alive? Why hadn't they just let her die so she could be with Johnny and their baby? And why hadn't they called someone to help?

Silently, Tara crept past them and inched her way across the concrete slope to the grassy levee. Every scratch, cut and bruise screamed in protest as she groped her way to the street above. She remembered climbing frantically up the levee to save the man she loved. She could hear echoes of herself screaming his name, trying to warn him. She heard him yelling her name, the sound of three deafening shots in the air, the shouts of the heinous men...and the thud of Johnny's body when he collided with the ground.

Shadows of Spanish moss swaying from outstretched tree limbs cast a ghostly impression against the asphalt street like slithering snakes made of soot.

Weary and pain-stricken, Tara stumbled aimlessly through the inky darkness of the abandoned road.

Why did we come here, Johnny? Why didn't we stay where we were safe?

Numbly, she ambled along the street's edge until she finally reached a vacant gas station. A blue and white ancient pay phone protruded from the right side of the empty building. Did the phone even work anymore? And she had no money. Did she have to pay to call 911? Tara staggered to the phone, grasped the receiver and pressed the number nine. As her finger moved to the one, she caught her breath. A photograph on the front page of *The Times-Picayune* made her heart stop. The bright orange newspaper dispenser displayed the Sunday morning paper, a breathtaking picture of Johnny on the front page. Tara gasped as she read the headline, *Mardi Gras Murder Remains Unsolved*, and the subtitled article, *Victim's Wife, Tara Blessing Boudreaux, Prime Suspect, Remains at Large.*

Tara's shaky hand dropped the telephone receiver.

The body of Jonathan Rene "Johnny" Boudreaux, thirty-eight, was recovered from Lake Pontchartrain late Wednesday afternoon. A native of Baton Rouge, Mr. Boudreaux had most recently resided in Peachtree City, Georgia. Mr. Boudreaux and his wife, Tara Blessing Boudreaux, had been vacationing in New Orleans since last Friday. Witnesses claimed to have seen Mr. and Mrs. Boudreaux at approximately 1:30 a.m. Wednesday morning when they apparently were breaching a parade barrier near Veterans Boulevard in Metairie. Mr. Boudreaux's abandoned 2000 red Dodge Ram was found on Williams Boulevard in Kenner at the levee for Lake Pontchartrain. After learning that Mr. Boudreaux had purchased a considerable life insurance policy with his wife, Tara, as beneficiary, the New Orleans Police Department has focused on Mrs. Boudreaux as the prime suspect in...

Tara stared in horror at the article. Her thoughts drifted back to the day Johnny had brought the insurance papers home. He hadn't wanted Tara to ever hurt financially if something should happen to him. Now Johnny's thoughtfulness was resulting in her being suspected for his murder.

She gathered her thoughts. She had to decide what to do. Telling the police the truth was the only logical answer, but she wasn't sure they would believe her. From the article, they believed that if they simply found Tara, they would have the murderer. More than likely, they wouldn't believe her at all. She couldn't risk calling them now. Instinctively, Tara picked up the telephone receiver and dialed *0*. When the operator answered, Tara requested a collect call then recited the number. Within a minute, Jade picked up.

"Jade, it's me," Tara said, as soon as the connection went through.

"Tara. Thank God! I thought you were dead. Where are you? What happened? Tell me."

"Johnny. Johnny's dead," Tara cried.

"I know, honey. I know. They think, well the idiots think that you did it."

"I'm looking at the paper now," Tara acknowledged. "I need help, Jade."

"Anything. Anything at all. I've been waiting for a call from you. Last night I decided that the police obviously weren't looking in the right places and I would just come down there and find you myself. Are you okay?"

"I—I need you here. It's too much to tell over the phone. I don't know exactly where I am now, but I'm pretty banged up and I don't have anything. No money, no clothes, and most of all, no way to prove that I didn't kill Johnny. I really need your help," Tara whimpered into the phone.

"Calm down, now. I'll be right there. I need to be able to find you, though. Do you know where you are? An address?"

"No," Tara moaned.

"Okay, look around. What do you see?" Jade requested, quickly finding her laptop and booting it up.

"It's dark here. The street is deserted. I'm at an old gas station."

"Look for a street sign. Is there a number on that station?" Jade said, pulling up a map of New Orleans.

"I can't see anything. I'm scared. I found this old pay phone. I don't have my cell. It was at the hotel."

"The pay-phone. Tara, look on the pay phone. The address should be on the phone somewhere," Jade instructed.

"I've got it. It's 537 Bissonet."

"All right. I'm looking at it. Okay, Bissonet intersects with Irving beside that gas station. Do you see the intersection?"

"Yes," Tara sniffed.

"Okay. There's a playground five blocks east down Irving. Can you walk five blocks?"

"Yes," Tara whispered. She looked down the gloomy street. Cars were in the driveways, but at four o'clock in the morning, the street was deserted.

"I'll leave now, but it will still be several hours before I get there," Jade said apologetically.

"Nine."

"Nine what?"

"It took us nine hours," Tara said, remembering her drive with Johnny.

"I'll be there in seven. Just make sure the police don't see you first," Jade warned.

Tara looked at her thin, beaten body and tattered clothes. "They wouldn't know me if they saw me. They're not looking for a homeless woman."

"What?"

"I've got so much to tell you, Jade. Please hurry," Tara said, wiping away another stream of tears.

Chapter Six

Sunday Evening – Hattiesburg, Mississippi

Still shaken by everything her best friend had told her during their ride from New Orleans, Jade stared at the fragile, distraught woman who had finally succumbed to the sleep that her body so desperately needed. She covered Tara with a thick blanket, paced to the hotel window and peered into the darkness. Tara had told her everything she remembered about that awful night, those three horrific men and the homeless pair who had religiously cared for her throughout the past five days. From the investigations Jade had watched in Georgia, however, she knew it wasn't enough. Although Tara vividly remembered the faces of the men, she couldn't remember their names or any other details that would help them find the villains who were willing to murder Johnny and leave Tara to die. Jade's blood ran cold. She wondered how so many things could have happened since last week, when she hugged her best friend goodbye.

"Heaven help me," Tara whispered in her sleep. "Heaven help me, seven, eight, three." She stirred in the bed, then opened her eyes and stared at Jade. "I remember," she whispered.

"What?" Jade asked. "What do you remember?"

"I was dreaming," Tara whispered hoarsely. "Most of it was just a dream, but then, then I remembered something."

"Tell me the dream."

"I was dreaming that I was standing on the high-rise bridge between New Orleans and Slidell, the bridge we crossed this afternoon." Tara paused, unsure whether she should continue.

"I remember," Jade added. "Go on."

"I was thinking that there would be no way that someone would survive a fall from that bridge. I wanted to jump, Jade. I wanted to jump so bad that I could feel myself climbing on the railing. All I had to do was take one step..."

Jade's heart ached for Tara. "And then what happened?"

"Then I looked into the churning brown water below and I could see three images in the water. It was those men, those three hideous men, and they were smiling and laughing at me. They were calling me into the water. I could hear them talking. I heard them calling each other by name."

"I did. I heard them as clearly as I heard them that night. Chet, Dave and Billy. Their names were Chet, Dave and Billy," Tara acknowledged. "Billy was the one that had the gun. He's the one that shot Johnny." She shivered uncontrollably.

Jade leaned over to hold Tara's shaking body, knocking the hotel Bible off of the nightstand and onto the floor. She reached down and picked up the worn book. "Thank you, Lord," she whispered, placing it gently on the table beside the bed. "If you're really there, and if you're really listening, don't leave us. Help us," Jade prayed.

"That's the rest of it. That's it. Heaven help me," Tara mumbled into Jade's shoulder.

"What?"

"Once I remembered the names, I remembered even more. When I ran to their truck, I leaned against the back. I saw the car tag, Jade. I remember it."

"What is it? Tell me."

Tara sat up foggily and rubbed her head. "I could see it as plainly as I did that night. There was a rebel flag sticker on the bumper and the tag was HHM 783, Heaven help me, seven, eight, three."

"This is it, Tara. This is what we need." She grabbed her laptop and booted it up. "We have names and a tag. Did you notice the state?" Jade asked as her screen illuminated with a screensaver photo of Brutus. "I should be able to find it anyway, but did you notice?"

"I didn't think I knew what state they were from, but in the dream I did notice something. There was a shaded outline behind the numbers on the tag—in the center."

"Did you recognize the outline?"

"It was the state of Florida," Tara said. "It was definitely the state of Florida."

"You're incredible," Jade affirmed, quickly guiding her mouse across the screen.

"Can we find them? And, if we do find them, what then?" Tara asked.

Madly clicking her mouse through endless search engines, Jade finally located the web address she needed. "It's a good thing I was paying attention to those guys at work. Every now and then, they would have to identify a tag at the airport, parking violations mainly," Jade said, clicking her mouse. "Kind of tough to get into the state's computer, but I always dreamed of being a real computer hacker, anyway."

"Jade, what will we do?" Tara asked with more conviction. She picked up the Bible and thumbed through the pages.

Jade stopped tapping on the keys and looked cautiously at the woman now propped against the headboard reading a passage in the Bible intently. She wondered what Tara was implying. Why would there be a question of what to do? They would find out as much as they could about the men and take the information to the New Orleans Police Department; however, if Tara knew what they *should* do, then why was she asking? Jade thought about everything that had happened to her friend throughout the last week. Tara had left Peachtree City with only anticipation for the trip she was taking with Johnny. Now her husband was dead—murdered—in front of her. She had been at death's door for nearly four days before Jade had found her, she had dreamed of committing suicide. Jade abruptly realized that she couldn't begin to imagine the tornado of emotions Tara had experienced, was still experiencing.

Tara stared at the scriptures with immediate realization at what she had to do.

Exodus 21:22-25. "If men strive, and hurt a woman with child, so that her fruit depart from her, and yet no mischief follow: he shall be surely punished, according as the woman's husband will lay upon him; and he shall pay as the judges determine. And if any mischief follow, then thou shalt give life for life, eye for eye, tooth for tooth, hand for hand, foot for foot, burning for burning, wound for wound, stripe for stripe."

Tara closed the Bible.

It's all up to me. Jail is too good for them. A life for a life. That's what it must be. A life for a life.

"Tara, are you okay?" Jade's voice broke her thoughts.

"Did you find them?" Tara asked.

"I've got an address now, but are you all right?"

"I'm sorry, Jade. It's just that I can't stop thinking about it. I'm going to be okay, as soon as we find them," Tara assured.

"Well, the tag is registered to William Alexander Reynolds. Here is his address. It's in Tampa," Jade said as she handed a slip of paper to Tara.

"William. That must be Billy. He's the one that—that actually shot—"

"I know," Jade comforted her, gently wrapping her arms around her sobbing friend. "Well, we've got him now. Listen, you don't have to do this alone. I'll go with you. We'll give this to the police and let them do their job. Surely, this will be enough to get the investigation moving."

Tara pulled away from Jade's grasp and stared intently at her best friend. "That's not good enough. I don't want there to be any way that they will go free, none of them. I want all three of them to hurt the way they have hurt me, the way they hurt Johnny!"

Jade's eyes widened. "What do you want to do?"

"We need to know where all of them are, not just Billy," Tara declared.

"You don't think the police will be able to find the other two once they find Billy?"

"I don't know if they will or not, but I know that we found Billy's address. I think we could find the other two also, so there would be nothing for the police to speculate. We could tell the police where all of them are, then they could get them all. That's what I want. Say you'll help me find them all," Tara pleaded.

"I still don't know what you're asking me to do."

"Trust me, Jade. I have an idea…"

Chapter Seven

Tampa

Chet paced anxiously in front of the substantial glass window that composed an entire wall of Billy's office. He stared blankly at the customers shuffling about on the lower floor of Reynolds Sea and Ski. Sporadically, he ran his ruddy hands through his strawberry hair, disheveling the curly locks until he resembled a Troll doll.

Dave peered over last Sunday's issue of *The Times-Picayune* he'd picked up before they left New Orleans and looked fixedly at his nervous friend. He had read the entire article about the murder of Johnny Boudreaux five times. Obviously, the New Orleans Police Department was convinced that Tara Boudreaux murdered her husband. The article didn't even mention the possibility of another party being involved. Dave felt fairly secure that they were home free as long as they kept cool; however, Chet's uneasiness perturbed him. If Chet couldn't pull himself together, he could single-handedly convict them all. Dave shot an intense look at Billy, trying to determine if Billy was also concerned about Chet's loyalty.

"There's nothing here that remotely suggests that anyone murdered that guy except his wife." Dave tossed the paper onto Billy's desk. "It's over."

"What happens when they find her, Dave? What happens when they find her body? Why would she murder the guy, toss him into the Pontchartrain and throw herself into the canal? They'll know something's wrong. And how long do you think it will be after they find her body before they start asking questions? How long?" Chet asked.

"Calm down," Billy instructed as he stood. "Have a seat."

Hesitantly, Chet sat in a leather chair on the opposite side of Billy's desk. Billy casually strolled to the front of the desk and sat in the chair beside Chet. He nodded to Dave, indicated the door. Dave instinctively moved to the office door and turned the lock. Chet shifted in his seat.

"I can do it. No problem," Chet said, a definite tremor in his voice.

"What can you do?" Billy asked, leaning closer to Chet's troubled face.

"I can keep quiet. We're in the clear, right? There's nothing to worry about. The police—they'll find her body and they'll think— they'll think—"

"Let me tell you exactly what they'll think," Billy started. "*If* they find her body, and I'm seriously hoping that a couple of gators find it first, but, *if* they find it, they will think that the couple obviously had a heated argument after a full day of drinking their way through Mardi Gras. Mr. Boudreaux evidently beat his wife immensely before she finally got the courage to shoot the miserable fellow and discard his body into the lake," Billy continued as Dave nodded. "Devastated by what she had done, Mrs. Boudreaux jumped from the overpass, pummeling her head against a large block of concrete in the Esplanade canal, thus leading to her own untimely death."

"Sounds good to me," Dave smirked.

"It doesn't all fit, Billy," Chet whimpered. "How would a small lady like that lift a large man to get him into the lake? Why would she leave his truck instead of driving it to the canal? And, if she didn't drive the truck to the canal, how did she get there?"

"Not our problem to figure out," Billy said with an exaggerated shrug. "Let the police do their job, Chet. Undoubtedly, it will be tough to put the pieces together, but they'll figure it out. Trust me." He walked to the large window and stood beside Dave.

"What do you think?" Dave whispered, peering out of the large glass.

"He'll be okay. Give him time," Billy answered.

"I—I guess I was overreacting. They can't find us, can they?" Chet asked.

Billy smirked at Dave. "No, Chet. Everything will be just fine. You'll head back to Colorado tomorrow, Dave will go back to Mexico, and I'll stay here. We'll return to life as we know it. Business will run as usual. We'll get back together next year for Mardi Gras, just like we always do. Nothing's changed since high school. This isn't the first time we've dodged trouble."

"But we've never—we've never killed anyone, Billy," Chet stuttered.

Dave stuffed his hands in his pants pockets and shot a worried look at Billy. He wasn't about to go to jail for this. He, Billy and Chet had been together since elementary school. As adults, they had established their credential livelihoods apart from each other, yet still remained tied through Billy's numerous operations. On the surface, the three weren't linked at all and were totally on the up and up, which was good, because their real business was anything but legal. Billy had taken over his family's business in Tampa, running three Sea and Ski shops locally and an additional twenty shops throughout the state of Florida. Chet had pursued a career providing a front for Billy's west coast operations, an elaborate ski resort in northern Colorado.

Dave had found his niche in Mexico. He loved Mexico, and had jumped at the opportunity to keep Billy's business on the Mayan Riviera running smoothly. Dave was so enamored by the country, and moreover by the endless supply of beautiful women, that he had vowed to live in Mexico indefinitely. For the past twelve years, he had controlled a well-managed monopoly on the tourist activities of Playa del Carmen. Dave thought about his condo on the beach, about Maria, his present live-in lover and the job he loved. He couldn't let Chet jeopardize everything. He *wouldn't* let him.

"I can see you are having a hard time with this, Chet," Billy said. He moved away from the window and propped against the mahogany desk. "Dave, why don't you go browse the store for a few minutes. I want to talk to Chet alone, okay?"

"Sure, Billy." Realizing that Billy had no intention of being caught, Dave wondered what he was willing to do to maintain Chet's silence. He ambled out of the office, listening intently to the low rumble of Billy's steady voice while he spoke to Chet. Dave thought he heard Chet whimpering as he started down the circular wrought iron stairway that led to the floor below.

"Mr. Danielson, so good to see you again. I wasn't sure if y'all were still meeting. There's a lady here who was asking about Mr. Reynolds. She says that she was a friend—well, she says she was one of Brighton's friends," the female employee said.

"I see," Dave said. His thoughts turned from Chet to his memories of Billy's brother. "Where is this lady, Mrs.—"

"Miss. It's Miss Hill. You can call me Joanie, Mr. Danielson."

Dave eyed the perky little brunette while she spoke. Obviously, this pretty young girl knew Dave as a friend of the owner. Perhaps she might even be interested in entertaining him for a night or two in order to have a good word put in to the boss. Dave considered altering his return flight to Cancun while Joanie continued her description of the curious customer. Dave barely heard the young cashier. He was too busy mentally undressing her, imagining what she would do with a real man. He was sure she had probably never experienced anything beyond a teenage boy. Satisfied with his visualization of everything he could do to her, and everything she could do to him, Dave finally drifted back to reality and listened to her continual rambling about Brighton's friend.

"All right, Joanie. Where is this lady?" Dave focused on the customer-filled store.

"She was here just a minute ago. Let's see. Oh, yes, there she is. Over by the dressing room, trying on the swimsuit. Yes, that's her."

"Thank you. I'll make sure that she meets Mr. Reynolds, Joanie. Now, you should probably go open another register. Things are picking up."

"Yes, sir, Mr. Danielson."

Dave casually moved across the large store, eyeing the woman Joanie had indicated. She stood in front of a huge mirror, observing every angle of the turquoise and gold bikini. Dave selected a golden sarong from a nearby rack and approached the woman.

Jade had nearly fainted when the friendly cashier informed her that Billy Reynolds was upstairs meeting with two of his acquaintances. She hadn't expected to actually meet Billy, Chet or Dave. Planning to disguise herself as an "old friend of the family," Jade had searched archives of *The Tampa Tribune* online and easily learned of the fatal boating accident that killed Billy's brother, Brighton, last year. She'd determined it would be safe enough to disguise herself as one of Brighton's old flames, since Brighton wasn't around to say anything to the contrary; however, she had merely planned on asking questions in one of Billy's numerous Sea and Ski locations. She would have never entered this particular store if she had known the killers were actually here. Now she had no choice but to continue her charade, hoping and praying that they didn't see through her lies. She tried to maintain her composure as she saw the cashier point her out to the man, and then watched as he proceeded to walk toward her, unabashedly looking her over as he neared.

"That suit was made for you. Of course, you'll want this too," he said, handing her the matching sarong.

"Thank you," Jade replied, gracefully knotting the sarong and positioning it to slant down her hip.

Stay calm. Stay calm for Tara.

Dave stared admiringly at the woman now twirling in front of the mirror. She was striking. Not beautiful, but striking. She had short, spiked blonde hair, almond-shaped blue eyes and the body of a long-distance runner, thin, muscled and tanned. Standing in the turquoise and gold bikini, she could easily pass for a model, the kind that would make it big because she was so unique. The spiked blonde hair actually accentuated the woman's athletic appearance, and she looked so sure of herself, so confident. Most women would have stayed in the dressing room to decipher whether a swimsuit, especially a bikini, had the right look. This woman not only came out in full view, but also welcomed any advice or comments from admiring onlookers. Dave was instantly intrigued.

"Joanie tells me that you were a friend to Brighton," Dave initiated.

Why did I have to say I knew him? Okay. I can do this. I can't stop now.

The young woman turned to face Dave. Her eyes sparkled as she answered, "I knew him well."

Dave noticed that a tear now fell from one of those beautiful blue eyes. She turned back toward the mirror and ran her hand across her face, brushing the tear away.

Don't cry! Don't get nervous. You always cry when you're nervous. Not this time.

"Are you William?" she asked, turning back toward Dave and extending her hand.

"No, and he actually goes by 'Billy' now. I'm one of Billy's friends, Dave Danielson."

"Jennifer Robinson," she replied and was instantly pleased that the lie came so easily.

"Billy is upstairs in his office. He's talking to—a friend of ours, but I'm sure he would want to meet you. He thought a lot of his brother, of course."

"Brighton was truly amazing."

Okay. Remember everything. What did the article say? Brighton was twenty-eight. He was on the family boat. What was the name of that boat?

"I tell you what. You go back in the dressing room and change. I'll let Billy know I'm bringing up one of Brighton's friends," Dave instructed, pulling his cell phone from his pocket.

"Sure."

Dave phoned Billy while he stared at the dressing room door where the woman was changing. Instantly, he recalled Billy's thoughts about installing two-way mirrors in the dressing rooms as a means of detecting shoplifters. He wondered if Billy had ever authorized the installation, and how he would love to watch Miss Robinson as she stepped out of the skimpy bikini.

Surprised to hear that a woman claiming to be one of Brighton's friends was in the store, Billy cut his talk with Chet short. Basically, he had informed Chet that he should either give up the notion of confessing or accept the fact that he could also experience an untimely death if necessary.

Chet had no doubt that Billy would hold no reservations in doing exactly what he'd threatened if he determined that Chet was a liability, so he had earnestly tried to convince Billy that he could be trusted. Unfortunately, he couldn't tell whether he had succeeded, or whether he had just managed to make himself Billy's next target. Still shaken, he made his way down the circular staircase. Halfway down, he met Dave, with a woman in tow. Chet barely noticed her at first; his mind still hovered on his previous conversation with Billy. Had he said the right thing? Or would Billy see fit to bid Chet adieu.

"Chet, you okay?" Dave questioned.

"F-fine. Just fine."

"You sure?" Dave tried to determine whether Chet was scared enough to keep silent. He liked Chet; they were friends. But friend or not, he wouldn't go to jail because Chet was weak.

"I said I'm fine," Chet snapped. His gaze finally captured the blonde beside Dave. "Who's that?" he asked, "and where're you taking her?"

"She was one of Brighton's friends. I'm taking her to meet Billy. I texted him and told him I was bringing her up."

"Jennifer Robinson," she said with an outstretched hand.

"Chet Garrison." He grasped her hand. "You knew Brighton?"

Jade shook the clammy hand, immediately noticing the beaded line of sweat on the ruddy man's forehead. "Yeah." She attempted a confident smile, but her lip quivered and she suspected it came across as watery and nervous. "He was a friend of mine. More than a friend, actually."

Dave raised a brow at the woman's last remark. "I'm sure Billy will be anxious to meet you," he said.

She noticed at once the ornate décor of the flamboyant office. Along with the complete glass wall overlooking the store below, it had a well-stocked wall of book shelving filled with an endless assortment of aged classics as well as modern literature. With furnishings of leather, dark mahogany and an enormous blue marlin mounted directly behind the desk, the room was an overpowering shrine to testosterone.

Billy Reynolds sat behind his vast desk, eyeing her intensely, like a cunning hawk stalking a field mouse. Jade couldn't help but notice that he had the stern look of a judge prepared to issue sentencing, and in her case, the death penalty. The hair on the back of her neck stood on end as she looked at this man. At this murderer.

"So, you knew my brother?" Billy queried.

"I knew him well," she replied.

Don't talk too much. Just answer his questions.

Billy motioned for her to sit down, but didn't bother standing to welcome her to his office. Dave noticed Billy's jaw tighten. He wondered briefly if Billy hadn't wanted him to bring this woman to his office; however, Billy had been so grief-stricken at the loss of Brighton that Dave couldn't imagine him not wanting to meet someone who obviously knew his brother well.

"You can leave, Dave," Billy instructed.

Dave exited the office with confusion apparent on his face. He wondered if Billy was upset with this woman—or with him for bringing her. No. He was just aggravated by the confrontation with Chet. His mood shift had nothing to do with this girl, this attractive girl who may have been more than just a friend to Brighton.

As soon as Dave left, Billy cut his sharp eyes at her. "How well did you know him?" The questions sounded almost...accusing.

"You could say we were very, very close," she answered with a slight smile. Then, as her eyes watered slightly, "I miss him."

Jade had always hated the way she cried when she was nervous, saw it as a sign of weakness. But now, the tears were an asset, adding credibility to her claim that she had a relationship with Brighton Reynolds.

Completely unaffected by her show of emotion, Billy probed, "Did he ever mention me to you? Did you know anything of our relationship?"

"He just said that he had a brother named William. I know a year has passed. I thought about trying to find you before, but it was just too hard," she sniffed.

Believe me, murderer.

Emotionless, Billy interrogated, "Did he mention our business to you? The family business? He was running everything quite well until, well, until the accident. It was a shame, a real shame."

Although Billy attempted to sound sincere about the unfortunate accident that took his brother's life, Jade easily detected the venom beneath his words. Brighton had been running the family business, the business left to Brighton, not Billy, after the death of their parents. And, Jade remembered from the newspaper article, Brighton was the younger of the two brothers. She stared into the eyes of the killer, and then she knew, knew exactly what this man was capable of, knew exactly why he pounded her with questions.

You killed him, didn't you, Billy? You killed your brother!

"He never mentioned business. We were in more of a personal relationship. To tell the truth, I didn't know much about his family. He had told me about your parents—"

"What did he say about their death?" Billy interrupted.

A thick drop of nervous sweat trickled down her chest and settled at the center of her bra. "Just that they had passed away and that the two of you were left on your own," she lied.

"I see," Billy said, studying her to determine just how much this woman knew. And whether she was a threat. He remembered vividly the scene of the car accident that took the lives of both his parents..after he'd chased them and forced their Jaguar down the ravine.

Brighton had mourned for months. Brighton, so pathetically emotional, had actually loved the power-hungry lunatics. Then, when he and Brighton had learned about the will, Brighton had actually tried to console him when they learned that their parents had left everything to Brighton. And nothing to Billy. Brighton told him that he would always give Billy his rightful portion of the business. He'd actually shown pity toward the older son, the one who should've received everything, but who had been hung out to dry.

Abruptly, Billy's thoughts turned to struggling with Brighton on their boat, plunging into the cold water, holding Brighton under and watching eagerly, excitedly as the fool struggled for air. Feeling his brother's body go limp.

Jade watched his face carefully, struggling to read the array of emotions that played across his features.

He's trying to determine what I know. He's not sure what to do with me.

"Perhaps I gave you the wrong idea. I met Brighton just a couple of weeks before the boating accident. I was just getting to know him, but I had hopes—"

Billy's thoughts returned to the woman in front of him. At once, he smirked wickedly. "Oh, now I see. You were Brighton's 'flavor of the month' at the time. Trust me honey. If you had been with him a couple of weeks already, it wouldn't have been much longer till he'd have given you the boot. I thought you said you were a friend of his." He stood and headed for the office door. "You can find your way out, I'm sure. I have another meeting, now. You understand."

"Completely," Jade said, when he ushered her into the outer corridor and slammed the door. "I understand completely."

Chapter Eight

Steamboat Springs, Colorado

Matthias McClain sat on the front pew of the small auditorium that composed the majority of the building for the Community church in Steamboat Springs. Scanning his sermon notes, he breathed in the strong smell of pine, or perhaps cedar, still evident from Sister Madeleine's thorough cleaning on Thursday. For a building this size, an hour's worth of cleaning would undeniably be sufficient; however, Sister Maddie's feebleness kept her from moving through the building any faster than a snail's pace. As a result, she generally arrived around six o'clock in the morning every Thursday and remained until time for her afternoon nap.

He smiled as he thought of the delightful elderly lady gradually working her way through the pews with her cotton cloth and a bottle of polishing oil in hand. Each week, he protested when the aged woman grasped the back of the last pew and worked her way into a crawling position on the floor, just to make sure the baseboards were as shiny as the wooden pews. Regardless of Matthias' weekly objections, however, Sister Maddie insisted on making the journey to the hardwood for her baseboard survey. Matthias looked away from his sermon plans to view the gleaming baseboards and made a mental note to remind the congregation of Sister Maddie's weekly service.

Glancing at his watch, he realized that his Sunday morning class should begin in three minutes. As usual, all fifteen pews were completely vacated. A sermon on promptness was probably in order; however, he couldn't risk losing one of the mere thirty-five members that composed his congregation simply because they weren't able to make it to the Bible study on time. Besides, things were different in Steamboat. Everything moved at a slower pace in the popular ski town. The residents were typically at a comfortable place in life, not concerned with everyday worries such as schedules and promptness. Thus, Sunday morning Bible studies generally started approximately ten minutes after the time displayed on the wooden sign posted by the street.

Matthias' congregation was composed of thirty-two permanent residents of Steamboat and typically three temporary residents. The temporary residents of the town, usually skiers and snowboarders, were definitely not bothered by everyday concerns. As a matter of fact, Matthias hadn't determined that they were concerned with much of anything at all, except how much fresh powder was available on the mountain.

Currently, three young women in their early twenties who had part-time positions at one of the local ski resorts composed the only temporary residents that attended the Community church. Evidently, the women had taken the positions in Steamboat immediately upon college graduation from the University of Tennessee. It seemed as though more and more recent college grads were coming here to have one last bit of fun before settling down and obtaining permanent jobs. These particular females had the strongest Southern accents Matthias had ever heard, "sweet enough to melt butter," as one of the elderly men had put it upon hearing the girls speak.

One of the young women, a petite brunette named Hallie, had set her sights on Matthias from the first time she and her two companions had stepped through the church doors. Hallie had wasted no time at all in obtaining the friendship of Sister Maddie and Sister Evelyn, the two most knowledgeable women on the comings and goings of everyone in the Steamboat Springs vicinity. The two mature women were more than willing to inform Hallie of every detail of the preacher's life, beginning with his ever-lingering bachelor status which, according to Sister Evelyn, was "such a waste of a wonderful creation of God." When Hallie asked Sister Evelyn if she was referring to marriage, Sister Evelyn had directly replied, "No indeed, child. I'm talking about the man!"

Of course, Brother Brantley, a seventy-year-old who had never married, happened to overhear the comment and immediately informed Matthias that those "conniving females" were after him. Matthias had merely reminded Brother Brantley that God created male and female, and that nothing God created was bad.

"Don't believe it. Never have, never will. You won't catch me running to the altar," the old man had responded. The image of Brother Brantley running anywhere made Matthias grin; he'd never seen the feeble old man without his cane, and a limp.

The auditorium doors creaked open. Matthias stood. Sister Maddie and Sister Evelyn eased their way down the center aisle to their predictable perch, the third pew.

"I made some homemade biscuits for you, Brother Matthias. I put them in the foyer," Sister Evelyn informed.

"You made them for everyone, didn't you?" Sister Maddie asked, with a noticeable punch of her elbow into Evelyn's side.

"That's what I said, isn't it?" Sister Evelyn replied with a giggle.

Matthias grinned at the two ladies while he pulled the wooden podium to the front center of the auditorium. "I'm sure the congregation will appreciate the biscuits, Sister Evelyn. That was very sweet of you."

Sister Evelyn's smile broadened as she beamed at the young preacher. "Have you seen that sweet Hallie this week?" she prodded. "Such a nice girl, isn't she?"

"Evelyn!" Maddie gasped. "Please forgive her, Brother Matthias. That's none of our business, is it? I mean, unless you want to talk about her. Or ask questions, you know."

"Actually, I haven't seen Miss Hallie since our Wednesday evening Bible study." He didn't feel the need to inform the overly inquisitive women that Hallie had been calling him nonstop on a daily basis.

Matthias was still unaccustomed to the forwardness of today's females, and Hallie was quite bold in her pursuit. She seemed to have no problem at all with the fact that she was barely twenty-two and Matthias was thirty-five. As a matter of fact, when he'd pointed it out, she had merely laughed and said that she could use some stability in her life. Matthias had almost expected her to propose marriage on that particular day.

It had happened just two weeks ago, when she caught him off-guard by breezing into his office while he was preparing a sermon. Unabashedly, she waltzed directly behind the desk where he sat, leaned over and kissed him intensely. Intimately. Matthias still flushed bright scarlet when he thought of the incident. What disconcerted him even more than the precocious woman's action was his own response. He had originally tried to push away from the aggressive female, but found himself enjoying the lingering invasion of his mouth, her warm lips, the smell of her that close to him. Finally breaking the heat of the moment, he pointedly told her that this behavior was unquestionably inappropriate to say the least then ushered her out of the office in an effort to catch his breath. He'd heard her giggle of triumph as she left the building, and he immediately prayed for the strength to resist temptation. Obviously, any relationship that would result between them would be based on mere physical attraction. As much as Matthias desired to have a woman in his life, he wanted it to be more than just physical. He longed for a relationship with a woman that would strengthen him spiritually, emotionally *and* physically. At thirty-five, he was beginning to wonder if such a woman existed.

Standing at the podium with his Bible and notes in front of him, he smiled and greeted each member that straggled into the Bible study throughout the next ten minutes. Hallie mingled into the auditorium with her friends, but quickly left them and moved toward the front to sit with Sister Maddie and Sister Evelyn. She wore a flaming red dress with matching heels and purse, pearl earrings and necklace, and the same perfume she had on that day in his office. Matthias could barely smell the sweet aroma, but he knew it was there. Lingering in the distance. Tantalizing his senses.

He silently prayed for strength.

Hallie Davenport noticed the red flush on Matthias' face. She wasn't positive, but she thought it happened when she walked into the auditorium. Excellent. She couldn't look at the handsome young preacher without remembering that surge of passion that he'd shown during their brief kiss. She wondered exactly how deep that passion went. He was denying it, but she knew he wanted her as badly as she wanted him. Surely, he didn't think that it was a sin to kiss, did he? No. He was scared of what he felt. Well, she was bound and determined to break through that fear. She could do it. He was trying to resist, but she knew he felt something for her too.

Hallie knew that she wouldn't be able to have him totally, completely, without marriage. Fine. She could handle being a preacher's wife. What girl wouldn't want a guy who looks like that and who truly believes that he should be committed to one woman monogamously until death. How romantic. How wonderfully romantic.

She glanced at the attractive man now speaking to his congregation. The fact that he didn't even realize the effect he had on women captivated Hallie. If Matthias McClain had been an option for a dorm poster, he would have been the one to adorn her wall, hands down, and life-sized. She watched him pace as he made the morning announcements. His sandy colored hair, buzzed extremely short, drew even more attention to his crystal blue eyes. His smile was genuine, with blinding white teeth accentuated by naturally olive-toned skin. He wasn't very tall, perhaps five-foot-seven, which was one of Hallie's favorite things about him. She had always laughed about her attraction to men who were virtually the same height as she. "Who wants to stand on their toes every time you want a really great kiss?" she had joked to friends.

Additionally, Matthias had a body that made her heart skip a beat. She could tell by the way he filled out his dress shirt and khakis that he was impressive, but when she had leaned against him that day in his office, she had felt every inch of hardened mass that composed the exquisite man. She thought of last night's dream. Matthias hovering over her, his shirt off, muscles tense, eyes intense...

She shook the memory away as she heard the beginning of the morning's first hymn and said a quick prayer for God to help her keep her mind pure, at least while she sat in the pew at church.

Matthias saw the flushed look on Hallie's face as he sang from the podium. He said another prayer for the Lord to help him resist worldly temptation, and in particular, Hallie Davenport.

As the song ended, Brother Matthias McClain announced the sermon topic to the congregation.

"As we completed our study of the husband in the home last week, we will begin this week's study with scripture regarding the wife's role in the home."

Brother Brantley groaned in dismay.

Chapter Nine

Jade set the cruise control on her Mustang to eighty miles-per-hour, crossed the Georgia state line on Interstate 20 and continued into Alabama. Any state trooper should allow ten miles over the speed limit, and although she was definitely in a hurry to get back to Hattiesburg, she didn't want to get stopped with Tara's things in the back seat.

It had been five days since she'd left Tara in that small hotel room. Jade knew better than to call and check on her friend. If the police happened to suspect that she knew Tara's whereabouts, they would definitely be tracking her calls. However, when Jade had asked Sergeant Billingsly for an additional week off to continue searching for Tara in New Orleans, he had informed Jade that the New Orleans Police Department had started searching the Pontchartrain and the surrounding areas for Tara's body. Sergeant Billingsly also told her that the police had an alternate theory that Tara had committed suicide after realizing the implications of what she'd done to her husband.

Jade had practically lost all control upon this remark from her superior. Standing in the middle of the International Concourse at Hartsfield, she'd yelled emphatically that her friend was not capable of murder or suicide. Billingsly made a genuine effort to console her, constantly telling her that he didn't believe the theory and that the truth would come out in the end. Jade just hoped that her performance wasn't too extreme. The sergeant couldn't suspect that she knew exactly where her friend was, and what actually happened on Mardi Gras.

She swerved to avoid a stalled dump truck in the middle of the interstate in Birmingham. "Dang it, pay attention," she said to her empty car. She grabbed a cold Coke from the mini cooler she'd stocked before leaving home and held the icy can against her cheek. She had to stay alert. With barely any sleep since she left Hattiesburg, she was utterly exhausted, but now wasn't the time to let exhaustion prevail. She wondered if Tara had been able to sleep at all throughout this nightmare.

Tara. Jade's eyes filled with tears as she thought of her beautiful friend. Just two weeks ago, she had been the most carefree, happy-go-lucky woman, living a life that Jade had merely dreamed existed. Now Tara's entire world had been ripped apart. She was actually hiding from the police! And if they found her, she would be accused of murdering the person that she loved more than anything.

Jade shivered. Tara was not only in danger of being located by the police, but also by the three vile men who had killed Johnny. Just three days ago, Jade had been face-to-face with Billy Reynolds. Tara had asked her to visit Tampa, ask questions and try to determine the names of Billy's friends. Jade had taken it upon herself to not only learn the names of Billy's accomplices, but to find out as much as possible. She shuddered with a vigorous frisson of cold fear, realizing how stupid she had been when she had visited Billy's store. She should have anticipated that Billy could have actually been in the store she chose to visit.

She recalled each of the three men. She had been surprised when she met Dave Danielson. Her affiliation with the police department had taught her that there wasn't a certain "look" for a killer, or an accomplice, but he certainly didn't appear as she had expected. Dave Danielson was about five-foot-nine at best, perhaps weighing a hundred and seventy pounds. He had wavy, black hair, deep-set eyes, and was dressed in tailored khakis and a pale blue golf shirt. For all purposes, his appearance resembled more of a preppy tourist than a cold-blooded killer, but Jade knew something wasn't quite right.

As she continued to drive south of Birmingham, she pictured the man vividly and realized what was wrong. His eyes. Dave Danielson's eyes had told a story of their own. Although he appeared cordial, his eyes exposed the hidden shrewdness underneath his courteous façade. As she thought about it further, Jade realized that she had felt uneasy the moment he had suavely introduced himself and offered her the sarong. Yes, Dave Danielson was the smooth operator of the group, appearing debonair while successfully camouflaging his cruel intentions.

Billy Reynolds, conversely, demonstrated no desire whatsoever to conceal his crude activities. Jade had felt as though she had entered a snake pit when she stepped into the fiend's office. A writhing mass of venom that would've put Indiana Jones into a coma. The presence of evil loomed imminently around the malicious man, and he didn't care how she perceived him; his foremost concern was obviously whether Jade knew of his past sins.

Although she hadn't known prior to their meeting, Jade now had a nagging suspicion that not only had Billy Reynolds murdered Johnny, but he had also killed his parents and his brother. Undoubtedly, he wasn't concerned with anything regarding Jade's fictitious relationship with Brighton; he was merely trying to determine whether she should be his next victim.

Jade adjusted the heat thermostat in the car as she shuddered with the cold reality of how close she had been to the murderer. She thought of the look on Chet Garrison's face when he met her on the stairway leading to Billy's office. He was scared. Scared of Billy. She wondered how the red-haired, nervous man could have become involved with Dave and Billy. He seemed so anxious, so tense, even panicky. Yes, that was it. Chet was panicked, afraid of getting caught. That was why Dave kept asking if he was okay. And that must have been what Billy was talking to him about in his office.

Well, maybe Chet would crack. She'd seen it before. All it took was one weak link and the entire criminal chain would turn brittle. Crumble completely. And if he was the weakest link, then Chet could be the key to proving Tara's innocence. Jade popped open the top of the Coke and took a gratifying swallow of potent caffeine. She would definitely make sure the police located Chet first. He would be the most likely candidate to give them every bit of ammunition they needed to arrest not only himself, but also Dave and Billy.

Jade glanced at the small notebook she had placed on the console. Three addresses were written on the overturned page. She had been surprised that the three men hadn't all resided in Tampa. On the contrary, they lived vast distances away from each other. Billy and Chet would be easily located, both living in the States; however, the last known address for Dave Danielson was in Mexico. That could definitely pose a problem for the New Orleans Police Department, but Jade continued to believe that justice would be served and that these men would all pay for what they'd done to Johnny and Tara.

Not realizing that Jade would come face-to-face with the murderers, Tara had requested the information that had put Jade in the depths of the lion's den. Jade had already decided that she would never tell Tara about actually meeting the killers. She would give Tara the names and addresses, just as if she would have given them to her had she not met one-on-one with Billy Reynolds. The meeting need never be mentioned. Jade didn't want to further upset her friend. In any case, she did get the information. Now, she and Tara could take the addresses to the police with the knowledge that they would be able to find the real killers. Then, hopefully, Tara's name could be cleared and perhaps she could return to a normal life.

Would Tara's life ever being normal again? When her parents had died, a part of Tara had died also. Now Johnny had been murdered, cold-blooded and in front of his wife. How would she live normally after that? A tear streamed down Jade's cheek as her heart ached for her friend. She glanced in her rear view mirror to observe a police car pacing her. Acutely aware of the large box in the back seat, Jade watched as the black-and-white slowed and turned toward the median to set up a radar position.

The large box filled the back seat. Two additional boxes that Tara had asked her to retrieve from her disaster stash were in the trunk. Jade wondered vaguely what could have been so important that Tara asked her to drive back to Georgia before meeting her again in Hattiesburg. She hadn't asked any questions. No doubt the contents of the boxes were important to Tara, and Jade wasn't going to begrudge her friend anything that she wanted now. Or ever.

Chapter Ten

Tara gripped the hotel Bible tightly as she remembered Jade's warning when she left Hattiesburg five days ago. Jade had reminded her to be careful, not to leave her room unless absolutely necessary, never make eye contact with anyone, pay for everything in cash, and most of all, don't leave a trail that the police can follow. The last thing they needed right now was for the police to find Tara hiding out in a hotel room in Hattiesburg. In that case, she might as well write an editorial to *The Times-Picayune* confessing to the murder.

Tara had heeded Jade's advice. Thanks to the small dorm-sized refrigerator that Jade had requested from the hotel and the supply of food and staples she purchased before she left, Tara had everything she needed to hold out here for quite a while. Jade had also purchased several hair coloring kits to help Tara camouflage her identity from anyone who had seen her picture on the television or newspaper. Tara had opted for a color labeled *Knock Them Dead Red* and had been shocked at how well her hair had accepted the hue. Her previously auburn locks were now flaming crimson, and her appearance was quite altered by the vivid color that now framed her face. Jade was smart to suggest the dye; it definitely provided the façade Tara needed.

Tara wondered how Jade was faring in her quest for information about Dave and Chet. She had suggested that Jade visit some of the local stores near Billy's address in Tampa to see if anyone knew the trio. Tara thought about her spirited friend and realized that she probably wouldn't have been satisfied to merely learn the names of the malevolent men. For the first time, Tara realized that she had put Jade in danger by asking her to go to Tampa. She gripped the Bible tighter and opened it to John 15.

"Greater love hath no man than this, that a man lay down his life for his friends," she said aloud. Her throat closed in. "No, Jade. Don't you dare do that for me. They can't take you too. God, don't take her too. She doesn't deserve to die. Johnny didn't deserve to die! Our baby didn't deserve to die!" Tara wailed. "You know everything, don't You, God? You know what I'm planning, don't You? Can You blame me? Tell me why I shouldn't do it. They don't deserve to live." She slammed the Bible on the bedside table and collapsed into a fit of tears on the bed. "Keep her safe."

Along with spending the majority of the past five days crying into the pillows of the hotel bed, Tara had also spent many hours praying to God, screaming at God, wondering if He had deserted her, or if He even existed. She had continually fought sleep. Sleeping meant dreaming and dreaming meant seeing those three repulsive faces laughing, always laughing, and sneering as the bullets hammered against Johnny's chest. Helplessly, she watched in horror as Johnny screamed her name, crumpled to the ground and became lifeless. Lifeless. His life was gone, stolen from him, and her life had been taken too.

The image of Johnny on that fateful Mardi Gras night was burned into her memory. If anything, the dreams only made her memory sharper. Everything replayed itself again and again in slow motion. She heard every word that had been screamed or whispered, saw vividly the gun at Billy's waist, heard the rumble of truck engines, felt the sting of the concrete attacking her flesh as she tumbled down the embankment. Tara relived it all every time she closed her eyes.

To keep herself awake, Tara read. Although the hotel Bible was her primary source of reading material, the hotel also provided a copy of *The Hattiesburg American* each morning, and she read it religiously to stay aware of any new information regarding Johnny's murder. Unfortunately, the newspaper had barely mentioned the murder, so Tara wasn't any more informed than she had been when Jade left five days ago. She supposed that the paper wouldn't have any room left for local news if they gave credence to every murder in New Orleans. But this murder was different; this murder was her husband, and Tara wanted to make certain that the murderers paid, and paid dearly.

She scanned the second page of today's paper and an article caught her eye. She read aloud, "Judge Orders Prisons to Relieve Crowding of Inmates." Tara finished reading the article then proceeded to tear the paper into shreds and throw it into the garbage. Bitter tears flowed as rage built within her. "How dare them let criminals go free. How am I supposed to feel secure that justice will be served when our judicial system has the audacity to order criminals back on the streets? How long will it take to put those three men behind bars, and then how quickly will they set them free? I can't—I won't—let this happen. Even if they go to prison, what does that mean? Three meals a day, television, clothes on their back. What kind of society lets murderers live better than fellow Americans, better than homeless Americans who have committed no crime?" She slung a pillow into the wall. "One nation under God? God isn't with this nation. He has left us. He has left us all."

Tara remembered the elderly homeless couple who had cared for her under the overpass in New Orleans. She hadn't thought of them since Jade had brought her here, but now her memory of the caring twosome was clear. That couple had taken great risks to help her when she unquestionably was at death's door. Now she wondered why they didn't just let her die. Then she would be with Johnny and their baby. Why hadn't God allowed her to die? Surely her life wasn't worth living now. Surely He knew that she didn't want to live anymore. Why hadn't she told Jade to let her out near that high-rise bridge, taken the walk to the top, and jumped?

Four hours later, Jade slowly opened the door to the small hotel room and saw Tara's petite frame sprawled across the bed.

"Dear God, No!" Jade threw her bags on the floor and darted to the bed. Dropping her head to Tara's chest, she breathed a heavy sigh when she heard the heartbeat and felt her friend's chest rising with a sharp intake of breath.

"What—What are you doing?" Tara shrieked, forcing her eyes to focus.

"I thought you had—well, I thought you were—forget it. I'm so glad you're okay," she said, hugging Tara tightly.

"I was worried about you, Jade. I sent you to ask questions, but I realized after you had left that you would never be able to stop there. What did you do? Tell me everything, and don't leave anything out."

Jade sat beside her dearest friend and told her about her trip to Tampa. She didn't exactly lie to Tara; she just didn't tell all of the truth. Handing Tara the names and addresses of Dave, Chet and Billy, Jade explained that she had visited one of the stores in Tampa near Billy's address and asked a few questions, just as Tara had instructed. She said it was fairly simple, and that most of the time she'd been gone had been spent in Peachtree City, gathering the boxes Tara had asked for, making arrangements for work and checking on Brutus.

Tara held the small piece of notebook paper containing the three names belonging to the faces that terrorized her nights.

"Mexico? Colorado? Are you sure?"

"Positive. Those were their addresses as of last month and should still be accurate. You can give them to the police when you tell them what really happened." Jade wanted to tell Tara to ask the police to locate Chet first, since he would be the most likely to cave under pressure, but that would mean telling Tara what she had done, and she couldn't let her ever suspect how close she had been to the killers. Jade reasoned that she would go with Tara to the police station and personally inform them of what she'd learned of the three men.

"Were you able to locate the boxes I needed?" Tara asked, continuing to stare at the list in her hand.

"They're in the car. Do you want me to get them?"

"No, it can wait until morning. I'm sure you're tired. We'll have a hectic day tomorrow when we take the information to the police.

Why don't we get some sleep?" Tara knew she wouldn't be able to go back to sleep again, but she could see Jade's lids were heavy. She had never lied to her friend before now, but she couldn't risk having Jade try to help with the rest of Tara's plan. She hadn't been able to protect Johnny, but she could keep Jade safe from those horrible men.

Jade hugged Tara tightly once again before climbing into the opposite bed. Tara watched in silence as she turned out the light and whispered, "Don't worry. Things can only get better, Tara."

"I know," she answered. "I believe they will."

Within ten minutes, Jade's breathing had steadied and she slept soundly. Tara edged out of the bed, easing her bare feet across the paper-thin carpet covering the concrete floor. She located Jade's computer bag in the dark and withdrew the laptop. Then she crept to the bathroom and eased the door shut.

When she was certain she hadn't heard any stirring from Jade, she powered on the computer then quickly connected to the hotel's wireless Internet. After only forty minutes of thorough queries, her mission was complete and she returned the computer to Jade's case.

Easing through the room again, Tara carefully picked up Jade's car keys from the nightstand and made her way to the door. This was it. So far so good. Glancing to the darkened parking lot below, she located Jade's emerald Mustang parked directly beneath the balcony outside their room. She walked briskly to the stairs and headed to the car. Seeing one box in the back seat, she began to panic. Surely Jade would have told her if she hadn't found all three boxes. Tara moved directly to the trunk, used the keyless entry to open it and flooded with relief when she saw the two additional boxes perched inside. Hurriedly, she opened the box marked "S1-Tara". An old turquoise towel she had once used for washing the car lay across the contents. She scanned the parking lot for movement. When she was sure the coast was clear, she plunged her hand under the towel and felt the bounty of plastic bags.

"Thanks, Dad," she whispered. She withdrew two of the old, bright blue Wal-Mart bags and shut the box again. After closing the trunk, she briskly moved back up the stairs to the room where her best friend slept. Jade hadn't moved an inch while Tara had been downstairs. Tara entered noiselessly, trying to keep the bags from rattling as she gently eased them on the bedside table. Then she hurriedly scratched out a note to Jade and laid it atop the bags of cash that her friend would find tomorrow.

"Please forgive me," she whispered, leaving the tiny room and her best friend, forever.

Chapter Eleven

If Jade would have realized that she was carrying exactly what Tara needed to leave her, she would have never brought the boxes from Peachtree City. Tara remembered her parents packing each of her survival boxes near mid-1999 when they anticipated the technological world would possibly halt on the date predicted to begin millennium madness, or Y2K. Contrary to that theory was the fact that the millennium madness actually occurred prior to January 1st, 2000, because of the media frenzy that had been building steadily throughout the 1990's. Tara had only been seventeen at the time, but she remembered it like it was yesterday.

Tara's parents had been particularly affected by the need to survive past the unknown. Her father was prepared to assist the mystified multitudes by seeking to bring their souls to Christ. He felt if their money was gone and their computers were useless, then who better to turn to than the Lord? Matthew Blessing was actually looking forward to the date and filled most of his survival boxes with small New Testaments and carefully prepared sermons. Of course, none of Tara's family had assumed that Christ would return on that day. The Bible told them in 2 Peter 3:10 that, "The day of the Lord will come as a thief in the night," and in Matthew 24:36 Christ said, "But of that day and hour knoweth no man, no, not the angels of heaven, but my Father only." There was no doubt in

Tara's mind that Christ would therefore not return as everyone expected, on January 1st, 2000. Obviously the people who were professing that date didn't know much about their Bible to begin with.

Tara, on the other hand, knew her Bible. Her parents had as well. And where had that gotten them? They were dead, and she was accused of murder.

Her eyes stung with tears as she continued driving Jade's Mustang through the darkness of I-20, leaving Mississippi behind as she entered Louisiana and continued driving. Remembering her family's preparations for Y2K only reminded her of how awful that day had actually been. It was much worse than she could have ever expected; she had lost both of her parents on that horrible New Year's Eve.

They had filled their old station wagon to the brim with tiny Bibles and were bringing the last load home when a drunk man drove his car head-on into the old wagon. Tara had been waiting on their return at the house when the sheriff arrived to tell her the news. According to the medics, they died instantly; they hadn't suffered. Tara hadn't seen the comfort in their lack of suffering. They weren't alive; that was what mattered. They were dead. The millennium had left the banks intact, kept the computers churning at impeccable speed, but had managed to steal something more precious than anything material. Matthew James and Betty Jo-Ann Blessing.

Pulling the Mustang into a rest area, Tara promptly dropped her head to the steering wheel and cried, sobbing in fits of gasps and coughs. She slid her hand across her face to remove the final batch of tears that streamed from her swollen eyes then placed her forehead against the cold steering wheel. Her mind ached with the memory of Brother Williams' lessons, of the multitude of scriptures she readily knew, of her parents teaching her to do God's will. "I know. I'm supposed to love my enemies. But, how can I? Do I just give up? Let them merely go to jail to be released to the world again? Johnny isn't getting to live again, is he? And neither is our baby!" Tara slammed her fist against the dash then drew her stinging hand against her chest. The skin, still torn from her attempt to escape the men, had busted open again with the force of the impact.

Tara didn't know how long she cried before shaking herself from misery and turning her thoughts to the task at hand. Getting to Dallas. She had known exactly what she needed from Jade's computer, and it had willingly obeyed her every command. She'd retrieved directions identifying the exact driving instructions from Hattiesburg to Dallas. The total estimated driving time was nine hours and forty-eight minutes; the total distance, five hundred eleven miles.

Her driving instructions included every highway, every street, and every turn from Hattiesburg to the Dallas Fort Worth International Airport, and she was grateful. American Airlines Flight 1211 would depart at 5:36 p.m., arriving in Cancun at 8:13 p.m. And she would be on that flight.

After carefully surveying the other vehicles parked at the rest area for the Louisiana Welcome Center, Tara decided it was safe to push the trunk release and extract her additional two survival boxes. Each of their family members had marked their ultimate survival boxes with S1 and S2.

S1 was to be their cash source. Matthew James Blessing had produced a small fortune in his lifetime, primarily from lack of spending. Other than his generous gifts to the church, orphanage and homeless shelter, he had never afforded himself a luxury item in his life. He perceived that things much more luxurious would be waiting in Heaven, and he could wait. Therefore, his ample supply of cash was kept to help those in need during the Y2K frenzy, such as it was. Tara had no idea exactly how much money had been stored in her S1 box, but she knew that it was filled with as many plastic bags as it would hold, and that each bag contained a minimum of five thousand dollars. She had left approximately ten thousand dollars cash for Jade to find at the hotel room, along with a note apologizing for buying her car without asking. Tara had also told her friend that she regretted lying to her, but that she had to leave. Hopefully, Jade wouldn't put the full picture together until everything was over. Tara hoped that Jade would surmise that she had simply fled for fear of the police not believing the truth.

S2 was filled with every bit of paperwork needed to prove her identity. Several copies of her social security card, birth certificate, driver's license, etc. were included in the box. Her parents had thought proof of identification would be important, should the computer systems actually fail. But Jade had talked to her enough about criminals obtaining fake ids and passports that Tara knew it wasn't that difficult to get both. She'd need to do that today, because she'd already booked her flight. According to Jade, she merely needed to find the seedy part of town and ask about a fake id. She'd do that this morning...in Dallas. Because by the time she got on that airplane later today, she'd need to be Ann James. The combination of her parents' names brought memories of when her world had been normal and made her throat thicken. She swallowed through the pain of bitter reality.

Resolving that she wasn't going to stop what she had to do, Tara looked at the final survival box. She'd positioned the S3 box in the passenger's seat. This was the one that summoned her interest most. Tara and Johnny had added an S3 to their stash of survival boxes, the final box being filled with the unknown. Johnny's final box had been filled by Tara; Tara's final box had been filled by Johnny. She knew it would tear her very soul to see what was hidden in the third box. For this reason, Tara drew a deep breath as she tore the tape from the top and peered inside. A rich, navy and gold silk fabric lay on top of the additional contents. Tara removed the beautiful cloth. It was one of the most exquisitely intricate, undeniably sexy pieces of lingerie she had ever seen. She tenderly brought the soft sheen of silk from the box and brushed the smoothness against her face, imagining what it would have been like to have worn this for Johnny. Tears spilled onto the fabric, and she laid it aside to keep from further staining the precious treasure.

Four glittery golden scarves were the next items Tara removed. She peered inside to see that the remainder of the box was empty except for a single, manila envelope that had been taped to one side. The envelope was labeled "My Life, My Love, My Tara."

Shakily, Tara removed the yellow envelope and located the letter inside. She stared disbelieving at Johnny's undeniable handwriting, his last message to her. Did he suspect it would be? Tara held back the tears that urged to spill onto the page.

My Dearest Tara,

I can only hope and pray that I am beside you as you read this, My Love. The negligee is merely a diversion from the true gift contained within this box (the negligee and scarves are more of a gift to myself—to help us celebrate after you have read this letter). This was the only thing I truly needed to put in our final survival box—my promise to you of the never-ending, unsurpassable love that is yours, yours alone. I know you, Tara. Therefore, I know that mere material things wouldn't mean a thing to you, not as much as my words, my love, my promise, but most of all, my soul. You have never asked anything of me, yet you have tried to teach me, to teach me of the God you love, of the Heaven you believe in, of the goodness that you have known since childhood, but a goodness that had escaped my life, until you. I want you to know that I believe. I believe it all! I believe in your God, the one true God—omniscient, omnipresent, and omnipotent. I believe it, Tara. Not only that, but I know it is true, just as true as the love I have for you. My love will not fail you. I have no doubt, no doubt whatsoever, that our love will see us through this life and into the next—the eternal life! I'll be there with you, Tara! I'll be there, because I believe in God, and I believe in you! All of my undying love, Johnny

"It isn't fair," Tara cried, holding the letter to her heart. "He should be here. We would be happy. We would have our faith, our love and our baby. Those men stole it all when they took you, Johnny. They took it all away."

Blinking past her tears, Tara returned to I-20 to continue her mission. She looked once more at the addresses on the tiny paper beside her on the console. "Dallas, then Cancun, then Playa del Carmen...then Dave Danielson."

*****

Jade twisted and turned on the lumpy hotel mattress before opening her eyes in the darkness. She tried to make out the shadow of her friend lying on the bed across from her, but her eyes were slow to adjust to the darkness of the room.

"Tara?" she whispered into the gloom.

Noticing that something on the night table obstructed her view, she reached out to feel the cool plastic bags. "Tara?" she repeated into the night. She pushed the switch of a small table lamp. The faint light dimly lit the room, but allowed Jade to examine the blue plastic bags more closely. She quickly spotted the single paper above them. Bolting upright from the bed, she gaped at the vacated spot where Tara should have been sleeping then she grabbed the paper and read the note. "Oh, Tara, why? I would have helped you. We could have made them believe you!"

Jade dropped the note to the floor and fell to her knees. Moaning, aching in disbelief that her friend was gone, she bowed down and prayed. Her voice cracking, her throat stinging, her mind throbbing from fear for Tara, Jade pleaded, "I've never asked anything of You. I haven't had the faith that I should. But she has. You know she believes. You know she is good," Jade's stomach knotted as she continued, "God, be with her. And, please, let me find her, let me help her!"

Chapter Twelve

Straining to hold her swollen eyes open as she made her way through the lunch hour traffic of Dallas, Tara breathed a sigh of relief when she merged onto Texas Highway 183, less than twelve miles from the airport. She had made the drive in roughly eleven hours, due to the frequent stops at rest areas and gas stations to momentarily rest her eyes, drink a soda, or use the restroom.

Choosing to drive the extra distance to Dallas, rather than take a flight from New Orleans, was a minimal sacrifice compared to what she would have given up if someone had recognized her in the New Orleans airport. Plus, she had booked a later flight, giving her ample time to obtain a fake id. It'd been even easier than she thought, once she ventured toward one of the shady sides of town, though the kid that helped her out looked more like a college freshman than a crook. In any case, she had enough time to also locate a shopping mall, purchase a bag for traveling and buy appropriate clothing for the trip. She desperately needed to blend with fellow tourists in order to learn more about Mr. Danielson before she actually met the man—again.

As Tara entered the parking lot of a local mall, she visualized the driver, Dave Danielson, climbing out of the truck, ogling her as though she weren't human, as though she were a helpless animal caught in their dreadful trap. She shook her head to stop the images before she was forced to watch Johnny die again.

Trying to stay focused, Tara took some cash from her S1 supply, checked the mirror to make herself as presentable as possible, and headed into the Dallas stores. She thought of the large box of cash in the back seat of the car and shook the thought that someone would find it. "What kind of lunatic would leave that much cash in a box on the back seat?" she muttered to herself as she entered the mall. In no time, she had located a nice piece of luggage, not too large to carry on the plane, with plenty of compartments for storing cash. She purchased only a few clothing items, deciding that she needed more room for cash in the carry-on and that she would be able to buy most any clothing item in Mexico.

After an hour of shopping, Tara headed back to the Mustang, immediately acknowledging that all of her survival boxes were intact. She removed the tags from her new purchases and packed the suitcase with her clothing and cash. Placing the passport and identification for Ann James in the outer pocket, she was ready to go. Adding the scarves and negligee to the luggage, Tara began to feel as though she could actually accomplish what she'd planned; in a way, Johnny would be with her, and she needed all the help she could get.

Parking the Mustang at a long-term parking lot near the airport, she quickly moved the two survival boxes to the trunk. She had placed the S3 box, now empty, in a stack of other broken-down cardboard boxes behind the shopping mall to be burned with the remainder of the pile. Johnny's letter was tucked safely in a zippered compartment within her bag, easily accessible whenever she needed to feel close to him. She boarded the shuttle bus from the Park and Fly thinking of the two survival boxes remaining in the trunk of the green Mustang. "It'll be okay," she mumbled, sitting on the hard aluminum bench.

Misunderstanding her remark, the friendly driver assured her, "First time flyer, huh? Don't worry. It's a piece of cake. Here, chew this when the plane goes up. Helps the ears," he said, handing her a stick of gum.

For the first time since that horrible night, Tara smiled.

God, please take care of this kind man.

She stared blankly out the shuttle bus window as it neared the airport. She had prayed to Him again. It was such a natural thing for her to do. Her entire life had been spent praying to God, acknowledging Him, thanking Him, and glorifying His wonderful creations. Now, He had left her, and yet she still prayed. Why? He knew what she'd planned. Certainly He didn't listen to her prayers anymore. So why did she still pray to a God who let Johnny die? Tara bit her lip as the driver nudged her arm and abruptly halted the thoughts that were plaguing her mind.

"We're here, ma'am. Don't worry, now. You'll be fine."

Tara handed the man a rolled bill and thanked him for his kindness. She left the bus and headed to the ticketing line to pick up the boarding pass she had reserved last night.

Leaving the airport, the shuttle driver unrolled the wrinkled bill to place it with his small gathering of tips for the day. "Goodness," he exclaimed, his mouth falling open at the sight of Benjamin Franklin.

Ten minutes later, Tara handed the passport to the ticket attendant and waited. The man stared at the photos, glimpsed up to compare Tara to the picture and began keying in the appropriate information.

"Okay, Ms. James, you will board at Gate C-7." The young man handed the identification and boarding pass to Tara.

Relieved, she picked up the bag and prepared to walk away.

"Ms. James—"

Tara looked back at the attendant. Surely he hadn't recognized her, had he? Trying to remain calm, she politely answered, "Yes?"

"The hair color, nice change," he said with a bright smile.

"Thank you," she said, turning to leave the counter. She hadn't even thought about the drastic difference in the picture she had supplied for the identification and her new look. She glanced at the small passport photo. "That girl is gone," she declared, following the signs to Concourse C. "She's gone."

Boarding began promptly at 5:20. Tara looked at the boarding pass she held. Her seat assignment was 20-A. She had neglected to request an aisle seat; hopefully, fate would place her in the aisle. She liked having the ability to get up at her leisure, without having to rely on the passenger who'd been blessed with control of the aisle. Plus, the window seat always left her feeling claustrophobic and trapped.

She entered the plane and immediately noticed that the seats marked "A" were against the window. Well, at least it was a short flight. Maybe the seat next to her would remain vacant. Idle conversation with a stranger was not what Tara needed now, and the close proximity of seats on an airplane, in Coach class at least, somehow made strangers assume that you were instantaneously friends.

Luckily, the seat next to Tara was empty when she placed her bag in the overhead compartment. She sat in the assigned seat and peered out the window at the luggage truck parked below. As she watched a plane taxi in to dock at a nearby gate, Tara felt the seat give as a body plopped down next to her. She hesitated to look. Maybe the person would just let her be, leave her to think, and perhaps even let her sleep.

No such luck.

"Good afternoon," sang the voice.

Tara reluctantly turned. A rather large woman with an undeniably round face, wearing the loudest floral ensemble Tara had ever seen had plopped in the next seat. Jewelry adorned every appropriate body part. Rings on every finger, dangling earrings, multicolored beaded necklaces, and Tara was sure there were probably some toe rings on her feet, though she didn't verify the assumption. Hot pink blush formed two Raggedy Ann circles on her cheeks and her eyes were painted cyan.

As she took in the whole appearance and musical voice, Tara couldn't help but think that it must be nice to feel so good about life. A month ago, she would have welcomed conversation with a woman so perceptibly happy. Now, however, Tara didn't want to be reminded of the happiness that she'd lost. She didn't want to acknowledge that life was good; it wasn't. It never would be. Never again.

"Hello. Sally Albright. Nice to meet ya!" the floral woman sang. She shoved a plump hand toward Tara.

Tara took the hand and shook it, barely.

"What's your name, honey? Seeing as we're gonna be buddies for at least this part of the trip, we might as well start out the introductions, don't ya think?"

"Ann," Tara lied. "Ann James."

"Well, Ann, won't be much longer now, will it? Be up and soaring out of here in no time. Goodbye Lone Star State! See ya in two weeks!"

Tara turned her attention to the books provided in the pocket of the seat in front of her. Feeling a large one, Tara hoped that someone had left something she could read, or appear to be reading, to avoid talking to this woman for the duration of the nearly three-hour flight. Tugging the thick book from the pocket, Tara was stunned when she realized that the large book was a Bible.

Why are You doing this to me? Why put this here now? How many people bring their Bible on a plane? And why would they have left it? You meant for me to find this, didn't You? You're trying to change my plan. Well, I won't. I can't.

Chatting endlessly about everything from the weather to professional football, the flamboyant woman finally stopped talking when she noticed Tara thumbing through the pages of a Bible. Tara noticed the gap in the woman's conversation, but wasn't sure whether she had said something that required a response from Tara, or whether she had merely stopped to inhale.

"Now, that's something you don't see every day," the woman marveled. "Reading your Bible. That's what the world's missing, yes it is. We need to bring God out there for the world to see now, don't we? Well, good for you, little lady." She patted Tara's knee. "Good for you. You know I carry mine with me when I travel. I figure if the plane goes down, it wouldn't hurt to have Jesus there with me," she said with a giggle. "But you've got the right idea, yes you do," she said, waiting for the *Fasten Seat Belts* sign to go off as the plane ascended.

After hearing the bell acknowledging they could stand from their seats, the loud woman stood, stretched, opened the overhead compartment, and to Tara's surprise, extracted a giant print Bible that appeared to be brand new. "Now then, I think I'll just have a go of this too." She opened the book. The new pages crackled to life.

Tara kept her head ducked into the pages of the tattered Bible and hoped the lady would start reading her own, if only to leave Tara alone.

After about two blissful minutes of silence, Tara was pain-stricken to hear the lady take a deep breath and begin rattling on again. This time, she attempted to show her knowledge of scripture, which, Tara quickly observed, was quite limited.

"So, my favorite passage is the twenty-third Psalm. I've been able to recite it from memory since I was just a young girl in Beaumont. Don't you just love the twenty-third Psalm? Do you have a favorite verse? What would it be? Can you quote it, or would you like for me to look it up for you? This Table of Contents really helps you to find the books easily; there are so many of them! I'd be lost without this wonderful list to guide me."

"Sixty-six," Tara said without looking up.

"I'm sorry, dear. Sixty-six what?" she asked.

"Sixty-six books in the Bible."

"Well, I knew there were plenty of them," the woman marveled again. "What about that favorite verse of yours? What would it be? You seem to really know your stuff."

Tara thought of her favorite Bible verse, or what had always been her favorite verse. She answered the woman, "My favorite verse had always been John 11:35."

Immediately, the woman located the page number for John, found the verse and read, "Jesus wept." She stared awkwardly at Tara. "That's your favorite verse? It's—well, it's short—easy to remember, I guess."

"It's the shortest verse in the Bible," Tara affirmed. "Jesus cried when he learned his friend Lazarus had died and that the sisters of Lazarus, Mary and Martha, were so grievous over the loss of their brother."

"So, your favorite verse is when Jesus showed the human quality of sadness because of the death of his friend," the lady said, nodding her head.

"No," Tara said plainly. "It was my favorite verse because Lazarus had finally left this sinful world and was in a much better place, and Jesus cried because he had to bring him back, back to the world of sorrow, hurt and pain, in order for others to see God's glory. Jesus showed how wonderful Heaven is by showing how distraught he was to bring someone back to Earth. That is why it was my favorite verse."

Startled by Tara's remarks, the woman composed herself enough to ask the obvious. "You said it 'was' your favorite verse. Is it no longer your favorite?"

"No."

"Well, what verse could mean more to you than that?" she asked impatiently. She chewed on a cuticle beside a flaming hot pink nail.

"If I had to have a favorite verse now, it would be—" Tara began as she knowledgeably turned the pages, "Deuteronomy 32:41."

Eagerly, the woman located Deuteronomy, found the verse and recited, "I sharpen my flashing sword and my hand grasps it in judgment, I will take vengeance on my adversaries and repay those who hate me."

Tara continued thumbing through the pages and peering over scripture.

Rendered speechless, the large woman stared straight ahead for the flight's duration.

Chapter Thirteen

Steamboat Springs

Three weeks had passed since Chet had left his two best friends in Tampa; four weeks had passed since Mardi Gras. He had no doubt that Billy's frequent phone calls weren't merely to chat; Billy was checking up on him. Evidently, Billy knew that Chet wouldn't be able to lose the recurring memory of that awful night. The girl's body had yet to be found. Billy assumed they would find her eventually; they were just looking in the wrong places. The police were probably concentrating on Lake Pontchartrain and the surrounding streets near the location where Johnny Boudreaux's truck was found, at least that's what Billy thought. Chet wasn't so sure. What if the police were merely letting people *think* that they had no real leads? What if, somehow, they knew exactly who had killed them, and eventually, they would find the murderers.

Chet walked aimlessly through the village shops of downtown Steamboat, letting his mind wander through the endless possibilities of what was actually occurring in New Orleans. Did the police suspect anyone? Did they suspect him? He tried to tell himself to be reasonable. If the police had any leads, they would have acted on them. Nevertheless, Chet tensed each time a local policeman met him on the busy street.

Maneuvering through the masses that crowded the normally calm street, he realized that the town was saturated with the Spring Break crowd from the east coast. Spring Break was here and he hadn't even noticed. He would need to oversee several of the activities that his resort had planned for the hectic week. He tried to concentrate on remembering exactly what he had scheduled for the week, but he couldn't recall one activity. Perplexed, he stopped to sit on a street bench and think.

"Mr. Garrison, is that you? Yes. Mr. Garrison. It is you, isn't it?" the extremely southern, undeniably female voice hummed.

Chet looked up to see three attractive women approaching him. In vain, he tried to place them. They were young, probably college-aged and drop-dead gorgeous.

Drop dead. Chet winced, saw the big man's body as it fell to the pavement with a colossal thud. Saw the dark waters of the Pontchartrain open up and swallow him whole.

The spokeswoman for the chatty females, a lean blonde with an alluring smile, leaned toward Chet and offered a friendly hug.

"Mr. Garrison, are you all right?" she asked. "You're not even wearing a jacket and you look—well, you're sweating!"

Chet thought of his appearance. He had been so preoccupied when he left the resort that he had forgotten a jacket. His red hair had probably grayed instantly from the falling snow, and he always perspired profusely when he was worried. He realized how peculiar he must have looked sitting alone on a bench in the middle of the day, as though he had nothing better to do.

"I—I guess I'm feeling a bit under the weather," he stammered.

"Would you like some help?" the blonde offered.

"Well, I've seen you before," he admitted, "but I'm at a loss for the names."

"That's okay. I only met you once. My name is Georgia. We met when I registered for the 'Strings of the Springs' contest."

Chet suddenly recalled flirting with the gorgeous southern belle when she'd registered for the newest contest hosted by The Summit. "I remember now," he said. "You're Georgia from Tennessee."

Flattered that he now remembered her, she giggled before she introduced her friends. "We're all from Tennessee, actually. This is Shelby; she has also entered the contest," Georgia said, gesturing toward a shapely red-haired beauty who looked remarkably similar to a centerfold Chet kept in his desk. "And this is Hallie; she didn't enter the contest though. She's got her eye on a preacher in town, and I guess she figures he'll be turned off if she heads down the mountain wearing just a bit more than dental floss. That is what it takes to win, isn't it? The smaller the better in a bikini contest, don't you think, Mr. Garrison? I mean, you are one of the judges, aren't you?"

"Georgia, you are atrocious!" the petite brunette exclaimed. "Please forgive her boldness, Mr. Garrison. Sometimes it's hard for me to actually believe she's from the south at all!" Hallie continued.

"Did you say something about a preacher in town?" Chet said, still staring at the stunning trio.

"Oh, yes. Hallie is interested in Brother McClain, Matthias McClain. He preaches at the small Community church here. You know, the charming building on the hill as you're leaving town," Georgia informed.

"I'm sure he isn't interested in my social life," Hallie said, her face reddening.

"Oh, but I am," Chet said. "I may need to talk to him. To a preacher, I mean. To discuss some things for The Summit, of course." Chet tried to remember the last time he had stepped foot in a church, but couldn't.

"Is your resort going to start performing marriage ceremonies or something like that? What a novel idea, getting married on the mountain!" Georgia exclaimed.

"Yes. Well, you never know what tourists will be interested in, do you?"

"No, you don't. I would have never thought of skiing down a mountain in less clothing than my—"

"Georgia, please, stop," Hallie commanded, while Shelby burst into a fit of girlish giggles.

"Well, ladies, I really have to be going. It was good seeing you, Georgia. Nice to meet you, Shelby, Hallie," Chet said. He briskly walked away, intent on catching the city shuttle to the church.

*****

Matthias had completed his notes on the fourth chapter of Luke and his sermon outline entitled "The Temptation of Jesus." He wondered how many members of his congregation had noticed the number of lessons emphasizing fornication and temptation since Miss Hallie Davenport had arrived. If they had, perhaps they would think that the sermons were entirely for the beautiful brunette, instead of primarily for Matthias.

Of course, Matthias had never been one to insinuate that his sermons were not meant as much for himself as for the fellow church members. However, this particular group of lessons had been most certainly taught for his own benefit. Hallie had been tempting him more than he thought possible, but he couldn't give in to physical temptation. He wanted more, and he didn't feel anything more than physical attraction for the young girl. Matthias prayed daily, not only for God to give him the strength to resist the temptation, but also for God to send the right woman. He was thirty-five. God had acknowledged that Adam needed a woman in Genesis. Surely He knew that Matthias needed one too.

As he closed his Bible and put his notes away, Matthias heard the church door slam. He stood and made his way to open the door to his office wondering who might need help from him, or from God.

For a moment, he thought that a homeless person in need of shelter had entered the building. He stepped toward the man and noticed that his clothing was soaked, his hair damp and disheveled, and that he seemed to be shaking.

"Can I help you?" Matthias asked, approaching the nervous visitor.

Chet turned to face the preacher, his face showing surprise at the preacher's appearance. No wonder the young brunette seemed so captivated. "Are you Brother McClain?"

"I am. How can I assist you?"

"My name is Chet, Chet Garrison. I needed someone to talk to. I thought you might be able to help."

"With the Lord's help, I'll try," Matthias answered. "Why don't you come sit in my office? Would you like a cup of hot cider? I have some already made."

"No thanks," Chet said, following Brother Matthias into his tiny office. The furniture was mismatched, but still fairly comfortable when he sat down. He wasn't sure exactly why he was here, but it couldn't hurt.

"Now, you said you needed to talk. What is bothering you, Mr. Garrison?" Matthias pleasantly inquired. In the light of his office, he now noticed that the man was definitely not homeless. He was dressed impeccably from head to toe. Obviously, he wasn't in need of shelter; he was distraught, and in desperate need of the Lord.

"About a month ago, I—well, some friends and I—we did something. Something really terrible," Chet stuttered.

Matthias stood from his seat, walked around the desk and sat in the chair across from Chet. Knowing that this poor soul was undeniably bothered by a past sin, Matthias wanted to help him feel secure as he confessed, and help him realize the power of God's forgiveness.

Chet chewed on his lower lip. His eyes darted wildly around the room. "I can't. I was wrong. I don't need to talk. I can't talk to you about it."

"It's okay, Mr. Garrison. Perhaps you aren't ready to talk about it to me, but you can still talk to God. If you feel that you've done something wrong in God's eyes, pray to Him. Talk to Him. Tell Him how you feel," Matthias advised.

As Matthias spoke, Chet realized that this preacher, this man of God, had no idea what he had done. He didn't know about New Orleans. How could he? No one else knew either. Pray to God? He hadn't prayed to God since—since—well, he couldn't remember when. Besides, he wasn't even sure God existed. If He did exist, why would He have allowed them to commit that murder in the first place? No. He didn't need to pray to God. He didn't need to talk to this preacher either. What he needed to do was claim his life again. Why should he sit around worrying about whether or not he was going to get caught? He should be as calm about what happened as Dave and Billy. Yes, things were going back to normal. Forget Mardi Gras. If anything, now he knew that he could get away with just about anything.

Even murder.

Maybe he had looked at this all wrong. Maybe Dave and Billy had the right idea.

He cleared his throat. "I'm sorry. I wasted your time. I don't need to talk, preacher."

Matthias saw it at once. This man, Mr. Garrison, had changed before his eyes. He had been looking at Matthias, but his mind was somewhere else. Somewhere evil. He had actually smirked. Demons were definitely at work on this man's soul.

"I would be happy to talk to you at a more convenient time, perhaps after you've had some time to talk to God, to think and pray about—"

"I don't need to pray. I was wrong to come here. Sorry to have bothered you," Chet said, promptly heading for the door. "I'll find my way out."

"If you ever decide you do need someone to talk to, I would be glad to help," Matthias called.

Chet stepped out of the small building feeling ready to go back to the life he had before New Orleans. "No more fear," he said as he walked across the church parking lot to wait for the city shuttle.

A bright red 4-Runner pulled into the lot directly in Chet's path. Immediately, Chet recognized the driver and grinned.

"I thought I might find you here. Need a ride?" Georgia yelled.

"You just made my day," he said. He climbed into the truck, leaned over, kissed the gorgeous woman and added, "Maybe you can make my night as well."

Georgia smiled at the rich resort owner, laughing as they left the church.

And Brother Matthias McClain.

Chapter Fourteen

Playa del Carmen, Mexico

Three weeks had passed since Tara had stepped off of the plane in Cancun. Mexico wasn't foreign to her; she had been here several times for mission work with her parents and once with Johnny, but that was another life ago. However, even though she was familiar with the people, culture and language, she had never seen the commercial aspect of Mexico.

Cancun, with its endless stretch of high-rise condos and American fast food restaurants, seemed shockingly like any beach town on Florida's panhandle. On the other hand, Playa del Carmen, merely forty miles from Cancun, still had the image of pristine Mexico, definitely set apart from the decaying locations where Tara had performed endless work projects, but still radiating the splendor of the country without all of the neon.

When she hadn't been watching *him*, or memorizing his daily routine, Tara had taken time to walk the village streets of Playa del Carmen. Similar to the outdoor flea markets of Alabama and Georgia, the village was jam-packed with locals displaying their possessions for sale, varying from hand-painted Mexican pottery to brightly colored, intricately woven hammocks, to exquisite jewelry. Prices were intensely negotiable, which made everyone who entered one of the breezy shops feel as though they had found the deal of a lifetime. Tara enjoyed speaking with the shop owners; it gave her peace, and put her mind off the task at hand.

Once she had learned her way around Playa del Carmen, it hadn't taken her long to learn about "Mr. Danielson" and the affluent American's lifestyle. Although many of the locals resented the young, handsome man who reaped the most benefit from every tourist that ventured into Playa, no one seemed willing to challenge him for the position.

Tara had quickly learned that Dave Danielson owned the one company that scheduled all tourist activities for the Playa locale. Evidently, whenever a similar corporation attempted to begin business in the area, something would happen to impede the progress, until finally the business plans would halt, leaving the hopeful entrepreneur to wonder what went wrong. Or, more accurately, why Dave Danielson wouldn't let them be. If it wasn't enough deterrence to make their business license impossible to obtain, Danielson would simply make the actual business location disappear, usually by having it burned to the ground. Although Playa Police suspected his guilt in the matter, it had never been proven, and the sleek American continued getting richer due to the monopoly.

Armed with the knowledge that Dave Danielson had made far greater enemies than friends, Tara felt strengthened by the fact that most Playans wouldn't mind it if something were to happen to the wealthy crook, some sort of odd, unaccountable tragic accident.

Helping Tara in her preparations was the fact that Dave Danielson, like most people, was a creature of habit. She had been relatively surprised at how easy she had pinpointed his daily routine, which was implausibly predictable, once she had studied him enough. Watching him wasn't even a problem; everyone watched Dave Danielson. From the way he smiled, laughed and waved to those he met throughout the day, Tara assumed he was quite unaware that the returned smiles hid gritted teeth, jealous eyes and loathing. That would prove a definite advantage.

Quite a ladies' man, the dashing Danielson wasn't shaken at all by the female stares he received as he jogged through the village streets each morning. Tara had seen him even glance her way a time or two as she sat sipping mango juice or reading a book on a local shop's terrace. He had flexed his bare pectorals and smiled; however, when she returned to her juice or book, Dave promptly increased his speed in search of the next admiring onlooker.

His morning routine began promptly at 6:30 a.m., when he left his lavish beach condo, and the ebony-haired beauty he shared it with, to begin a five-mile run down the beach, through the village and back to the condo. By 9:00 a.m., he'd leave the condo again, always dressed casually but impeccably, to drive to his nearby office.

Precisely at noon, Dave Danielson's assistant would leave the office, making her way to either of three local restaurants to pick up Danielson's choice of lunch for the day. And at exactly 4:00 p.m., he left the office and returned to the condo. It was simple. His days were virtually the same. For three weeks she surveyed his every move, and the days never varied. His nights, conversely, were another story entirely.

As methodical as Dave Danielson's days were, his nights were as chaotic. Each night was another chance to try out a different party and partake of another female's charms. Although Dave ended every night, usually between 1:00 and 2:00 a.m., by going back to his lover at the condo they shared, his evening hours prior to that were virtually his own, and he took advantage of every minute.

He usually turned up at one of several popular clubs known for enticing visiting tourists to "let their hair down and let loose." At these clubs, he'd determine which female would share a portion of the evening exclusively with him. Tara had watched him make his exit, arm-in-arm with whomever he surmised was the most striking woman present and proceed to romance her as they slowly made their way to the beach.

Occasionally, the two wouldn't even make it to his Mexican villa, which sat merely a couple of miles from his condo. Tara had actually witnessed one of these encounters from the rooftop of the hacienda she had rented, just five doors down from Danielson's villa. With her hand covering her mouth and her stomach buckling at the disgust of it, she saw them. His hand was on her waist, sliding lower, lower. The woman turned to face him, allowing him to kiss her, allowing him to do whatever he pleased. In less than two heated minutes, Dave had easily undressed the woman, placed her own dress between their bodies and the sand, and proceeded to have sex with her under the moonlight. Tara had barely made it into the bathroom before vomiting.

*****

Tara knew that the best time to approach Dave Danielson was during those late evening hours when his schedule was uncertain. Patience would be the key to success. She would have to wait for the perfect night, the perfect moment, the perfect place.

Tara watched him for five weeks before it finally happened. As had become her usual routine for the evening, she located the bar where he was aggressively partying inside, found a table hidden in virtual darkness on the veranda and proceeded to sit, sipping on a virgin pina colada. Silently, she watched, listened, waited.

Tonight's bar, *El Futbol*, was covered in soccer paraphernalia, primarily for Mexico, in vibrant color combinations of green, white, and red. A soccer ball rolling down the back streets of Playa del Carmen followed by hordes of excited children was a constant daily reminder of the enthusiasm for the game. Boisterous cheers and applause roared from *El Futbol* as tourists and locals shared in the excitement of the nearing World Cup.

On this particular night, a large group composed primarily of European tourists cornered Dave Danielson and were visibly upset with the American. Even with music blaring and televisions booming, Tara still heard every word of the intense conversation.

"You said these tickets were TST Category One, valued at two thousand four hundred U.S. dollars. You said these were the same tickets that FIFA restricted to four tickets per household," the Frenchman said. He waved a handful of tickets toward Dave. Tara shifted her chair to get a better view of the display taking place inside.

Danielson smiled at the bulky man, who appeared to be about the same size as Tara imagined Olympic wrestlers. If Mr. Danielson was nervous, he wasn't showing it. Instead, he tried to explain.

"That's exactly what I told you, because that is exactly what they are. You are holding fifty TST's, team-specific tickets, meaning that you can follow the team of your choice all the way to the final game, if they reach it. And France, of course, should be there."

Glaring at Danielson, the Frenchman argued, "I know that France will be there, you fool! I also know that they will win, as they should! But, what I also know is that these tickets, for which I paid you two thousand U.S. Dollars each, are Category Three tickets, valued at less than two hundred U.S. Dollars, not Category One! Did you not think I would verify the tickets? Did you not think I would learn of your scheme, filthy American?"

Dave's face tinted scarlet as the blood rushed to his head. "I am sure there must be some misunderstanding. I was sure that these were Category One. Give me a couple of days to check into the mistake. I'll make sure that you get the tickets you paid for. Let's just be reasonable about this."

"I do not want tickets from you, thief! I want my money. I want it all. One hundred thousand U.S. Dollars by tomorrow morning, or you will see first-hand the wrath of France," the colossal man bellowed as he stormed out of the bar.

Tara watched Dave retrieve a starched white handkerchief from his back pocket and wipe his forehead. His face still reddened from the heat of battle, he looked exceedingly bothered as he began ordering straight shots of tequila.

For the next hour, Dave drank steadily, while the additional patrons of *El Futbol* talked up their favorite teams. Tara remained patient, biding her time, until finally he staggered onto the veranda and collapsed to the ground, not three feet from where she sat, where she had been all night, silently stalking her prey.

Chapter Fifteen

Disturbed by the fact that his and Billy's latest scheme had started to unravel, Dave resolved to drink himself into a stupor before stumbling home and calling his friend. Worse than Dave loathed giving the money back to the Frenchman, he dreaded telling Billy that their plan had failed. Luckily, Billy was far enough away that Dave didn't have to worry about him taking out his anger personally.

Or did he?

Dave had told Billy that this scheme wouldn't work. Anyone who had been staying on top of the soccer world knew the difference between the varying categories associated with the team-specific tickets. Granted, the team-specific tickets had only been available the past few years, but what kind of idiot would pay a hundred thousand dollars for fifty tickets without verifying that he had the real deal? Billy should have known it wouldn't work. He should have known.

Dave propped himself against the railing of the porch and tried to decipher which direction he should walk to get home. And where should he go? The villa, without a woman to share it with? Or Maria at the condo? He had been so busy with that crazed Frenchman that he hadn't been able to spend any time with the gorgeous beauties that had originally attracted him to this bar. Why should he go to the villa? But he wasn't really ready to go home to Maria either.

For a moment, Dave pondered simply sleeping the worst of the tequila off on the porch. Holding the railing, he slowly edged his way down to the deck and sat, propping himself, trying to maintain his balance.

"Hello, Mr. Danielson," a very soft, very sensual, very female voice purred.

Dave tried to clear his thoughts as he turned to view the pair of beautifully sculpted legs in high navy heels. He smiled as he realized the night might not turn out to be a total disaster, and he wished he hadn't taken in quite so much tequila.

"Hello," he answered to the beautiful lady now crouched down beside him. She stared at him with the most vivid eyes he had ever seen. How had he missed this one tonight?

"You seem to be feeling poorly. Can I help?" She put her arm around him and helped him stand.

"I'd never refuse the help of a lady," Dave whispered, trying to sound as though he weren't totally intoxicated, though his slurring betrayed his attempt. He couldn't help but stare at the exquisite woman. Her hair, a vivid red, accented dark eyes. Creamy skin shone in the moonlight against her silky navy cocktail dress. Her figure was petite, but curved. Just right. Perfect. Stunning.

Dave desperately wished he weren't inebriated and hoped he would sober up soon. He knew that he would have her, but he wanted to make sure he remembered it afterwards. Such a beautiful stranger, yet something about her seemed almost...familiar.

"Can I help to get you home?" the striking woman offered.

"Anything you'd be willing to help me with would be just fine," Dave responded. "I don't live very far away. It's just—"

"I know where you live," she whispered into his ear as she led him from the bar.

"Do I know you?" he asked, stumbling alongside Tara.

"We're neighbors, so to speak. I'm renting a house five doors down from your villa. I've seen you around," she enlightened.

Feed his ego. Keep his guard down.

Dave's chest swelled with the knowledge that practically everyone knew him as a prominent businessman. Excellent. This deal with the Frenchman was a minor setback. Dave would give him the money, forget about it, and move on to bigger and better things. Like more women, like *this* woman, tonight. He tried to take an eager step forward, but stumbled again as the tequila took its toll.

"It's okay. I'll help you," she soothed, guiding him down the walkway and helping him into a cab parked on the cobbled street.

"We don't need a cab. It isn't far. We could just—" he began.

"I don't think you're in any condition to walk the beach right now, Mr. Danielson," Tara reasoned.

Not the beach. Not with me. Besides, I need you to stay as drunk as possible. I can't let you walk it off. I need all the help I can get.

"I guess you're right," he muttered as he listened to her recite his address to the cab driver. "My address, how did you know?"

"I told you," Tara answered, patting his arm reassuringly, "We're neighbors."

"Right," Dave responded, his head swaying slightly as they drove the short distance to the villa.

Tara paid the cab driver and helped Dave from the car. His breathing had steadied, and he walked more assuredly now. She wondered if this might not have been the perfect night. Perhaps he didn't drink as much alcohol as she had originally thought; but then again, it was too late to turn back now.

Dave pulled the villa key from his pocket and fumbled with the lock. Tara brushed against him to help him with the key. Dave instinctively leaned toward her, breathing in her scent, running his arm around her waist and then slowly, slowly moving it down the curve of her hips. His hand slid against the silky fabric of her skirt until he finally reached her bare legs. He pressed against her, pushing all of his weight alongside her, feeling every wonderful curve.

Tara wanted to scream, but she didn't dare. She wanted to stop him, but she couldn't. This was part of the plan. This was the part she dreaded most, even more than what she would do later. He had helped murder Johnny and yet he was here, touching her, wanting her. She finally managed to turn the key.

"There now, we're in. It's just the two of us now," she whispered into his ear. Opening the door, she created a hint of distance between them as she slid her hand down the wall to find the light. She flipped the switch, instantly illuminating the entire villa.

"No," Dave whispered, kissing her neck.

Tara tried not to cringe.

"Watch," he continued. He switched off the light and pressed a knob beneath the switch. Immediately, the room was illuminated again, but it was softer, intensely romantic. Tara observed the tiny star-like lights that had been embedded into the walls and ceiling. The entire villa had been transformed to a vision of outdoors, a place for the most intimate of moments, an evening under the stars. The type of place she would have loved to have spent a night with Johnny.

Tara's stomach quaked.

I can't. I can't do it. Why am I here? Dear God, I'm scared!

"What do you think?" Dave purred into her ear while his arms continued to wrap around her, gradually moving down her spine, then up her back, gathering the silken fabric of the dress within his hands. Tara felt the bareness of her legs as he easily glided the skirt upward, grabbing handfuls of the shimmery fabric and pulling her closer, closer.

"I have a surprise for you," she said anxiously.

"I love surprises."

"Not here. The bedroom."

"Bedrooms are so—ordinary," Dave challenged, now running his tongue under her shoulder strap, working it slowly but surely down her arm.

"Trust me," Tara said. She stepped away, pushed the strap back in place and took his hand, "It will be anything but ordinary."

Dave stumbled a bit as he attempted to lead Tara to his room. "Well, then, that's different. The bedroom it is, but I must tell you— there isn't much I haven't seen. Of course, I haven't seen anything of you yet, now have I?"

"Oh, I'm sure you haven't seen anything like this," she said. "I would bet my life on it."

I am betting my life on it, aren't I? Oh, dear God. No. I can't pray now. Why am I here? Why don't I just leave?

"Well, what do you think?" Dave asked, indicating the elaborate décor of the master bedroom.

Tara already knew exactly how the room would appear. She had a perfect view through the patio doors of her own rented hacienda into Dave's illustrious bedroom, with its marbled columns and mirrored wall. She had seen the room illuminated several times when Dave allowed his female guests a view, before turning out the lights and turning his attention to his guest.

Now, as Tara examined, she understood exactly why he wanted them to see the magnitude of this room. It was remarkable. Combinations of creamy marble with golden accents gave it a look of sheer opulence. Dave stumbled across the floor, eventually locating a knob placed to the right of the bed. When he slowly turned it, Tara understood exactly why the light had never stayed on for long when she'd viewed the room before. With a twist, the bright lights were extinguished, and several simulated candles glowed from all sections of the room. As incredible as it was when fully lit, Dave's elaborate boudoir was even more beautiful in the subdued candlelight. Each sparkling light stood atop an elegant pewter candlestick. Although the candlesticks hadn't stood out when the room was fully lit, now they seemed to be everywhere, and the scene was absolutely breathtaking.

Johnny would have loved this.

"Well, what do you think?" Dave whispered. He leisurely moved closer to Tara.

"It's amazing," she whispered.

"Yes, it is, isn't it? Now, you said you had a surprise for me." He sat on the end of the bed and motioned for her to come to him, patting his lap to show her exactly where she should sit.

Tara edged her way toward Dave, stopping just before reaching the bed.

"I do have a surprise for you, one you'll always remember, but you have to lie down first."

Dave smiled wickedly as he pushed his body back on the large bed and, propping a pillow under his head, prepared for the show. "I'm ready," he said, tossing an eager grin at the sexy lady. He thought of the many women who had earnestly tried to satisfy him by trying to be unique; it was extremely rare for one to actually do something that he hadn't seen before, but somehow, he thought this one might be able to pull it off.

His smile broadened as he looked at her and anticipated what she'd planned. She was definitely more exquisite than anyone he had slept with in quite a while. He tried to pinpoint it exactly, and then he decided—she was alluring. Yes, that was it. All of the women he brought here were pretty; some were beautiful. But this one was different.

Generally, he brought women here simply because he wanted to be with a woman, not a particular woman. If he wanted a particular woman, he could go home to Maria. No, he brought women here because he simply wanted to experience the variety of women that the world had to offer. It had never really mattered what woman was here, merely that he had one to fulfill that need. But this time, he wanted her. As he watched, she opened her beaded navy evening bag and began to withdraw something golden, sheer and glittery, and he realized that this woman had every intention of making this night unforgettable.

Tara laid the golden scarves on the edge of the bed.

You're with me now, Johnny. You're helping me. I can do it. I can do it because of what he did to you.

Tara took one of the flowing scarves and tied it around Dave's right wrist. Forcefully, she pulled the scarf toward the headboard, leaning slightly to tie it securely around the marble post. Dave twisted toward her, playfully nudging his face against her chest, licking the small curve of her breast exposed by the shifting fabric. He mischievously offered her the other wrist.

"Here, by all means, let me help," he whispered.

Without a word, Tara tied the second scarf around the other wrist. She seductively stretched herself across the bed, allowing her chest to hover less than an inch above Dave's face as she fastened the second scarf to the opposite marble post. Unable to resist the temptation, Dave lifted his head and began wildly kissing every inch of Tara's exposed flesh, trying desperately to move the silky navy barrier.

"Not yet," Tara said, reaching for another scarf.

Moving to the foot of the bed, she gently removed Dave's woven leather shoes before wrapping the soft scarf around his ankle.

"Aren't you forgetting something?" Dave asked when she secured the scarf to the third marble post.

"What would that be?" Tara asked intently, knowing exactly what he was going to say.

"My clothes. Your clothes. Did you forget about them?" Dave chuckled, thinking he had found a fault in her plan.

"I haven't forgotten anything." She climbed onto the bed and reached for his cotton shirt. "I just thought it would be more fun this way," she said, grabbing the thin fabric and pulling it from his chest to send the tiny buttons popping free.

Dave's body lifted slightly with the sudden movement, partly because she had pulled him upward, more accurately because he was aching with desire to be closer, much closer to the intriguing woman.

Tara moved to grab the last scarf, aware that her last move may have been too intense. However, she knew that to keep him off-guard, to keep the upper hand, she had to convince him this was all part of the sexual fantasy. She had to keep up the charade until she was sure he couldn't escape.

Dave stared at the beautiful woman as she wrapped the final scarf around his ankle. He still wore his khaki shorts, the only article still clothing him and was eagerly anticipating the moment when she would rip them off too. He smiled when he imagined how surprised she would be when she learned that he wore nothing underneath.

After securing the last scarf, Tara knew she still needed to make absolutely certain he couldn't get free.

"Now," she purred, "we're going to play a little game."

"I love games."

"This one's fairly simple. If you can free yourself from one scarf, I will remove one article of clothing. If you can free yourself of two, I'll remove two. If—"

"I get it," Dave said with an evil grin. "Now, you and your clothes should get ready for a quick parting of the ways. And I want you to take them off very slowly, by the way."

He began violently twisting, turning, and pulling at the scarves, trying to free himself. After several minutes of intense effort, Tara started to feel comfortable with her position. Then the scarf on his left leg, the last one she had tied, loosened and ultimately fell to the floor.

Tara gasped.

"Okay," Dave panted, "I'm too drunk to keep trying, but I've earned one thing to come off now. I'm going to assume the rest will come later."

Tara wished desperately that she hadn't already removed her heels when she entered the villa. But, she had to keep up the façade. She had to keep him off-guard, so there was no other choice. She crossed her arms in front of her chest and pushed both index fingers underneath the silky straps of the dress, gently pushing them off her shoulders. The silken material slid easily down her arms and rested on the curve of her hips.

Dave stared in wonder as he saw the sexy, sapphire and golden lace negligee she wore underneath. It was practically translucent, not really covering her body, but accentuating it. The look of her in that sheer fabric, shimmering in the candlelight, was more erotic than anything he had imagined. Then he noticed that she hadn't made an effort to slide the dress past her hips.

"You haven't removed it yet," he observed, trying to mask his anticipation.

"I will," Tara answered, slowly making her way to the fallen scarf. "I just have to make sure we can continue the game."

She knotted the scarf around his ankle and then to the marble post.

"Now, try to get it free," she instructed.

Still fairly exhausted from the last effort, Dave tried to liberate the leg. "I can't. I'm completely at your mercy now. And now that you've got what you wanted, lose the dress," he commanded with an evil smirk.

Tara gently shifted her hips, allowing the navy fabric to slip down her legs to the marble floor. The negligee was cut high, allowing a mere sliver of lacy material to pass through the center of her legs. Dave moaned at the vision. She was perfect, and he wanted her. Now.

Feeling assured that he was confined by the scarves, Tara casually picked up a torn piece of fabric from Dave's shirt and climbed onto the bed.

"I can only imagine what you're planning to do with that," he teased. He was thoroughly enjoying himself. Even if he was painfully aware of his desire for her, he had decided that this woman knew exactly what to do to give him a night to remember, and he fully intended on letting her do whatever she desired. Much to Dave's surprise and delight, she moved her body on top of him. His heart beat rapidly as he felt the heat of her body against him, with only a sliver of fabric between them.

"Just one more part of the surprise," Tara whispered into his ear as she slid the torn fabric across his neck.

"I can't wait," he responded, eager to see what else she had in store for him.

Tara brought the long scrap of cloth up to his face, covered his eyes and tied it securely.

"No peeking," she said. "Can you see anything?"

"Not a thing. But I can feel everything, everything, pretty baby," Dave growled, shifting his hips underneath hers.

Pretty baby.

"Looks like we've got ourselves a live one, Chet. What's the matter, pretty baby, haven't found anyone to give you what you need lately? Looks like this fellow here is the only thing between us and that little vixen, what do you think, Billy?"

Tara cleared her thoughts and reached for a pillow. Still moaning, Dave waited for her to make her move. She took a deep breath, grabbed tightly to the pillow and pressed it to his face.

Confused about this part of the game, Dave shifted, trying to free his mouth, trying to ask her what was going on. And then…understanding.

Tara felt his body shudder with realization and she put all of her weight against the pillow. She could hear his muffled voice as he attempted to yell, but his screams could not be heard. She continued pressing, pushing with all of her might, as his restricted body lurched violently, fighting for air. He was strong, very strong, but the tequila and the confinement of the scarves were rendering him virtually helpless.

"How does it feel," she hissed, holding the pillow down with all of her strength. "How does it feel to realize you're dying? How do you think Johnny felt? How do you think I felt when you took the one thing that made my life complete? How does it feel? How—does—it—feel!" she screamed as she struggled to press the pillow tightly against his limp body, against his *lifeless* body.

Tara stopped.

Dave Danielson lay motionless on the bed, pillow still resting on his head. She collapsed to the floor and cried.

Trying to determine what to do now, she grabbed the side of the bed and stood, staring at his body, seeing what she had done, but still not believing.

Tara swiftly found her dress and put it on. She grabbed her evening bag, opened it and walked toward the bed. She had to get Johnny's scarves. Trying not to look at Dave Danielson's still body, she frantically untied the knot connecting one of the glittery scarves to the headboard. When it was free, she moved to the wrist. Within seconds, she held the first scarf. She was stuffing the scarf into her evening bag when she felt something brush against her back. She turned just as his hand reached again, swinging through the air. He caught her, and then violently, aggressively closed his large hand around her neck.

Pillow dislodged, Dave Danielson glared at her, intent on what he had to do. His free hand tightened the grip on her neck, pulled her down to the bed, and gripped her throat powerfully.

Tara brought both hands to her throat, trying to pry his hand off, but he held firm. His hold seemed to grow stronger, as she felt herself getting weaker. She crumpled to the bed as he held her there.

"Johnny? I heard you! I remember you, the little vixen! You thought you could hurt me? Actually believed you could kill me, didn't you? Well, there will be a death here tonight, but it won't be mine!" Dave roared, tightening his hold.

Tara struggled hysterically, trying to get free. She removed her arms from her throat and began flinging them wildly, kicking her legs, thrashing her body, anything to get free.

Dave held her as tightly as possible while she fought. He eyed the bonds that held his other arm and his legs. If he could just get the other arm free, he wouldn't be struggling at all. He wanted the other arm free, if for no other reason so that he could hurt her more intensely as she died.

He never saw it coming. Dave turned from staring at the captive arm to see a blur of silver as it crashed into his forehead. Tara fell to the floor when he released the grip. She scrambled to her feet, whirling the pewter candlestick again, this time connecting with his cheek. Dave's free hand instantly moved to shield his face, but Tara's momentum triggered a fury of blows to his head that he couldn't defend.

When she had finally finished, Dave Danielson was dead, his body lying in a mass of bloody sheets.

Still holding the pewter candlestick, Tara stood and turned away from the awful image that she had created. She grabbed her bag, removed the one golden scarf, and wrapped it around the candlestick before dropping it to the floor. Slowly, mechanically, she left Dave Danielson's villa, stumbled down the street to her hacienda, and showered. Then she gathered her things, packed her suitcase and stepped into the night.

Chapter Sixteen

Chelem, Mexico

Kaleb Andrews stood on the porch of the supply house waiting for the youngest members of the teenage group of volunteers to catch up. He had guided them through their daily work projects for the past ten days and enjoyed every minute of it. The enthusiasm of this group was awe-inspiring to say the least, and he hadn't heard one complaint. As a matter of fact, the teens kept thanking him for letting them be a part of something so worthwhile, something so life-altering. This group was going to have a special place in his heart; but then again, every group he had helped throughout the past forty years had a special place in his heart.

Like most missionaries, Brother Kaleb Andrews had begun his mission work as a young child alongside his parents. He had performed work projects in many countries as a youth, but his heart belonged to Mexico. He had met his wife, Liera, while helping his parents start a church in her hometown of Ensenada. It wasn't as though he was planning to fall in love; he couldn't help it. It was definitely God's plan. One simple "Hola" from Liera and he was smitten. Together, they had shared their lives, created three beautiful daughters and saved countless souls from sin. She had grasped Christianity with a passion, eagerly studying, learning and teaching, and he loved her even more because of her Godly desire. They were inseparable, committed to their God and to each other. Now, four years since she left this earth to be with the Heavenly Father, Kaleb still felt her presence. She was a part of him when she was living; she was still a part of him now. He was nearing seventy. It shouldn't be too much longer until he would be with her again. Kaleb smiled.

The young group assembled outside of the supply house to listen to the wisdom of the older man. They had seen several slide presentations prior to making this particular mission trip, and their respect for the accomplishments of Brother Andrews was tremendous. He had steadfastly worked to build and minister to churches throughout Mexico. In addition, he had started numerous work projects to benefit the people of Mexico, while also showing them the power of God's love through the help of Christians.

For this particular work project, Brother Andrews had recognized the problem of inadequate roofing on houses throughout Mexico. During the hurricane season, roofs were ripped off of houses as easily as the aluminum on a can of sardines. Traditional Mayan huts had thatch roofs that never withstood hurricane winds. Older houses with roofs made of sticks and corrugated tarpaper were also wiped away easily. To prepare the houses for the impending storms, Brother Andrews issued a plea for volunteers to help build the concrete roofs that had proven to be the ultimate safeguard from hurricanes.

Under his instruction, and with him always pitching in to help, the groups mixed cement, sand and gravel with water to make the concrete. Using a shovel, they mixed the concrete then shoveled it into buckets and passed it to the roof. The group then dumped the bucket on the roof and continued the process until the entire roof was covered with about two inches of concrete. It was hard work, especially for the teenagers who composed the majority of the volunteers, and it truly amazed him how many kids used their vacation time each year to come and sweat in the heat of Mexico for a week or two. It amazed him even more to see how many of them would return, year after year, because of the way it made them feel to help.

God was truly at work here.

After leading the work group in prayer, Brother Andrews returned to his small office in the rear of the supply house to begin preparations for next week's volunteers. He had barely started writing when the phone rang.

"Hola," he answered.

"Hello, Kaleb. How are you?" the familiar voice sang.

"Sister Rebecca. It has been too long. How are things at the shelter?"

"Everything is going well here. The Lord has been good to us and to the homeless of Merida. How are things in Chelem?"

"The same. More and more work groups are signing up; more and more are returning to work again. The people of Chelem are very grateful. They are eager to learn of the type of love that causes people to help so willingly. As a matter of fact, another member of the community was baptized earlier this week. The small church building that we built is now a regular meeting place for over twenty brothers and sisters in Christ."

"That's wonderful, truly wonderful," she answered, though her voice trembled.

Kaleb heard the shift in her tone and immediately sat forward in his chair. "What's wrong, Rebecca?"

"I hate to trouble you. I know that the summer months are a busy time for the roofing project," Sister Rebecca started.

"Tell me what's wrong. Perhaps I can help," Kaleb assured.

"I'm not sure if you can help, but I do need some advice. It's about a young woman who is here at the shelter," she continued.

"One of the missionaries or one of the homeless?" Kaleb asked.

"She's homeless. I mean, I do not know where her home is, though I am sure that someone is missing her. She's such a dear woman," Rebecca added.

"Tell me why you are concerned."

"You see, Kaleb, she came here early one morning about ten weeks ago. She's been here longer than any of the other homeless individuals now, but she doesn't seem to have anywhere to go. When she entered the shelter, it was as if she knew everything about it, almost as if she had been here before. But I've never seen her. She looked terrible, not malnourished or poor, like most of the homeless individuals we attend to, but emotionally wounded. I had assumed that perhaps she was in mourning, suffering from the loss of a dear friend or loved one."

"And you are no longer under that assumption?"

"I do think that she is in mourning; however, I believe," she paused, dropped her voice to a bare whisper, "I believe she mourns for her soul."

"She mourns for her soul," he repeated.

"She prays fervently every day, for most of the day, actually. She doesn't know that I've heard her pray. I've heard her cry out to the Lord, begging for forgiveness. She barely eats, and she only sleeps when she has cried herself into exhaustion."

Brother Kaleb removed his glasses and rubbed his eyes, silently saying a prayer for the woman's soul.

"There's more," Rebecca said as he sat silently listening. "She talks in her sleep. She quotes scripture. She truly knows the Lord."

"She recites Bible verses in her sleep?" Brother Kaleb asked.

"Not just verses. She quotes word-for-word full chapters of the Bible. She recites scripture more fluently than anyone I've ever heard. But it isn't just the fact that she can recite scripture that has me so concerned; it is the scripture she recites. It all has the same theme."

"And the theme?" he asked, perplexed as to what it could be.

"Murder."

Chapter Seventeen

Ordinarily, Brother Andrews would never leave a city in the middle of a work project; however, this situation wasn't ordinary. A soul was at risk of being lost, and he was going to make every effort to save it, to save her, from whatever tormented her spirit.

He arrived in Merida just before midnight exhausted from the day's work but eager to help. Sister Rebecca met him and took him immediately to the hallway outside of the young woman's room. She stood nearby as he leaned against the outer wall, listening. The words were mumbled at first, then spoken with more clarity and emphasis. Sister Rebecca held her Bible, mesmerized by the woman's accurate portrayal of scripture.

"She's nearing the end of Romans, chapter one," Rebecca informed.

"I know," Kaleb responded, still listening.

"And even as they did not like to retain God in their knowledge, God gave them over to a reprobate mind, to do those things which are not convenient; being filled with all unrighteousness, fornication, wickedness, covetousness, maliciousness, full of envy, murder," she whimpered, then continued, "debate, deceit, malignity; whisperers, backbiters, haters of God, despiteful, proud, boasters, inventors of evil things, disobedient to parents, without understanding, covenant breakers, without natural affection, implacable, unmerciful: Who knowing the judgment of God, that they which commit such things are worthy of death, not only do the same, but have pleasure in them that do them."

Kaleb glanced at Rebecca, who mouthed "Word-for-word" as a tear spilled onto her cheek.

They walked together, quietly reflecting on what they had just witnessed. Brother Kaleb had been overwhelmed with emotion when he listened to the woman. Her knowledge of the scripture coupled with the emphasis of pain that she uttered with every word had touched his heart. He wanted to help her; he wanted to save her.

Rebecca broke him from his thoughts when she stepped in front of him and opened the door to a small room containing a cot, a small table and a sink. Fresh flowers were arranged in a paper cup on the table. Although the room was tiny, it was warm and clean.

"I will take you to meet her in the morning," Sister Rebecca said with a tender smile.

"You didn't tell me her name."

"I do not know her name," she answered. "She brought a bag with her. I suppose some identification is inside, but I wouldn't look without her knowledge."

"She hasn't told you her name?" Kaleb asked, bewildered.

"She gave me a name, but I have no doubt it isn't her given name," Rebecca answered.

"What name?"

"Mara."

"Mara. I see. And, with her obvious knowledge of the scripture, she knows exactly the origin of that particular name. Poor soul. I hope I can help, but even if I can't, I know the Lord can. Thank you for asking me to come. Also, thank you for the room. It is just right," he added.

"You should know," she said. "You built it."

"With many fine Christians and the Lord's help. I was just a small part of the whole picture, but it does warm my heart to see it being used to help others. It is exactly what we intended it to be when we poured the foundation thirteen years ago. I suppose we should have made the walls a bit thicker, so we wouldn't be able to hear—"

"If we weren't able to hear, we wouldn't be able to help her. God's power is at work here. We were meant to hear her. We were meant to help. He has a plan. We just need to make sure we do our part," Sister Rebecca said as she left the room.

Kaleb kneeled beside the cot and prayed, "Lord, help us to do your will. Help us to save this woman's soul. She is troubled, Lord. But she knows You. She knows Your Word. I have heard her speak it with moving conviction. Please, dear Heavenly Father, help me to do my best. Don't let us lose a precious soul. In Jesus' Holy Name, Amen."

The next morning, Kaleb awoke earlier than usual. He hadn't slept well, spending the majority of the night thinking of the woman who slept down the hall. His thoughts returned to his conversation with Rebecca.

"But it isn't just the fact that she can recite scripture that has me so concerned for her; it is the scripture that she recites. It all has the same theme...murder."

"Murder," he whispered, shaking his head. Brother Kaleb knelt beside the cot and again prayed for the woman's soul. After he finished, he cleaned up, dressed and carefully picked up his Bible from the small bedside table. He tenderly thumbed through the pages, not sure what scripture would be needed today, but certain that whatever he needed would be provided within the worn book. Stepping outside of the room, Kaleb immediately saw Rebecca sitting in a chair at the end of the hall reading her Bible.

"Have you been waiting long?" he asked.

"Not really. I wanted to let you get the sleep you needed, but I assumed you would be up early, and I wanted to be ready to introduce you to her," she admitted.

"Is she awake?"

"Yes. She is engrossed in her Bible, as always. I took her a plate for breakfast, but I'm sure she hasn't touched it. Are you ready?" Rebecca asked eagerly.

"With the Lord's help, I believe I am," he answered.

They walked together to the woman's room. Rebecca motioned Brother Kaleb to stand in the hall while she entered. He listened to her speak.

"Mara, we have a visitor today. He would like to meet you. I thought you would enjoy a bit of company. He's a kind man, a missionary, who has spent the majority of his life doing the Lord's work in Mexico. I think you will like him."

She gave no response.

Rebecca peeked into the hall and nodded her head for Brother Andrews to come inside. He entered cautiously, not wanting to startle the woman. Rebecca took his hand before leaving the room and faintly whispered, "God be with you."

"I'm going to leave you two to visit," she said upon leaving.

Kaleb observed the small room that had been this woman's home for nearly three months. It was a bit larger than his room, with the same furniture, except a small chest of drawers was placed against one wall and an additional chair sat cater-cornered to the bed. Tiny paper cups containing wild flowers were placed spontaneously around the room and on the windowsill of the single window. Rebecca was obviously trying to help the girl feel comfortable.

She hadn't moved since he entered. She was turned away from him with her chair facing the window, her head bowed, following her finger as it guided along the page of scripture. She wasn't clothed as a homeless person. She wore a pale yellow linen dress, nicely made, that flowed to her ankles, exposing her bare feet. Her hair was red, deep scarlet, pulled into a high ponytail, tied with a creamy yellow ribbon, which was in direct contrast to her vivid red locks. He had noticed a small piece of luggage sitting next to the chest of drawers. She must have brought her clothes with her, probably bringing everything that she needed. Like Rebecca had mentioned, she seemed to need a place to stay, having nowhere to go. Brother Kaleb's heart ached for her—and her soul.

Carefully, he picked up the extra chair and moved it to sit closer. She stared at the Bible in her hands.

"Hello, Mara," he greeted.

The woman slowly raised her head, turning to look at Brother Andrews. Her cheeks were tear-stained and further tears quickly gathered in the corners of her dark eyes. She flinched as the next batch fell due to the movement of her head, spilling against the already damp pages of her Bible.

Kaleb Andrews caught his breath. "Tara."

Chapter Eighteen

Memories flooded Kaleb as he looked into the heartrending face of Tara Blessing. He hadn't seen her in several years, but he knew her instantly. Matthew James and Betty Jo-Ann Blessing had been monumental in organizing the volunteer groups that built the Merida Shelter for the Homeless. Their daughter had enthusiastically joined in their efforts. Singing hymns and quoting scripture as she worked, she had been the breath of fresh air when the hot, humid days of Mexico took their toll on the volunteers. No one would dare complain about the burden of their work when they saw the petite girl laboring so diligently, thoroughly enjoying every sweaty minute of it. He recalled how impressed he had been by the teen's strong spirit; now he wondered what had happened to break that spirit, and how he could help it mend.

"Tara Blessing," he spoke tenderly.

"Hello, Brother Kaleb," her voice quaked.

He handed her a tattered handkerchief from his pocket and watched as she carefully patted the damp pages of her Bible before dabbing at her eyes and face.

"I didn't realize you were the woman Rebecca told me of. She is concerned for you, Tara, as am I."

"I didn't know where to go. I remembered the Merida shelter. I thought perhaps I could come here," Tara paused, not sure what to say. She didn't know how to express the magnitude of emotions she had endured daily for the past three months, since the night she murdered Dave Danielson.

"I know something is troubling you, child. I'm also sure that the Lord helped me to find you. Together, we can pray, and let the Lord help you through this," he pleaded.

Tears fell freely, but she didn't respond. Kaleb ached for the distressed young woman.

Through watery eyes, Tara stared at the older man. She and her parents had worked alongside him to build this shelter. Now, nearly fifteen years later, she noticed the changes in the gentle missionary. His eyes were still tender, but even more wrinkled than she remembered. His hair, though gray then, was now completely white. His body also appeared to have taken its toll during the years of working outdoors to build countless shelters, houses and churches. But even with the added wrinkles and his darkened, leathery skin, his face still carried the look of care and concern that she remembered. He was a man who determinedly lived his life for God. The love of God shone through him.

As a teen, she repeatedly came here to help Brother Kaleb, basking in the love he had for humanity and all of God's creation. His love for the Lord had made her faith stronger. It made her feel good simply to be around someone so dedicated to his faith. Now, however, seeing the Godly man sitting next to her only reminded her of the condition of her own soul. The sharp contrast of her spirituality with his pierced her heart. She remembered that awful image from the day she'd been baptized. The ivory flesh, the red snake. The white obviously represented those like Brother Kaleb, pure like her soul had been at the time. And now she...

She looked away.

Kaleb watched the whirlwind of emotions cross her face before she turned her head. How could this have happened to Tara? And, what had actually happened? Rebecca had said— murder.

"Tara, your parents, how are they?" he asked, hoping to encourage her to talk. "It has been several years since I've heard from Matthew."

"They've passed on," she whispered. "I miss them. I've needed them."

"I'm so sorry," Kaleb responded. "They were strong in their faith, and I deeply cared for them. I didn't know."

"New Year's Eve of the millennium. A drunk driver—" she stopped, unable to finish.

Tears gathered in Kaleb's eyes, spilled to his wrinkled cheeks. "I'm so sorry."

Tara tried to push the memories of her parents into the recesses of her mind and focus on the scripture in the Bible. Her emotions were already spinning out of control. She couldn't start thinking of her parents too. It was too much. She wanted to die. Obviously, Brother Andrews tried to change the subject to something positive, but he didn't know that the other subject that would have been dear to her heart was also a sharp reminder of her loss.

"So, you're in your twenties now. I remember you said you wanted to marry young and have a house full of kids," he said with a soft smile. "Did you marry?" he asked, still trying to get her to communicate.

A low moan involuntarily crept from her throat. She rocked unconsciously in the chair as her cries echoed through the room. Her head throbbing from the onrush of memories, Tara couldn't stop it anymore. Her parents. Johnny. His screams. His body collapsing. Their baby. Those men. Those horrible men. "They murdered him!" she wailed. "They murdered him! And I—I—"

Kaleb quickly moved to comfort her. Wrapping his arms around her, he cried. He couldn't have imagined. This poor child had been through such tragedy, lost her parents, lost her husband. And even worse, he had been murdered. He rocked with her, silently praying to God, begging God to comfort and heal her aching heart.

"I'm so sorry," he finally managed to speak as he held her. "I'm so sorry." He tried desperately to comfort her.

Gradually, Tara's tears slowed as she listened to the kind man speaking. He was crying. His body quaked from his concern. He was trying to help her, but he didn't know. He didn't know what she had done, that she had taken another person's life. She was no better than those men. They murdered, and she murdered. Now a Godly man was trying to help her, and she didn't deserve to be helped. She didn't want him to care. She pushed away from him and stood staring out of the window.

Kaleb wanted her to confide in him and release the pain, but he knew that she wasn't ready. She wanted him to leave. He stood from the chair.

"I'm so sorry for everything you've been through, Tara. But I want to help you get through this. The Lord can help you. Don't give up on Him now. He will see you through. Let Him help, Tara." He gently closed the door behind him as he left the room.

Tara dropped to the floor and cried, "God forgive me. Forgive me."

*****

Kaleb found Rebecca sitting outside studying her Bible. She watched him sit down beside her, his mind obviously lost in thought. He held his Bible gingerly, placed it in his lap and brushed the dampness of a tear from the leather cover.

He shook his head in disbelief at what had happened to the young vivacious girl who had worked so hard for the Lord.

Rebecca continued watching as another tear passed down his weathered cheek before he wiped it away. She waited patiently for him to speak.

"Her soul is indeed in agony," he finally began.

"Do you know what happened to her? She is so knowledgeable in the Word. What has upset her?"

"I do know. I know so much more about her, Rebecca, and it pains me to see her like this. I've known her for years. Her name is Tara. Tara Blessing."

Rebecca leaned back in her chair and thought about the name. She knew the name. She could almost picture it. She had seen it recently, in the shelter. "I remember now. Her name is listed on the dedication plaque."

"Yes. She and her parents were here for the entire summer when we built the shelter. They also returned at every opportunity to help with its maintenance. Tara never tired of the work. She was so enthusiastic about helping others. She was even more enthusiastic about spreading God's Word."

"What happened to her? Why is she so troubled that she recites scripture when she sleeps? Scripture about murder?"

"She has been through more turmoil than most people will endure in a lifetime. She lost both of her parents when a drunk driver hit their car. Then, her husband was murdered. I do not know exactly what happened, but she is still reeling from the agony of it, and I fear—" he stammered as another tear fell.

"You fear she is blaming God," Rebecca concluded, nodding her head in agreement.

"Yes."

"And she is tormented by the murder when she sleeps. That is why she quotes those particular scriptures. We've got to help her, Kaleb. We have to help her see that she needs God now, not as the One to blame, but as the One to save her from her sorrow. We cannot let her lose her soul."

"Her precious soul. I agree. But I do not think we will be able to do anymore today. The memories that flooded her while we met...well, they tore through to her very soul. She was in such pain, such horrific pain."

"We should let her rest until the morning. But after that..."

"We *will* save her soul."

Chapter Nineteen

Feeling the coolness of the concrete floor against her cheek, Tara woke just before midnight. She had cried herself into complete exhaustion, not even having the strength to climb onto the cot to rest. As a result, her entire body ached from the hardness of the cement. Slowly, she sat up, causing her Bible to drop from her chest to the floor. She picked it up carefully and remembered the last thing Brother Kaleb had said.

"The Lord can help you. Don't give up on Him now. He will see you through. Let Him help, Tara."

"Why would He want to help me now? If Brother Kaleb knew everything, he would understand. God doesn't want to help me anymore. And I can't allow you to try to help me either, Brother Kaleb."

Instinctively, she stood, found her small suitcase and laid it on the cot. She opened the bag, checking to make sure the remainder of cash was still secure within the zippered compartments. She then retrieved her clothing from the chest of drawers and placed it in the bag. After writing a small note of thanks to Sister Rebecca and Brother Kaleb, she placed it on the bedside table and walked toward the door. "I'm so sorry. You wanted to help save my soul. If you only understood. It's beyond saving now," she whispered as she left the Merida shelter.

Seven hours later, Tara placed her bag in the overhead compartment on American Airlines Flight 265 from Cancun to Dallas/Fort Worth International. Even purchasing her ticket at the last minute, Tara had been able to get an aisle seat on the early morning flight. This particular flight had several vacant seats and, luckily, the window seat next to her remained vacant. Tara didn't know if she could handle idle conversation today. She closed her eyes and tried to put the past twenty-four hours, and the words of Brother Kaleb, out of her mind.

Johnny knelt in an airy room, glowing stark white. He held a beautiful baby girl in his arms. The baby reached for him, and Tara watched as he placed a finger just inches above her while her tiny hand instantly wrapped around it. He appeared to be—no, he definitely was—crying. Crying and praying. He prayed with all his might, with all his heart. Tara strained to hear what he said, but the words were muted and indistinct.

"Excuse me. I'm sorry to wake you, but we're here now," the flight attendant gently nudged Tara's arm.

Heavy-eyed, Tara tried to clear her mind and remember where she was. Glancing around the plane, she remembered; however, the memory of Johnny and their baby still burned on her mind as she extracted her bag and walked somberly toward the concourse.

She located the Park and Fly shuttle stop and sat on a park bench to await the next pick-up. Closing her eyes, she tried in vain to see Johnny again. Her heart ached to see him, but she couldn't regain the vision. When the shuttle stopped in front of her, she brushed a small tear away before standing.

"You've been gone quite a while. Have to admit, I was worried about you," the shuttle driver said, picking up her bag and helping her inside.

Looking into his kind eyes, Tara realized at once that this was the same driver that had taken her to the airport.

"I have been gone for a while," she said numbly, more to herself than to the kind-faced driver.

"Sure have. I've kept an eye on your car though. It's fine. We have a very secure lot, you know." He placed her bag on the shiny silver rack behind the driver's seat. "Hard to believe the summer's nearly over, isn't it?"

"Is it?" Tara asked, suddenly realizing that she had no idea exactly how long she had been away.

"Well, it'll be August next week. Kids already dreading going back to school and everything. I like the Fall best though. This hot weather is quite the bear, don't you think? Where did you go, by the way? Hotter or cooler?"

"Mexico," she replied truthfully.

"Hotter," he said with a grin. "And did the chewing gum help?"

Tara remembered the stick of gum he had given her prior to her departure. She remembered praying for him. "It did. Thank you for your kindness."

"Wouldn't have it any other way," he answered.

"Here we are," he said, nodding toward the dusty green Mustang. He parked the shuttle, stood and retrieved her bag.

Tara remained sitting. She had no idea where to go.

"You okay?"

"Yes," she answered. "I'm just a little tired, I guess."

"That's expected, with a trip as long as yours. Here, I'll help you with your bag." He grabbed the suitcase and helped her down the shuttle steps. Using the keyless entry, she unlocked the car doors and proceeded to open the door to the back seat so he could place the bag inside.

She handed him a rolled bill before getting in the car.

"You gave me too much last time," he said. He unrolled the hundred. "I can't accept this again, ma'am." He tried to return the bill to her, but she refused.

"You are too kind," he said.

"No, you are. God bless you," she said, shocked that those words slipped from her lips.

"Oh, He does, ma'am. He does."

Until He tears your life apart. Until He takes the one you love. Until He tests you beyond your power, when your soul gives up, and you abandon Him, because He abandoned you.

"God bless you, too, ma'am," the compassionate man added with a smile.

Tara closed the car door, waited for him to drive away and dropped her head to the steering wheel. She couldn't stop thinking about how much her life had changed since that awful night in February. It had been five months now. She hadn't even realized that the summer was nearly over and that Johnny had been gone for so long. She'd expected so many wonderful hopes and dreams to come true this year. Another year with Johnny and with their baby, a precious new soul that they could raise together. Now, Johnny was gone, the baby was gone, and she wasn't the person she used to be.

She was a murderer.

Tara gulped several deep breaths of hot air, fighting to calm herself. She had to think. Where would she go now? What would she do? She started the car and immediately thought of Jade. Surely, her friend was worried about her. She missed Jade, and she needed to talk to someone.

She straightened in the seat, rubbed her hands down her face. "A murderer," she mumbled, starting the car. Tara drove to the small, glass building where the cashier waited.

"Must have been some trip," the cashier commented when the huge amount flashed on the digital screen.

Without a word, Tara nodded and handed the lady the large amount of cash. Then she left the Park and Fly and pulled into the nearest gas station. She saw a woman talking on her cell phone at the next pump. It'd been a long time since she'd had a way to call Jade. Would the police be watching Jade's phone for calls from Tara? Did they ever learn of that call Tara made from the payphone in New Orleans the week Johnny died? Or did they monitor things like that so closely? Tara didn't know, but suddenly, she simply had to speak to her friend.

"Excuse me. I—I lost my cell. Can I borrow yours to make a quick call?"

The woman gave her a friendly smile. "Sure."

Jade would be at work, which meant her cell phone would be switched off and stored in her locker. Hesitantly, Tara punched in the number to Jade's office.

"Roberts," Jade answered. She waited for a reply. "Hello. This is Roberts," she said again. Then, somehow, Jade knew. "Tara," she whispered.

"Yes."

"Hold on. Don't hang up," she demanded as she hurriedly closed her office door. "Are you okay? I was afraid when I never heard from you. I've been so worried. Where are you?"

"I'm okay. I'm sorry for taking your car," Tara stuttered.

"I would give you anything. You know that. And besides, you paid me way more than the old thing was worth. Now, tell me where you are. I'll come get you. I can help you, no matter what you decide. We can go to the police, or I can help you hide, or whatever you want. Just let me help."

"I can't, Jade. Things are so complicated now. Don't worry. I'll be okay."

"No, Tara. How are you going to be okay? Let me know where you are. Let me help," Jade pleaded again.

"I'm sorry, Jade. I've got to go. I just wanted you to know that I am okay," she said before hanging up.

"Tara, don't—" Jade heard the click on the other end. Slamming the receiver down, she was shocked that she didn't think to remind Tara to be careful. She glared at the phone, enraged that she didn't have the caller identification feature on the ancient phone in her office. She tried to get a grip on herself and walked to open the office door. "Do any of you guys know what you have to do on the phone to find out the last number that called you?"

"Sure. Star-six-nine," an anonymous voice screamed from across the room.

"Thanks." She ran back to the phone and hit the numbers. Then she listened intently as the automated voice began reciting, "The number of your last incoming call was," and then paused.

"Come on!" Jade yelled into the receiver.

"214-555-0913," the message ended.

Jade dialed the number.

"Hello?"

"Tara?" she asked. It didn't sound like Tara on the other end.

"No, you must have the wrong number."

"I just received a call from my friend from this number."

"Oh, yes, she borrowed my cell at the gas station. But I've left the station, and she pulled out before me."

"Where are you? What city?"

"Oh, Dallas. I'm in Dallas."

"Thanks," Jade said, hanging up the phone. She dropped in her chair. "She's in Dallas."

Chapter Twenty

At the same time Jade boarded the Delta plane scheduled to fly directly from Atlanta to Dallas/Fort Worth, Tara crossed the Texas state line heading into Oklahoma. She knew her best friend would try to find her, but she also knew that she would be gone before Jade arrived.

Tara wasn't sure where she was going. She'd started driving north on Interstate 35, and she simply stayed on that road. After four hours of driving, she entered Oklahoma City. Tara had only been twelve when the city was left in the devastated aftermath of the bombing, but she remembered it well. She had prayed for the survivors, for the victims' families and for the city itself. And then, with the twin towers, she'd seen once more how evil could take control. At that time, Tara had tried to imagine how each family felt, losing loved ones, having their lives ripped apart by violence.

Now she knew.

"So much evil in the world," she said as she drove through the streets of Oklahoma City. Tara wondered how the community would ever truly recover from the anguish of that day, and how New York would ever recover from 9/11.

She wondered how anyone recovered from losing someone they loved more than life. How did they live again? Or specifically, why they would want to live when they lost someone the way she lost Johnny.

A sign marked the way to the Oklahoma City National Memorial. She wasn't sure why, but she knew she had to see the monument. She wanted to know how they chose to mourn, how they chose to live and whether they blamed God.

Tara followed the signs until she reached the memorial. She parked the car and began steadily walking toward the large gate marking the entrance. She read the inscription on the east gate identifying the mission of the memorial, *"We come here to remember those who were killed, those who survived and those changed forever. May all who leave here know the impact of violence. May this memorial offer comfort, strength, peace, hope and serenity."* Tara read the statement twice, then again. "The impact of violence," she said aloud.

Stepping through the gate, she entered the memorial. Boldly inscribed on the inside of the structure was the time *9:01*. She remembered the Oklahoma City bombing took place just after 9:00 a.m., because she'd been in school at the time.

A reflecting pool, breathtakingly beautiful and at least four hundred feet long, stretched out in front of her.

Then Tara saw them. A myriad of glass and granite chairs. Even before reading what they stood for, she knew. The chairs represented the one hundred sixty-eight men, women and children who lost their lives on that horrible day. Tara's throat began to close as she visually realized the magnitude of lives torn by a single horrific event.

How could God have let this happen? Fathers, mothers, sons, daughters, babies—all gone. Why? What kind of God lets this happen?

Tearfully, Tara continued through the tribute. Memories of the countless pictures she had seen during and after the spring of 1995 resurfaced as she viewed remnants of the original Alfred P. Murrah Federal Building. She watched an elderly gentleman clutching a tiny bouquet of flowers and a pink teddy bear enter the grounds. He silently made his way to the reflecting pool then tenderly placed the items by the water's edge. Wanting to comfort him, Tara walked toward the man, but she didn't know what to say. As she neared him, the older man turned to look at her with swollen, tear-stained eyes.

"I'm sorry," she whispered.

He nodded, then walked away.

Tara looked at the tiny bear and bouquet of flowers. A white piece of paper pinned to the bear displayed the man's message of grief.

My Beautiful Daughter,

Today would have been your birthday. How I wish you were here to spend it with me. I miss you! I miss you, and the beautiful baby you were carrying, my first grandchild. But I will see you again, and I will meet the wonderful grandbaby that I never knew. Until we meet in Heaven, Daddy

Beneath the handwritten note, the man had added a statement made by President Clinton following the tragedy: "There are forces that threaten our common peace, our freedom, our way of life. Let us teach our children that the God of comfort is also the God of righteousness."

God of comfort? God of righteousness? What comfort does anyone have? That God will take care of us? That God will watch over us? What is righteous about allowing innocent people to die? What is righteous about letting that man lose his daughter and grandchild? What is righteous about allowing Johnny and our baby to die?

Tara exited the memorial through the West gate, reading the inscription there, the large bold numbers identifying the time after the explosion, *9:03.*

"Just two minutes, and so many lives were changed," she whispered.

After returning to her car, she continued thinking about the suffering that had taken place here years ago. Looking around her, she couldn't help but notice that the city seemed normal again. Life had continued, but they'd needed a place to reflect, a place to mourn. She watched as more visitors approached the east gate, some holding handkerchiefs or flowers. This was the way they grieved. Friends and family of those who had lost their lives would make the pilgrimage to the memorial to remember. Remember their life, remember their death. Tara left the car and returned to the memorial. She stepped through the gate and broke down.

She remained there until the heat of the afternoon expired and darkness prevailed. She sat beneath the Survivor Tree, an American Elm that had withstood the fateful explosion, and remembered her own life before that horrible night in February. She remembered specifically the day she was baptized and how much God had meant to her at the time. She remembered her parents and how they had raised her, teaching her right from wrong, and loving her unconditionally. Her wedding day and honeymoon blended together in her reminiscence. Johnny's arms around her, holding her, loving her. Then those memories, the ones in shades of pristine white, paled and stark red reality invaded her mind.

The sheriff telling her of the automobile crash on New Year's Eve. Rushing to the hospital minutes after both her parents had been pronounced dead. Crying in Johnny's arms.

Trying to stop the memories before she had to see Johnny die again, Tara left the Survivor Tree and walked to the reflecting pool. Staring into the still water, she began to feel peace. She closed her eyes, knowing that something felt different here.

It was Johnny. She could *feel* him, standing beside her, trying to comfort her. She quickly opened her eyes and turned, nearly losing her balance by the abrupt movement.

She was alone.

Tara found that she couldn't leave Oklahoma City as she had planned. She knew that Johnny's spirit had been there, beside her at the reflecting pool. She had sensed his presence, and she didn't want to leave him behind. Instead of continuing her journey north, she got a hotel room near the memorial and spent her days at the monument thinking of Johnny and hoping to feel him again.

It never happened.

Refusing to give up, Tara remained in Oklahoma City until the summer departed and the leaves on the Survivor Tree were tinged with red and gold. She faithfully visited the memorial for over three months, and Johnny's spirit never returned. Painstakingly aware that she would probably never feel it again, Tara's heart ached even more for the memory to return.

During the third week of November, she visited the memorial for the last time, prepared to bid her farewell to the place that had provided her respite from the storm of her memories. She knew that Johnny's spirit had been here with her, if only once, and for that reason she found it difficult to go. But Johnny hadn't returned, and she knew she should leave.

Tara walked to the reflecting pool and stared once more into the quiet water, but this time she didn't feel Johnny. Instead, she saw something horrible. The shadow of the survivor tree cast slithering shadows across the water's surface. Autumn leaves gave the picture an eerie hue, a bloody, red tint. Her mouth went as dry and scratchy as steel wool while she watched the red snakes mingle and converge until they formed—*faces*. Those horrible reflections that she had seen before in her nightmares. Except now, instead of three faces, there were only two. Billy Reynolds and Chet Garrison were laughing, gawking at her and laughing. Perhaps they didn't even realize Dave Danielson was gone. But Tara did. And now she knew exactly where she would go.

Chapter Twenty-one

Steamboat Springs, Colorado

Brother Matthias McClain had been awestruck by the flowers that arrived at the church. Truckloads of white roses accented by crimson ribbons had been delivered yesterday morning, and the arrivals hadn't slowed since. Guests from around the country, around the world, filled all of the hotels, condos and chalets of Steamboat Springs. Obviously, Grayson Eubanks intended to make the most of this, the wedding of his only child, his precious daughter.

Matthias had seen the guest list, definitely a "Who's Who" of the executive world. He had even noticed a few congressmen and two celebrities from the Hollywood A-list. No doubt the wedding would make the front cover of most newspapers around the country and would definitely be the major story for the *Steamboat Pilot*, the town's only newspaper, published weekly, every Wednesday.

He had informed the wealthy man that this particular church building was not built to accommodate the number of people anticipated, but that they would do their best. Mr. Eubanks had kindly told him not to worry about it; it was all arranged. Now, looking at the immeasurably large white heated tent that had been flown in for the occasion, Matthias understood exactly what he'd meant. It didn't matter the cost. His little girl was going to have the best wedding ever, and since she wanted it in Steamboat Springs, in the snow, in November, he would make it work.

And he did.

Matthias was delighted when the bride requested that he include his favorite passage regarding marriage:

"Husbands, love your wives, even as Christ also loved the church, and gave himself for it. That he might sanctify and cleanse it with the washing of water by the word. That he might present it to himself a glorious church, not having spot, or wrinkle, or any such thing; but that it should be holy and without blemish. So ought men to love their wives as their own bodies. He that loveth his wife loveth himself. For no man ever yet hated his own flesh; but nourisheth and cherisheth it, even as the Lord the church: For we are members of his body, of his flesh, and of his bones. For this cause shall a man leave his father and mother, and shall be joined unto his wife, and they two shall be one flesh."

Brother Matthias McClain was just completing the scripture when the dark green Mustang entered the opposite side of town.

Tara pulled into a service station and asked final directions to the address she had been given earlier. Within ten minutes, she had the directions, driven down Lincoln Street to Mount Werner road and located the Snowden Ski-in/Ski-out Condominium Resort. She parked the car, extracted her bag from the back seat and walked to the building marked Office. Her breath fogged in front of her face and caught in her throat as she viewed the ski slopes, shining with a fresh blanket of early season snow.

"Johnny would have loved this."

He'd taught her to ski. It was on the eastern coast, at Maggie Valley, the Cataloochee slope. The mountain there seemed huge to her at the time. Now that she viewed the massive slopes of Steamboat, she was glad that Johnny had started her out at Maggie Valley. She had been intimidated by the slopes there; she couldn't imagine what she would have felt if she would have seen the size of these slopes as a first-time skier.

Johnny had laughed at her rigid body when she strained every muscle and gripped the poles as if letting go would deprive her of air. Eventually, though, she kept up with him, and by the third ski trip, she progressed from green to blue and even tried a couple of black slopes too. He had loved the fact that she wouldn't give up. It thrilled him when she'd try anything simply to see him smile. And the love they would make after those days on the slopes was unbelievable. But that was when life was good, before God took him away.

She entered the spacious office to find one lady standing behind the large counter. She'd been reading a thick romance novel, Tara observed, and she flipped it upside down on the counter to mark her place.

"You must be Miss James," the pleasant lady remarked when Tara entered.

"Yes, I am. How did you—"

"Oh, because you were the only one calling here today asking if we had any condos for rent. Most people automatically assumed we'd be booked up because of the wedding and all. As a matter of fact, you got the only one we had, and that's just because the guy was called away to some big conference in London or something like that. Lots of important folks here this weekend, but they should clear out tomorrow."

"That's odd. It appeared that the town was practically deserted as I drove in. All of the hotels and condos are full?"

"For the wedding. Oh, honey, haven't you heard? Steamboat Springs is the site for Grayson Eubanks' daughter's wedding. It's the biggest thing here since—well, I can't remember anything this big before. You know who Grayson Eubanks is, don't you? He owns Eubanks Enterprises, which means, well, basically he owns a large portion of every industry in the United States, and a smaller portion of every industry anywhere else," the woman said with a chuckle.

"I've read about him," Tara admitted.

"Well, the reason you didn't see any traffic is because of the wedding. It's going on now," she said, glancing at the large black and white circular clock on the wall. "They may even be into the reception by now, depending on how many songs they do and how long-winded the preacher is and all, but I've never minded it when a wedding runs long. Might as well make the wedding last a while, chances are the marriage won't." Another chuckle.

"How much did you say the condo rents for?"

"It's a hundred seventy per night, but the price changes with the seasons, you know."

"That's fine. How long is it available?" Tara interrupted.

"Oh, let's see. Now, as I told you on the phone, we're a resort management company. We don't actually own the condos. We just rent them for the owners. Now, let's see. Ah, yes. Okay. The owners haven't rented out this one yet, at least not for this season. The season really hasn't even started, you know. So, you can have it as long as you want. What do you need?"

"Do they have a monthly rate?"

"There isn't one listed, but I could call them and ask," she offered.

"I want it for at least a month, perhaps even two or three. Ask them what price they want and let me know," Tara said. She handed the puzzled woman a stack of bills. "Here is enough for the first couple of weeks. I can pay by the week or by the month, whichever they prefer."

"Certainly," the lady replied. "Here's the key. The unit is on the second floor of Building B. Use your room key to access the building. Here's the layout of the resort," she said, handing a folded pamphlet to Tara. "This will show you where the gym is located, the sauna, heated swimming pool and hot tub. It also has some great coupons for places around town. It's not that big of a town, so you shouldn't find it hard getting around, but if you need me, just dial zero. It'll ring directly to the office."

"Thank you," Tara said as she left the building. "I appreciate your help."

The woman quickly annotated Condo B21 as *Occupied* on the dry erase board behind her before eagerly returning to her novel.

Tara entered the one-bedroom condo, dropped her bag on the plush sofa and took in the surroundings. Decorated with coral, turquoise and cream, the southwestern décor flowed throughout. She opened turquoise vertical blinds to reveal the mountain, white and luminous. Then she marveled at how incredible a world God had made, only to allow evil to prevail within it. Tara sat on the sofa, unzipped her bag and ran her hand along the inside, searching for the single piece of paper. Finally, her fingertips felt the fragile folds of Johnny's letter. She carefully unfolded the letter, read his words of love and cried.

On the other side of town, in a giant ivory tent, a toast was being made to the newlyweds.

"To my beautiful daughter and my new son-in-law. May your happiness endure forever, throughout this life and beyond. May God watch over your union, blessing you with limitless years of happiness, and many, many children," Grayson Eubanks said. He winked before continuing, "A toast, to my beautiful Georgia and her new husband. To Mr. and Mrs. Chet Garrison."

Chapter Twenty-two

Exhausted from the drive, Tara resolved to sleep and begin her search for Chet Garrison tomorrow. Before climbing into bed, she impulsively retrieved Jade's note identifying each man's address. She had already scratched through Dave Danielson's address in Mexico. Now, two addresses remained, Chet's and Billy's. Having no idea where Chet's home was located, Tara had been pleasantly surprised to find that the ski town was relatively small. It wouldn't take her long to find him, learn his daily routine and finalize her plans. She laid the note on the bedside table and went to sleep.

Chiming church bells woke her the next morning. She hadn't heard the sound in many years, since she was a child, and she strained her ears to listen. "Sunday," she remarked, crawling out of bed. She stumbled to the kitchen and surveyed the empty cabinets. Her stomach growled in anticipation. She hadn't eaten since lunch the day before. Aching with hunger pains, she quickly brushed her teeth, pulled her hair up and dressed.

She left the condominium and immediately noticed the fresh snow that had fallen during the night. Deciding to grab a biscuit from a drive-through rather than pick up groceries and return to the condo, Tara drove the car through the town. The appearance was more of an old-fashioned village than a modern city. Charming shops, similar to gingerbread houses, lined both sides of Lincoln Street, which ran through the center of town. The stores were already decorated for the holiday season, with tiny white icicle lights hanging from every rooftop and pine wreaths garnished with thick, red ribbon on every door and window. It was amazing, like stepping back in time to the way a town should look, without the smog and the high-rise buildings.

Continuing her drive, Tara couldn't help but notice the tiny church building perched on a hill at the edge of town. Hordes of snow-laden roses and shining red ribbon lined the steep driveway leading to the building. The white roses looked perfect, pure and full of life. But there was something about that red, curling ribbon...

The doors of the church were adorned with tulle, more roses and more of the horrid curling ribbon.

Wanting a better view, Tara pulled her car to the side of the road and parked. A large white truck was parked behind the building, with several men busy loading it with white chairs, tables and a variety of decorative fixtures. The vast white tent had been partially disassembled, and the snowy fabric lay strewn around the churchyard. Despite all of the activity going on outside of the church, the members had attempted to have service as usual. The small group filtered out of the church doors, pointing and exclaiming at the crew that worked diligently around their tiny building. She couldn't help but notice how happy they all appeared, laughing and hugging each other as they parted ways to enter their vehicles.

Saddened by the vision, she drove away.

Before returning to the condo, Tara stopped at a small grocery store to pick up some basic staples and enough food for the week.

She also purchased one of the city street maps displayed at the checkout. After returning to the condo and storing the groceries, she sat at the kitchen table to peruse the map. It was as she expected. The town was small and the streets clearly marked. She retrieved Jade's note from the bedside table. Comparing it to the map, she gasped when she located Chet's address. He was only a half-mile farther up the mountain, not far at all from Tara's condo. It looked as though the ski run that ran parallel to her condo ran directly beside his home. "Excellent," she said, folding the map and heading back to the car.

She ascended the mountain, climbing steadily past the collection of condominiums that lined the base, and viewed the exquisite chalets that were elegantly positioned on the side of Mount Werner. Locating Chet Garrison's residence wasn't hard; a shiny brass plate emblazoned with *Garrison* glistened on one of the brick columns steadying the electric wrought iron gate. Tara could only view the roof of the chalet from the road, but it appeared to be quite substantial. She turned the Mustang around in the paved area in front of the gate, then steadily guided the car back down the mountain and returned to her condo eager to start learning the daily habits of Mr. Chet Garrison.

At the condo, she visualized Chet. Even though it had been dark on that Mardi Gras night, she could still picture him perfectly. Although his hair had been plastered to his head with water, or sweat, she could tell that it was red. His face was ruddy, his mouth thin and his eyes—she couldn't remember what color his eyes were, but she would know him. She remembered him; she *would* recognize him. Tara suddenly stopped the imagery as she realized— he may remember her too. She quickly ran to the bathroom and stared at her reflection. The bright red hue had long since faded. As a matter of fact, she looked almost exactly as she did that night, with the exception of her hair being slightly longer. She had lost some weight, so she was thinner than he would remember, but no, he would remember. Tara thought about the night with Dave Danielson in Mexico. He hadn't recognized her, but he had also been extremely intoxicated. Tara stared intently at the mirror. "Okay, don't worry. It'll be okay. I'll just have to fix it."

She left the condo, returned to the grocery, and headed for the "Hair Care" aisle. She seized two boxes of *The Ultimate Blonde*, made the purchase and returned to the condo.

Monday morning, Tara stared at the new reflection. "Perfect," she acknowledged before showering and dressing to leave. "Let's see if Mr. Garrison likes blondes."

She took one of the condo's Steamboat Springs Information Guides and began her search. Pulling into a gas station, Tara set the pump to run and jumped back in the car to avoid the cold. While waiting, she flipped through the information guide. "Let's see. Your chalet says that you're not hurting for money. So where does a wealthy guy go during the day at Steamboat? Do you work? Or, do you just play?" she muttered to herself as she continued browsing the resorts, restaurants and activities listed in the guide.

The pump stopped abruptly at the precise moment she flipped the last page of the guide. "Well, I'll be," she said, staring at the undeniable face of Chet Garrison. Smiling, he had his arm draped around a woman wearing the skimpiest bikini she had ever seen. Tara's jaw was still hanging slack when she heard a car horn sound behind her. She glanced through the rear window to see an irritated man in a pick-up waiting to use the pump. Jumping out of the car, she mouthed an apology and quickly removed the nozzle, then immediately pulled the car out of the man's way. Then she parked beside the station and read the caption.

Mr. Chet Garrison, owner of the prestigious resort The Summit congratulates the winner of the "Strings of the Springs" contest, Miss Georgia Eubanks. The Summit hosted the well-attended event, which Mr. Garrison plans to make an annual festivity for the mountain."

Tara glared at the picture. The tall, gorgeous girl wore nothing more than a yellow ribbon, no doubt held in place with ample amounts of body glue. Chet Garrison smiled wickedly and, as Tara examined the picture further, had his hand tucked smoothly underneath the curve of tiny fabric resting on her waist. "Disgusting." She flipped to the cover of the book. "April Edition," she said. "Well, no doubt you're still at The Summit."

Within fifteen minutes, Tara had parked her car in front of the elaborate ski resort. Checking her reflection in the rear-view mirror, she determined that he would indeed have a hard time recognizing her. She exited the car and started toward The Summit. She didn't really want to see him today; rather she hoped to merely find out a little more about his daily routine. Did he come to his resort daily? Weekly? Did he come here at all, or did someone else run it? And, if that were the case, how would she be able to pinpoint his daily routine?

Tara viewed the impressive lodge, directly centered between four similarly styled buildings composed of condos. Although fashioned to resemble rustic log cabins, the buildings were undeniably new. A bright green roof and matching shutters provided a stylish contrast to the cedar-toned logs, and the dust of snow that the buildings had received during the night altered the entire appearance from attractive to spectacular.

Couples dressed in ski gear stood outside of the lodge sipping hot chocolate or snuggling in the cold. One particular couple, propped against the corner of the large building, grabbed Tara's attention then squeezed her heart mercilessly. They eagerly kissed, giggled and smiled at each other.

Honeymooners.

Tara entered the lodge to find more couples obviously enjoying a day on the slopes, dressed in ski parkas, laughing, visiting with each other, or simply sitting around the vast circular hearth encompassing the focal point of the room, a dramatic stacked-stone fireplace.

Not hurting for money, are you Chet?

Tara quickly surveyed the room and instantly realized Chet Garrison wasn't present. Undeterred, she approached the long, marble counter where several attendants waited.

"May I help you?"

"I'd like to get some information about your resort please," Tara replied.

"Certainly. I'm afraid we're completely booked right now, with the wedding and all, but things should begin to clear out later this week," the polite woman informed as she gathered information and rate sheets. "Normally, this is a slow time for us. The slopes just opened last week, but our owner, Mr. Garrison, caused the place to fill completely with his wedding guests."

"Wedding guests?" Tara stammered.

"Oh, my. You haven't seen the press footage? It was incredible! I'm sure I'll never see another one like it. That Grayson Eubanks sure knows how to throw a party!"

Okay, Tara. Breathe. Breathe.

"Are you okay?" the young woman asked as the color drained from Tara's face.

"Fine," Tara managed. "I suppose he and his wife are on their—"

"Off to Mexico, of course. For a six-week honeymoon. He said not to look for him until the New Year. And to think, we all thought he'd be a bachelor forever. Georgia sure won him over!"

Mexico. Mexico? Dear God, no!

Tara unconsciously gripped the edge of the marble counter, remembering the vision of Dave Danielson covered in blood. She wondered how long it would be before Chet Garrison and his new bride knew about Dave, and if he would figure out that she was responsible.

"Are you sure you're okay?"

"Just a bit under the weather," Tara panted. She turned to leave.

"Miss, you're forgetting your brochures. We would love to have you stay with us at The Summit."

Tara shakily took the brochures and left.

Twenty minutes later, she stretched out on the bed in her condo and willed herself motionless, staring at the ceiling as steady tears tumbled from her eyes. Some settled in the shell of her ear. Some dampened her hair. She didn't care.

Chet Garrison was married. Not only that, he was married to Georgia Eubanks. Tara remembered the picture in the information guide. Georgia Eubanks in the bikini. Then she understood. The big, fancy wedding at the small church, the white roses, red snake-like ribbon, fancy tent, white chairs…all for Chet Garrison. He had helped to take Johnny's life, helped to kill her husband, and yet he was living a dream.

"How could You do this, God? You did it, didn't You? He's married. If I do anything to him now, I will be doing the same thing to that poor girl that those three men did to me! You knew exactly what this would do to me! Why, God, why? He doesn't deserve to live! He doesn't deserve to be happy!" Tara screamed, as the tears continued streaming down the sides of her face.

Chapter Twenty-three

Tara alternated between hours of sleeping and hours of crying until finally, the next morning came. She rose from the bed still feeling exhausted. Fumbling her way to the bathroom, she started hot water for a shower. The steaming water pelted her back while she thought about everything she'd learned during the past twenty-four hours. She couldn't take Georgia's husband from her. She couldn't do the same thing to Georgia Eubanks that they had done to her, even if her husband was Chet Garrison.

She dried off, wrapping one towel around her body and another around her hair before walking into the small living room. Then she cracked the vertical blinds enough that she could see the presence of additional snow without intruders being able to peer in. Perplexed at what she should do now, she sat on the sofa and contemplated packing her things, putting them in the car and heading south. Toward Tampa. Billy Reynolds was the one that had actually shot Johnny, and she was willing to bet that *he* wasn't married by now, but then again...

"God, You could arrange that too, couldn't You? I would spend a week making my way down to Tampa just to find that he had moved, or married, or whatever else You have fixed to keep me from helping the world be rid of him. Why? You know what I did to

Dave Danielson. You see all. You saw it! Why do You care what I do? Maybe You want me to be the one to go. Maybe You're trying to show me that I'm the one that should die," Tara wailed into the silence of the condo. Tearfully, she stared around the room until her eyes landed on a worn Bible resting on the mantle. Instinctively, she crossed the room and picked it up.

"Show me. Show me what You want me to do," she said, taking the Bible with her to the sofa. She placed it upright in her lap, closed her eyes and let it fall open. Opening her eyes, she peered at the page. The owner of this particular Bible had underscored and highlighted a verse on the opened page. "No way," she said, reading the verse. "No way."

"Repent ye therefore, and be converted, that your sins may be blotted out, when the times of refreshing shall come from the presence of the Lord." Acts 3:19

"That your sins may be blotted out," Tara said aloud as she re-read the verse. "No way. No way can You forgive me. And besides, You know my thoughts. You know that I want them all dead—and I want them to die the way Johnny did—painfully. How can You forgive me when I feel this way? Give up on my soul, Lord, if You haven't already."

Quickly, she dried her hair, dressed and left the condo. She had no particular destination. She just wanted to drive. Without thinking, she steered the Mustang through town. Once again, she noticed the small church that had been the site of the elaborate wedding. Chet's wedding. All of the wedding embellishments were now gone, and the quaint church looked as if it hadn't had the "wedding of the century" there the previous weekend.

A lean, young teen balanced on a ladder, diligently altering the sign on the church marquee. As she passed the church, she read the beginning of his message, *"Don't give up. Mo"* and she wondered what the remainder would say. She continued driving, glancing back to see his image still faithfully working on the sign. She thought about turning the car around and asking the man if he knew anything of the wedding, specifically of the groom. Had Chet Garrison changed that much in the past nine months? Perhaps he had found peace with himself, forgiven himself for his part in Johnny's murder and moved on to a blissful life of marriage. Although Tara thought it near impossible, maybe that was exactly what had happened. She slowed the car to make the turn, then stopped.

"You're wanting me to go to that church, aren't You God? You're putting these thoughts in my head. He's probably as evil as he was at Mardi Gras, maybe even worse. I'm not going to that church, or any other church," she said, stomping the accelerator.

Tara had been driving for at least an hour before she finally relented and turned around, heading back toward Steamboat. She had spent the majority of the time thinking, wondering what to do about Chet Garrison and deciding that ultimately she couldn't do anything to him. She couldn't put another woman through the same thing that she had been through. Period. She finally re-entered Steamboat Springs when the dark shadows of late afternoon were taking over the sky. She could tell that evening was nearing because the chair lifts on the mountain were immobile against the white snow in the distance. The charcoal of the sky met the white capped mountains to produce a subtle gray glow that cloaked the city like a mournful whisper.

Taking in the postcard image of the town at dusk, Tara was taken aback when the Mustang neared the small church...and sputtered. She'd barely maneuvered it to the shoulder of the road before it died completely.

"Great," she muttered, locking the doors and getting out. The church sat on the hill in front of her, and Tara grudgingly began the climb up the steep driveway to the building.

"You were determined to get me here, weren't You?" she mumbled. Then, with more irritation, she added, "If You are so resolute in getting exactly what You want, why don't You just come down here the way You did for Moses and tell me. There's a bush. Make it burn!"

Matthias McClain had seen the woman's car as it slowed to a stop. From the stained glass window, he watched her make her way up the driveway obviously fussing about the situation. He couldn't help but smile. She forcefully yelled, at no one, and then turned to glare at the green metal that had left her stranded. She whirled around and continued her trek up the hill. She was agitated, annoyed and, surprised with himself for realizing it, beautiful. He opened the church door just as she had stepped onto the first concrete step.

"Hello," he said, noticing small beads of sweat dotting her forehead in spite of the November chill.

Tara stretched out her hand, immediately recognizing this man as the lean, young teenager that she had seen putting up the marquee letters. But now, looking at him closely, she realized he wasn't as young as she had originally thought. On the contrary, he was probably her age and nice-looking. Very nice-looking. Reflexively, she glanced at his left hand and noticed that it was bare. Just as quickly, she furrowed her brow at the realization of what she had done.

What am I doing? What am I thinking? I should be thinking of— Johnny.

"Having a little trouble? Come on inside," he directed, opening the door for her to enter.

Tara stepped inside the charming church. It was small but striking, with stained glass windows, shiny wooden pews and the strong smell of pine oil. Warmth gathered in her chest at the faded memories stirred by the vision.

"My car. It broke down, and I'm not sure what's—" she began.

The man had already located the thin phone book for Steamboat and held his cell in his hand. Making a small wave to Tara, he punched in a number and began talking.

"Mike, yes, this is Matthias McClain. Well, I'm glad you enjoyed it. Yes, it was a beautiful ceremony. Yes. Mexico, I believe. Six weeks. Yeah, must be nice. Well, her parents own a resort or two down there, and I believe the groom said he had a friend there as well, so perhaps they are visiting," Matthias started.

Tara's mouth went dry as she listened. They were planning to visit Dave. She was glad she hadn't stayed in Mexico any longer, and she wondered why Chet hadn't been previously notified of Dave's death.

Or had he?

Matthias continued, "Well, I have a nice lady here who has a bit of car trouble. It's a green Mustang, on the side of the road directly across from the church. Yes, I knew you could. Sure, I'll let her know. I appreciate it, Mike. See you Wednesday night. Bye."

Tara stared questioningly at the man, obviously the preacher, who had just helped her immensely. His hair was cut like the models on the front of a GQ magazine, so short on the sides that you could see his skin, but long enough on top to spike just a bit. It was—well, quite sexy, she had to acknowledge. His eyes were practically transparent, icy blue, like the water in a swimming pool. Tara tried not to stare. He was smiling at her now, and she wondered exactly how long she had been examining his face. Her cheeks instantly reddened, and her stomach tensed. She was betraying Johnny's memory. She didn't want anyone else. She never had. Especially not a preacher.

Matthias watched the myriad of emotions play across her face. He had, by the way, noticed the wedding ring on her left hand, and he merely wanted to help the woman. However, he couldn't deny that she was attractive. He was sure her husband was very aware of this quality. Matthias had trained himself so well that if he happened to ever feel an attraction to a married woman, he would continually tell himself about the husband. Tell himself what a wonderful man he was, even though, at times, Matthias would never meet the lucky man. Right now, he said a silent prayer to God to make the instant feelings he had toward this woman who had materialized at his very doorstep subside.

"A friend of mine, Mike Tolleson, owns an automobile service station in town. He's very good and very fair. He's going to come tow the car in, if that's okay."

"Yes, that's fine, but I will—well, can you tell me where the nearest city shuttle stop is?"

"There's one just outside of the church building," Matthias began.

"Thank you," she said, turning toward the door.

"But it has finished its last run for the day," he completed. "They stop running at six o'clock."

"Oh."

"Give me a minute. I'll take you. It can't be far. The other side of town is only three miles away," he chuckled.

Tara smiled at the kind man.

Matthias McClain locked the door to the church building and walked Tara to his car, a restored red and white '65 Mustang. She couldn't help but run her hand along the sleek fixture of a time gone by.

"Guess I'll always be a teen at heart," he reasoned when he saw her interpretation of the car.

"I think it's absolutely incredible," she exclaimed.

He opened the passenger door and she slid onto the red leather seat. "I do like it," he responded as he got in and turned the key. "Okay, tell me where to go."

"I'm staying in Snowden Condominiums. It's—"

"I know where it is. Remember, the town is not that big," he said and drove down the hill.

Tara looked at the marquee before they turned onto Lincoln Street.

"Don't give up. Moses was oncc a basket case."

Chapter Twenty-four

Matthias sat in his office the following morning trying to concentrate on his Wednesday night lesson, but continually finding himself thinking of the woman. She had literally walked in from the street, practically appearing out of nowhere, and yet somehow managed to grip his heart stronger than he would have ever imagined. Something was different about her. He could visualize her, sitting in his car, blond hair resting casually on her shoulders, piercing dark eyes occasionally casting nervous glances at him, delicate body hidden by a mass of wool sweater and thick jeans.

"Keep your thoughts pure," he warned himself.

When he'd dropped her off at the condominium, he had offered to take her car keys to Mike so he could begin work on the Mustang. She had given him the keys, along with her name and the phone number to the condominium. Before handing the keys and information to Mike, Matthias had copied the name and number, so he could make sure she was okay and didn't need anything while her vehicle was being repaired. He knew she could use the free city shuttle to travel around town, but he wanted to have the information, just in case. Now he found himself continually setting aside his lesson plan and staring at the name and number.

"Mara," he said. The name had haunted him the moment he saw it on the paper. She hadn't even written a last name. He wondered momentarily why parents who knew what the name represented would bestow that name upon their daughter. Then he had wondered if perhaps her parents hadn't known the story behind the name. Ultimately he had decided, particularly when she hadn't given a last name, that "Mara" wasn't her given name, and that perhaps she had given herself the title, because she had actually experienced the same tragedy as Naomi. That thought disturbed him. What if this beautiful young woman had actually experienced the ultimate loss?

Matthias reached for the phone.

"Hello," she answered.

"Hello. This is Matthias McClain, from the church," he began, in the same manner he used to call any visitors of Steamboat.

"Hello, Matthias. Any news on my car?" Tara asked.

"No. Sometimes it takes Mike a while. He's pretty much a one man show, but as I said yesterday, he's good, and he's fair," Matthias answered.

"Oh, that's fine. I can use the shuttle until it is repaired."

"Well, I was just calling to see if you were doing okay, or if you needed anything."

Tara noted the caring tone of his voice and her heart warmed. She wasn't sure why she felt so drawn to him, but undeniably, she did. "I'm doing fine, but I appreciate your concern."

"I also called for another reason. Today is Wednesday, which means we will be having our mid-week Bible study tonight at the building. I thought that you might like to come."

Tara sat, bewildered at what to say.

He's inviting me to church. A Bible study. How can I go after what I've done? But, he was so kind to me, and I don't have anything else to do until the car is repaired.

"Mara? Are you still there?" he asked.

Mara. Surely he knows that isn't my name.

"Yes, I'm here. I suppose I could come," she said with a sigh.

"Wonderful," Matthias exclaimed, forgetting to control his enthusiasm. "I'd be happy to pick you up and bring you if that's okay. The shuttle will have completed its routes by the time our service begins, and it wouldn't be any trouble."

"I'd appreciate that. What time should I be ready?"

"Six-thirty."

"I'll see you at six-thirty then. Thank you, Matthias," she said before hanging up the phone.

Matthias placed the receiver on the hook and stared at the phone. "She said yes," he said with a grin. And then, he returned to his lesson.

Promptly at six-thirty, Matthias pulled his Mustang into the parking lot of Snowden Condominiums. Tara, dressed impeccably in a creamy sweater and fitted skirt, waited in the foyer. She exited the building as soon as he entered the parking lot and readily made her way through the patchy snow to meet him. He quickly stopped the car, exited and walked around to open her door. Trying to get out of the cold as quickly as possible, she had already lifted the handle.

"I guess I'll need to speed up my pace if I'm going to be a proper gentleman." Matthias helped her open the door, made sure she was inside and then closed it.

Tara laughed at him. It caught her by surprise, how good it felt to laugh. She couldn't remember the last time she had.

They entered the church before anyone else had arrived.

"I'm afraid the congregation isn't known for punctuality," he explained, "but we've got a wonderful group here, small but wonderful."

Tara had brought the worn Bible she had found on the mantle in the condo. She took it and silently sat in a pew to await the arrival of the other church members.

Sister Maddie and Sister Evelyn were the first to arrive, though by the time they had slowly but surely made their way to their predictable pew, two additional members had entered the building, used the restroom, located a pew, and reviewed the lesson. All before the two elderly women had even sat down.

Tara smiled at them when they passed her pew. They reminded her of the elderly women who had faithfully attended church with her when she was young, always covering their heads, listening to Brother Williams.

Upon sitting down, Sister Evelyn shifted in her seat, nodded toward Tara. "What's your name, sweetie?" she yelled, obviously louder than she realized.

"Mara," Tara answered.

"Nice to have you here, Mara," she said before abruptly twisting around.

"What did she say her name was?" Sister Maddie asked, obviously louder than she realized.

"She said her name is Mara!" Sister Evelyn yelled.

"Dreadful name!" Sister Maddie responded, definitely louder than she realized.

Tara couldn't help but form a slight grin as she listened to their remarks. Undeniably, these two women knew exactly where the name originated. Well, she hadn't exactly lied to them. She could be called Mara, and the implications of the name were indeed true.

Matthias watched the entire exchange between the elderly women and was a bit worried that they had hurt her feelings. Then he saw the slightest of smiles when she heard their response.

There is hope for her, isn't there God? Help me to help her.

He had originally planned on studying about God's righteousness, but something compelled him to change the topic.

"Tonight's lesson is entitled 'The Amazing Forgiveness of God'."

Tara shifted in her seat uneasily.

You did this, didn't You? Here I am, and You are going to talk to me through this nice man. Well, I can't very well leave, now can I? If You still care anything at all about me, God, help me to be strong. Don't let me break down here, not in front of all of these people. Help me maintain my composure. Help me not to think of Johnny. Help me not to think of Dave Danielson.

"Let me ask you. When I mention the name of David, what saying comes to mind? He is said to have been a man after—what?"

"He was a man after God's own heart," an elderly man answered grumpily.

"That's true, Brother Brantley, but even though he was known as the man after God's own heart, he was a sinner, as we all are. As a matter of fact, David committed the horrible sin of murder. Who can tell us the story of David, Bath-sheba and Uriah?"

Tara's stomach knotted as she knowingly turned the pages of her Bible to the eleventh chapter of Second Samuel. She knew the story, and yet, now it meant more. She listened intently to the conversation between Matthias and the members of the church. Trying to keep her tears at bay, Tara began to realize what God had been trying to tell her...while Sister Maddie identified the horrible act that King David had performed.

"...and so essentially, he murdered that poor man," Sister Maddie completed.

"That's correct. King David had lusted after Uriah's wife, Bath-sheba. Not only that, but he desired her so much that he sent for her, slept with her and she became pregnant with his child. Afterwards, King David learned of the pregnancy. Knowing that her husband, Uriah, was a faithful soldier of his own army, David summoned the soldier to the castle and commanded him to go home. But Uriah, knowing that his soldiers were sleeping in tents at war, refused to go home; instead, he slept with the servants of the castle."

"King David panicked when he realized Uriah hadn't returned home and slept with Bath-sheba, allowing the opportunity for him to assume the baby she carried was his own. So David proceeded to keep Uriah from the war an additional night, attempted to get him drunk and tried to make him go home to his wife. Again, Uriah was faithful to his soldiers, refusing to accept the pleasures from his wife if his fellow soldiers were not able to be with their own wives. Finally, dismayed that his plan hadn't worked, King David, the man after God's own heart, sent Uriah to the front-line of battle and waited—and it was there that the faithful soldier Uriah met his death. Now, does this sound like a man after God's own heart?" Matthias rhetorically asked the congregation. The sound of turning Bible pages echoed through the small auditorium.

"Now, after giving Bath-sheba the time she needed to mourn her husband, David married her and they had a son. But the Bible clearly states that, 'The thing that David had done displeased the Lord.' Now, I ask you, can the Lord be displeased with us and still love us? Can he still forgive us? Certainly he can, just as he forgave David. God can hate the sin, yet love the sinner. However, David wasn't forgiven without having to suffer. He and Bath-sheba lost the child, and during the time that their son was sick, David fasted and suffered greatly. But he repented and asked the Lord's forgiveness. And God did forgive David. He loved David, and David and Bath-sheba were blessed with another son, the wise King Solomon. And, even though he committed a dreadful sin, David was forgiven, and was still considered truly 'a man after God's own heart.' Now, I will ask you again. Do you not think God can forgive us today, as he forgave David in the past?"

Matthias completed the lesson eloquently, occasionally shifting his eyes toward Mara. She had been staring intently at the Bible in her lap, but he had thought, at least once, she had brushed a silent tear from her cheek.

Dear God, please take care of her. Help me to say the right thing.

When the lesson ended, Matthias took the opportunity to introduce her to the fellow members of the congregation. Brother Brantley was shaking her hand and introducing himself when Tara overheard the conversation between Matthias and Sister Evelyn.

"So, I guess Hallie moved back to Tennessee last week," Sister Evelyn said matter-of-factly.

"Yes, I believe she did. Evidently, she received a job offer she couldn't refuse," he answered.

"Well, if you ask me, the only offer she was really looking for was your hand in marriage, but you didn't give her the time of day, did you preacher?"

"Evelyn!" Sister Maddie exclaimed as she patted her friend's arm. "Sorry, Brother Matthias. Sometimes her tongue gets away from her."

"Not at all. I understand that the two of you had high hopes for a union of myself with Miss Davenport, and I can assure you that I never gave her any indication—"

"Well, if you ask me—" Sister Evelyn started.

"He *didn't* ask you, Evelyn. That's the point. It was a good lesson, Brother Matthias," Maddie continued as she pushed her friend out the door.

Matthias sheepishly grinned at Tara as the two women left.

She thought he looked simply angelic.

Chapter Twenty-five

Brother Andrews was pleasantly surprised when Sister Rebecca entered his office in Chelem.

"Hello, Rebecca," he said, standing. "How are you?"

"I'm better now," she answered, indicating a postcard she held in her left hand.

"From Tara?"

"She wants us to know that she is okay. I've prayed for her continually. This was such a blessing to receive. I had to come share it with you in person." She offered the card to him.

He took the card and examined it.

Brother Kaleb and Sister Rachel, Thank you so much for allowing me to stay at the shelter and for the tender love and care that you gave to me. I apologize for leaving so abruptly, but I had to go. Perhaps God has not forgotten me after all.

"She didn't sign it, but I agree that it must be from Tara," he said, noticing the postmark. "The postmark is blurred, but I believe it says—"

"Colorado," Rebecca finished.

"Yes. And it sounds as though she has found the Lord again," he added.

"Yes. Praise Him," Rebecca answered with a tear. "May He continue to help the sweet girl."

"Lord, be with her now," Kaleb prayed as he continued studying the small card.

*****

Also on the Yucatan peninsula, Chet Garrison crept away from his new bride as she dozed on the beach in Cancun. When he was certain he was far enough away not to wake her, he fished his cell from his pocket, hurriedly keyed in the number and waited.

"Speak," Billy Reynolds answered on his private line.

"Billy. It's Chet. I just found out about Dave. Did you know—"

Fuming, Billy tried to control his voice while he answered, "Of course I knew. And you would have known too if anyone could get in touch with you. Where have you been the past six months? As if I didn't know," he growled as he picked up the Sunday issue of the *Tampa Tribune*, which clearly displayed a picture of Chet, Georgia and Grayson Eubanks.

"You said for us to lay low until Christmas, not to talk, not to email."

"I called your cell, and it was disconnected."

"I got a new one. All part of laying low after everything that happened at Mardi Gras. And I've been trying to keep Georgia out of my business stuff. She doesn't know about you and Dave..and everything. See, I'm—well, I'm married. We were busy with plans. She's—"

"I know you're married. The whole country knows you're married! Well, while you were off losing your head over the sexy little heiress, I've been trying to deal with more important matters, like the fact that Dave was murdered!" Billy screamed into the phone.

"I haven't lost my head, Billy. I probably did the smartest thing I could have done, considering."

"Forgetting to stay in touch with me was not smart, Chet. We've got to do some damage control. We need to know exactly what happened to Dave so we can protect our interests. Do you understand?"

"Of course I do. The paper here says that he got in a fight that night with some European tourist. The guy's name is—"

"I know all about the fight. He was fighting over one of our ticketing deals, but what the paper doesn't let you know is that he was okay after the fight and that he actually left the bar with a sexy redhead."

Chet concentrated on what Billy said while also watching to make sure his new bride hadn't missed him. "Do you know anything about her?"

"Not yet. I've got some guys checking into it, but Dave didn't make it easy to figure out. Evidently, he had been with a different woman every night since he left here. Could have been that he got hold of one that wasn't into sharing him, but it also could have been a set-up. Someone could have had the girl lure him away so they could nail him. Dave never was any good at watching his back. On the other hand, it could have been something else completely. Either way, I'll find out, and the redhead and anyone else involved will pay."

"What do I do?"

"You just make sure to keep yourself out of it. I know you're in Mexico. The whole world is keeping tabs on you now. Really, Chet, what were you thinking? Well, I'm telling you—no, I'm ordering you—don't go near Dave's place. I've got guys taking care of it, and I'll keep you informed. I shouldn't have to remind you, but—not a word to your new bride about your *real* business," he snarled into the phone.

"Billy, that's what I was trying to tell you," Chet lowered his voice to a whisper, "I have been thinking. I've got my own plan, and if everything works out the way I'm planning, we won't have any troubles—ever."

"Chet, don't do anything stupid," Billy warned. "Keep your nose clean, at least until we get to the bottom of what happened to Dave."

"Don't worry. I've got it all figured out," Chet said as he hung up the phone.

Billy slammed the receiver, trying to imagine what Chet had planned. Chet didn't have a clue on how to effectively run the business; if he did, he would have never married one of the most prominent young women in America, drawing the media to him like sharks to a bloodbath. How could he continue running the business on the west coast if he lived in a fishbowl? Billy grabbed the newspaper from his desk and slung it across the room, sending the pages flying in every direction.

Chet returned to find Georgia looking for him.

"Where did you go?" she said. She grinned, casually ran a hand up his thigh.

"Just planning a little surprise for you," he replied with a wink.

"I love surprises," she purred.

"You'll really love this one."

Chapter Twenty-six

Four weeks had passed since Tara had attended her first Wednesday night Bible study at the tiny church in Steamboat Springs. She hadn't missed a service since, partly because Brother Matthias McClain was so eager to bring her and partly because she just wanted to be there, reading her Bible and studying again. It was still difficult for her to comprehend that God could forgive her, but she was beginning to think that not only had He forgiven her, but He was allowing her to have new hope in life—in the form of Matthias McClain.

Matthias had called her daily since their chance meeting that Tuesday. He continually offered her a ride to and from town, acknowledging that she would be much more comfortable riding in his car than taking the city shuttle. He hadn't been aggressive in his friendship and that was something for which she was extremely thankful. She still missed Johnny terribly, and she wasn't ready for a serious relationship; somehow, she felt that Matthias understood.

Their time together was spent primarily attending church services and occasionally attending some of the local events, art exhibits and craft shows for the holiday season. During the week prior to Christmas, Steamboat Springs had a multitude of festivals and activities ranging from a living nativity to tree lighting ceremonies.

Matthias eagerly offered to take her to all of them, and Tara enjoyed spending more time with the handsome preacher.

Occasionally, as she and Matthias drove past The Summit, or when she saw an article about the famous newlyweds in the paper, Tara would regretfully be reminded of Chet Garrison. The articles displayed pictures of Chet and his beautiful bride enjoying the superb beaches of Mexico.

Tara remembered her own honeymoon in Mexico. She and Johnny had been so happy. They had planned to spend the rest of their lives together, to have children together, to grow old together—and Chet Garrison had helped to take that dream away. She was still so very outraged at what those men had done, but she was now hoping that at least one of them had changed his life.

Matthias had mentioned that Chet Garrison had attended a few Bible studies with Georgia, and although he didn't seem to enjoy the studies, he still came to make her happy. Tara prayed that he would continue to learn about God and turn away from his sinful life. She tried daily to forgive Chet Garrison, but just as soon as she felt she could, the memory of Johnny's death would overpower her willingness to forgive—and the bitter hatred would return.

Tara continued to pray to God for help. She knew that He was listening to her again, and she began to feel a trace of peace. She thought that possibly seeing Chet and Georgia when they returned to Steamboat would help her to view him as a changed person and would help her to forgive. She wouldn't have to wait much longer for the opportunity. They were scheduled to return after the New Year.

On Christmas morning, Tara awoke to the constant ringing of the phone. She stumbled out of bed, slowly made her way into the small living room of the condo and made an effort to stop the shrill sound.

"Hello?" she said, wondering if the croaking sound she heard was actually her voice.

"Still sleeping, huh?" Matthias asked.

"I'm up now. I should probably be up anyway," she said groggily. She strained her eyes to view the red digital numbers displayed on the microwave's clock. "Six o'clock? In the morning?" she asked, unsure now if she was dreaming or if Matthias was actually on the other end.

"Sorry it's so early, but I was wondering about something."

"What were you wondering?" she asked with a wide yawn.

"What did you do for Thanksgiving?"

"Thanksgiving?"

"Yes. What did you do? I hadn't met you then, and I was wondering what you did. You were in Steamboat, weren't you?" he continued.

Tara had to think for a moment to remember. "I was here," she recalled. "Okay. I watched the television parades, ate a turkey sandwich and watched a football game." She thought about saying that she had also cried for the majority of the day, feeling angry and miserable, but she refrained.

"That's what I thought," Matthias said, then paused. "One question first, and I don't need details, but I do need to know."

"Okay," she said nervously. "What is it?"

"I've seen your wedding ring."

"I lost my husband nearly a year ago," she said, not wanting to talk about it any more than that.

"I thought so, but I needed to ask."

"I know," she whispered, blinking past the emotion of everything that had happened in the past year.

"I'm sure the holidays aren't easy now, but I want to help if I can."

"I'm listening."

"The fact is, I have a proposition for you, Mara."

"Proposition," Tara repeated, still trying to become more accustomed to her other name.

"Yes. I want to help your Christmas top your Thanksgiving, and from what you've told me, the bar isn't that high."

She was glad he'd turned the conversation away from the somber and to the lighthearted. "Thanks," she said sarcastically.

"No, really," Matthias continued. "I want you to spend today with me, if you don't have any plans."

"I don't, but I thought you would be visiting your family for the holiday. Where did you say they live?"

"Oregon, but they're traveling with a mission team. I think they're actually scheduled to be in Germany on Christmas day. That's normal for them, so I'm used to planning my own holiday. And I've got this one planned, so what do you say?"

Tara had wondered how she would spend Christmas and had anticipated it being absolutely horrible. She knew that she would enjoy the time with Matthias, but part of her once again felt as though she'd betray Johnny to enjoy the holiday with another man, rather than thinking of him and that they should be spending it together.

"Mara?"

"I'm sorry. I was thinking."

Matthias really wanted to spend the holiday with her, but he hadn't felt confident in asking her during the previous weeks. Somehow, he knew that she didn't feel right about celebrating. He had hoped that she would tell him why she occasionally got upset during church, or why she didn't seem to let her guard down with him, or why she called herself Mara. In truth, he wanted to know everything about her.

He could sense a strength in her, a knowledge of things spiritual, of the true priorities of life; he knew that she put God first. And yet, he sensed the sadness lurking beneath the surface, something that troubled her soul, and he wanted to help. He wanted to help the Lord save her, and in truth, he desperately wanted the chance to love her. She had been in his every waking thought since he met her that day at the church, but he knew he needed to be careful. He didn't want to upset her, or by any means, scare her away.

During the past weeks, they had gradually spent more time together, and he had enjoyed every minute. But it was as companions, as friends, and he desperately wanted to begin building on that friendship. He wanted to take care of her—forever. He wanted to love her and more than that, he wanted her to return his love.

"Mara, please," he said, not knowing what the right words would be, but hoping she would know how much he wanted to be with her today.

He was pleading to her now. Tara thought of Johnny. He had loved her so deeply, but he wouldn't have wanted her alone on Christmas. He actually wouldn't have wanted her alone at all.

"Okay," she whispered.

Matthias said a silent prayer of thanks to God. "It will be a full day," he said excitedly. "Can you be ready by ten?"

"You woke me up at six to ask if I can be ready by ten?"

"I wanted to catch you off-guard," Matthias replied.

"And you did. Sure, I'll be ready."

Smiling, Matthias hung up the phone. "She said yes," he whispered as he started toward the shower. "She said yes."

Four hours later, he parked outside of Snowden Condominiums and anxiously waited. Finally, she exited the building. She looked stunning, wearing a bright red coat with matching hat and gloves, with two tendrils of blond hair delicately framing her face and bouncing slightly as she walked toward his car. Matthias was so taken by her appearance, he nearly forgot to get out and help her in. Suddenly remembering, he jumped from the car, slipped on a small patch of ice and immediately fell to the ground.

Tara quickened her pace to help him. "Are you okay?" she asked, watching her step as she neared the car.

"I am now," he said, trying to grin past the pain. He stood slowly, braced himself against the car, but the patch of ice was still beneath his feet. Slipping again, he tried to grasp the door handle, but only managed to catch Tara's hand on the way down. With a chorus of squeals, the two hit the ground with a thud. Tara immediately threw her head back and laughed. She looked at Matthias, and laughed some more. Matthias stared. He had never heard her laugh so hard. She edged her way to the side of the car, propped herself against it and laughed until she cried.

"I'm sorry," she managed. "It's just that, well—I guess I needed a good laugh. Are you okay?"

Matthias moved beside her, both of them now sitting on the cold patch of ice, with their backs leaning against the car. "I am. Are you?"

"I am," she giggled.

Matthias looked at the beautiful woman sitting next to him. She was happy. For the first time since he had met her, she looked content, and he loved the change. Snow started misting them as he continued staring at her. Jolted from the fall, her red hat balanced near the back of her head, releasing a sea of blonde locks to fall on both sides of her face. White snowflakes rested on her lashes, her nose and lips. Unaware of his examination, she continued giggling.

He wasn't sure what made him do it. He had tried to keep his feelings in check, but she was so incredibly beautiful, and he wanted her.

One moment Tara was laughing, feeling the cool brush of snow against her eyes, cheeks and lips. Then, she felt warmth, a wonderful invigorating heat that she knew, but hadn't experienced in nearly a year.

Matthias simply couldn't resist. Her lips were so inviting, glistening with the smallest amount of snow. He kissed her tenderly, not wanting to scare her, but needing to be close to her. He felt her tense and was about to pull back, but then—

Tara's mind spun as she tasted him, realizing he wanted her, realizing she wanted him. She parted her lips and let his tongue linger, not wanting it to end.

The increasing amount of falling snow, coupled with the frigid temperature, caused the two to ultimately part. Tara stared at him through snow-covered lashes, her eyes filled with tears.

Matthias brushed her tears away. "I'm sorry, Mara. I didn't mean to upset you. I just wanted to be close to you," he stammered as he helped her stand. "Please. Don't cry."

Tara continued to look into the crystal blue eyes that made her heart beat faster, simply because of the way they looked at her. She still tasted his kiss, still felt the warmth of him, the heat from him.

"I'm not crying because you've hurt me. I'm crying because I never thought I would feel anything like that again," she admitted.

"I care about you, Mara," he said as the snow continued to fall. "I want you to trust me. I know something horrible has happened to you, but I want you to talk to me. I want to help you. Honestly, I want to know everything about you."

"I don't know if I can," she said truthfully. "I don't know if you would want to know me at all if you knew everything."

"Believe me, there is nothing that you could say or do to change the way I feel. I don't want to push you. You can talk to me whenever you want, but you've got to give me a chance."

Tara began to shiver, partially because of the cold, partially because of the whirlwind of emotions running through her heart and her soul. She wondered if she could truly start over, if she would be able to tell Matthias about what those men did to Johnny, about the baby she lost, and most of all, about what she had done to Dave Danielson.

She shivered again.

"Come on, let's get you in the car. I shouldn't have kept you out here this long," Matthias said as they cautiously stepped past the icy patch and he helped her into the car.

He returned to the driver's seat and immediately turned up the heat thermostat. "Now we should get warm."

"Where are we going?" Tara asked, trying to get her mind off of the kiss and back on the day ahead.

"We're going to Mike's house. He has a couple of toys he asked me to try out for him."

"Toys?"

"You'll see," he answered with a wink.

"I've been a bit surprised that he hasn't finished working on my car yet. I know you said he's a one man show, but I would have thought that he would have been able to fix it by now."

"Oh, I was supposed to tell you that he's got it ready," Matthias said.

Tara noted the nervous tone instantly, and thought she knew why. "When exactly did he ask you to tell me?"

"Well, I can't recall exactly," Matthias said. He grinned, a little too broadly, a little too guiltily.

"Okay. About when?" She watched his neck flush crimson, and then the redness stretched its way to his face.

"Two weeks ago."

"You're terrible," she said. "Why didn't you tell me?"

"I wasn't sure if you were just waiting on the car to leave town. I had to make sure I had you thinking you couldn't live without me. I mean without a nice, long vacation in Steamboat, of course."

Still amazed that he kept it from her, she asked, "Does Mike know you didn't tell me?"

"He might."

"Then you're both terrible," Tara said, taking the red hat and flinging it at him and sending snowflakes against his chest in the process.

"We'll make it up to you today. I promise."

They pulled into a small farm on the outskirts of Steamboat. The driveway had been cleared of snow, and it wound through a long field to a fascinating log cabin completely surrounded by a wide porch. It was breathtaking. Tara saw Mike's two daughters working steadily at building a snowman. A carrot, scarf, buttons and gloves were scattered haphazardly on the snow around them.

"Hello!" Matthias yelled as he and climbed out of the car.

"Hello, Brother Matt," the oldest girl squealed. "Guess what we got for Christmas!"

"Tell me."

"Sticks!" the smallest girl yelled with a small giggle.

"No, we didn't. We got a new sled. Go inside and see it. We'll ride it after we're finished with Max."

"Who's Max?"

"Our snowman, silly."

Matthias and Tara made their way inside to the smell of pumpkin pie, baked chicken and yams.

"Glad you could come," Gina said from the kitchen. "Mike's out back getting your ride ready."

"Thanks," Matthias said. In his eyes, Mike and Gina had the perfect marriage. After over fifteen years together, they were still on their honeymoon. They held hands and even stole a kiss or two in public, had two beautiful little girls that they both adored, and they loved the Lord. Matthias enjoyed being around them; it provided him with a picture of the life he longed for, and it proved to him that it was possible to find that special person who can share your passion spiritually as well as physically. Matthias looked at Tara, wondering if one day they could share their lives together, and if she would ever let him in.

"Our ride is ready?" Tara asked as Matthias led her through the house to the back porch. He grabbed two sets of slick gloves from a hook by the back door, then, as Tara watched in amazement, he grabbed two helmets.

"What are we doing?"

"Snowmobiles," Matthias informed, opening the door to show her the two shiny ones parked outside. Mike walked out of the barn and smiled at his two guests.

"Okay, Matthias. Try not to get too wild for her first time. We want you to still be in one piece for dinner."

"Will do," Matthias said.

Mike showed Tara the basics before leaving them to ride. Matthias led the way through the glowing white fields behind Mike and Gina's home. Tara's blood pumped violently as they sped through the fields of snow. Matthias darted right and left, occasionally pointing out an elk or deer that had ventured to the edge of the clearing. He thoroughly enjoyed the ride and equally enjoyed the experience with Tara.

Tara loved the adventure. Although she had seen the beauty of the city of Steamboat, she now witnessed the pristine splendor of the land surrounding the city, and it was extraordinary.

After four hours of riding, they returned, exhausted and exhilarated, to have dinner with Mike and Gina. They breathlessly told the married couple about everything they had witnessed, from elk, deer and red fox to intricately frozen waterfalls, so well-preserved in their frozen state that they resembled lacy bridal veils.

Mike and Gina listened intently, knowing that they were witnessing something that they had wanted for years. Brother Matthias McClain, falling in love.

Chapter Twenty-seven

Steamboat Springs boasted one of the nation's largest New Year's Eve celebrations. Parties were numerous, with many taking place on the mountains. The ski slopes were splendid, lit with a massive amount of tiny sparkling lights that illuminated the fallen snow and made the entire mountain look iridescent and glittery. Tara couldn't help but think that this had to be the most superb way to bring in the New Year.

She and Matthias rode the gondola to the midpoint of the mountain and joined a group from church to perform their annual "Skiing in the New Year" ritual. It was something Matthias had started when he first became the preacher at the small church and was basically a way to let them get together and do something fun that didn't involve intoxication.

When they exited the gondola, the group gathered to sing a hymn and pray for the year to come. Then they each took the route most appropriate for their ski-level. The majority embraced the green run entitled *Why Not*, a scenic, easy route that wasn't too difficult on anyone. A few daredevils opted for a black run called *Concentration*. Ultimately, they all met at the base of the mountain, where the elderly of the congregation, including Brother Brantley,

Sister Evelyn and Sister Maddie, waited for a final prayer service with the group.

Tara thought the idea was marvelous and was thrilled to be a part of the tradition. She watched Matthias with admiration as he led the congregation in praise to God. Since Christmas morning, they had been inseparable, and although he hadn't tried to kiss her again, Tara found that she anxiously looked forward to midnight, because the New Year's Eve tradition would most likely define their second kiss, and she definitely wanted to feel that passion once more.

Matthias also found himself watching the clock as the night progressed. He had truly enjoyed Christmas with Tara. During the days that followed, he'd spent every day with her, mostly showing her the not-so-obvious sights of Steamboat. He had never even realized how many attractions the town had to offer and was disappointed in himself that he had taken so many beautiful things for granted. She had listened intently when he had told her about the Sleeping Giant, a vast mountain that had the acute appearance of a large man sleeping, who was said to be keeping watch over the town and protecting its inhabitants. Donning snowshoes, they had rigorously hiked the mountain, even venturing to see the infamous Rabbit-Ears Pass. And when he had informed her about the town vote that changed the name of Steamboat's bridge from The *Stockbridge* to the *James Brown Soul Center of the Universe Bridge*, she had absolutely loved the story. She'd laughed the most when she asked what his vote had been, and he'd answered, "James Brown, of course."

Matthias watched her gracefully glide down the mountain obviously quite comfortable on skis. He wondered what other sports she enjoyed, and if she would ever let him know about her life before she came to Steamboat. He prayed to God that she would. He wanted to know. He wanted to know everything, because he loved everything about her.

The final prayer service ended thirty minutes before midnight. Mike had offered to drive the elderly members of the congregation to their respective homes while Gina stayed to enjoy the festivities. Matthias helped to see them off, then returned to Tara.

"I've enjoyed tonight," she said.

"I have too. You're quite a skier."

"I've been skiing a few times, but never at night. The slope is so incredible with the lights reflecting from it."

"Mara, I've been thinking, and I want to ask you something. You don't have to answer."

"What is it?"

"Mara. That isn't your name, is it?"

"It is now."

"But why? I'm certain you know the history behind it. Naomi asked to be called Mara because the name meant 'bitter.' And she was bitter toward the Lord for allowing her husband and children to die," Matthias said grimly.

"Yes," Tara answered.

"That's what happened to you."

"Yes."

"Do you blame the Lord?"

"I did blame the Lord. I blamed Him, and I was angry with Him. I even felt that He had abandoned me, that He no longer listened when I prayed and that He didn't care. You're right, Matthias. I lost my husband and my baby. And I did blame the Lord, but I don't anymore. I blamed Him, and then I met you. But I must tell you that I've done something horrible, something I thought that the Lord could never forget, something I thought He could never forgive. But that first Wednesday night that I went to study with you, you taught me about God's forgiveness, of His unconditional love for us, even when we have done something so undeniably wrong. You have helped me so much, Matthias. I could never truly let you know how very much you have helped me—with your lessons, with your friendship, and with your—"

"Love," Matthias completed.

Tara's eyes welled with tears. "There's more that you have to know, but I'm just not ready—"

"It's okay. We'll have plenty of time. Just promise me that you'll let me help."

"I will," she promised as the clock struck midnight.

Matthias stepped closer to her. Slowly, he ran his hand along her cheek then traced her lips with a gentle finger. He leaned toward her and kissed her softly, then more firmly as he pulled her close. He locked his arms around her and gently kissed her neck. Matthias covered her neck, her throat, her cheeks and lips with soft, warm kisses. Tara moaned tenderly as her body melted into him. "Don't ever try to leave me. I can't let you go. Not now, not ever," he whispered as they continued touching, holding and kissing.

They were still embracing when Matthias heard his name screamed from the street.

"Matthias!" Mike yelled again.

Seeing Matthias and Tara, he quickly apologized. "Matthias, Mara, I'm sorry, but there's been an accident, a terrible accident. An assistant for Grayson Eubanks called the church looking for you, Matthias."

"Grayson Eubanks," Matthias repeated. "Why does he want me?"

"It's Georgia. There was an accident in Mexico, some kind of diving accident when she and her husband were diving. Matthias, she's dead."

Chapter Twenty-eight

Grayson Eubanks insisted that Matthias conduct the funeral service. Unbeknownst to Matthias, Georgia had never regularly attended any type of church prior to the church at Steamboat, and Grayson had been deeply touched by his daughter's sudden rejuvenated faith. Now that she was gone, Grayson could think of no one better to remind the world that his daughter still lived, not only in his heart, but eternally as well.

After learning of Georgia's death, Matthias had taken Tara home then left Steamboat immediately. Grayson Eubanks had sent a private plane to the small airport in Hayden, merely twenty miles from Steamboat, to take the preacher directly to Nashville for the two days of visitation and then the funeral.

Matthias had been so shocked at the news of the young woman's death that he hadn't noticed Tara's reaction as being more than warranted sympathy. Both of them had been silent during the drive to her condominium. He was thinking of the tragedy of a life lost so young; she was thinking of the possibility that Chet Garrison had murdered—again.

As Matthias' plane made its ascent in the first hours of New Year's Day, Tara sat on the couch in her condominium staring blankly at the television as the news station relayed the report.

This late breaking story. Georgia Eubanks-Garrison, daughter of prominent businessman, Grayson Eubanks of Eubanks Enterprises, died earlier this evening in a diving accident near Cancun, Mexico. At age twenty-four, Mrs. Eubanks-Garrison, the heir to the Eubanks fortune, was celebrating her honeymoon with her husband of one month, Chet Garrison of Steamboat Springs, Colorado when their honeymoon ended tragically. Please stay tuned for additional details."

Tara wondered what actually had happened in Mexico. "A diving accident," she said. Her mind returned to the honeymoon she had shared with Johnny. They had gone diving practically every day. She remembered how meticulous the diving instructors had been and how they carefully watched each diver to ensure safety. Even after she and Johnny had completed their certification requirements, the instructors had been extremely watchful, making sure that everything was perfect before proceeding with any dive. Surely with a diver that had the notoriety of Georgia Eubanks-Garrison, the utmost care would have been taken to ensure her safety. What could have gone wrong?

Tara's thoughts were interrupted by the newscast.

Additional details concerning the death of Georgia Eubanks-Garrison. For those of you just tuning in…Georgia Eubanks-Garrison, the daughter of prominent businessman, Grayson Eubanks of Eubanks Enterprises, died this evening in a diving accident near Cancun, Mexico. At age twenty-four, Mrs. Eubanks-Garrison, the heir to the Eubanks fortune, was celebrating her honeymoon with her husband of one month, Chet Garrison of Steamboat Springs, Colorado when their honeymoon ended tragically.

Channel Six has just learned that Mrs. Eubanks-Garrison was participating in an activity known as cenote diving when she and her husband were inadvertently separated from the remainder of their diving group. While attempting to locate the group, according to Mr. Garrison, Mrs. Eubanks-Garrison had difficulty with her equipment, and although her husband fought to get her to safety, her air supply quickly depleted, resulting in her untimely death. This station would like to offer its sincere sympathy to Mr. Garrison, and to all of the Eubanks family.

Please stay tuned for additional information regarding the death of Georgia Eubanks-Garrison and cenote diving.

"Cenote diving," Tara repeated. She and Johnny had been extremely interested in cenote diving while they were in Mexico. It was the main reason he had wanted to go there for the honeymoon. That particular type of diving required a special cave diving certification, which she and Johnny had obtained upon their arrival in Mexico. But, even with the certification, the guides would never have let them get lost. Tara's stomach knotted as she wondered what had really happened in the cave. She got up, went to the bathroom to wet a small towel then returned to the couch to continue watching. Placing the towel across her throbbing head, she continued to watch the broadcast.

Additional information on the death of Mrs. Georgia Eubanks-Garrison. Channel Six has just received information regarding the form of diving that Mrs. Eubanks-Garrison was participating in when she met her untimely death. Cenote diving refers to a specialized form of diving wherein the diver is actually diving within

*a cavern, or cenote. Cenotes may technically be considered
'sinkholes', but they differ considerably from what we generally
envision as a 'sinkhole.' The Yucatan peninsula has only a few lakes
and rivers above ground level. Below ground, however, the
peninsula is covered with a limestone shelf. When a portion of earth
above the river or lake collapses, it tends to stay that way, forming a
cenote. The water contained within a cenote is crystal clear,
allowing up to one hundred and fifty feet of visibility, thus providing
the diving enthusiast with an experience of a lifetime; however,
divers are strongly cautioned when performing a cenote dive. Divers
must be cave-dive certified to dive in these underground rivers.
According to authorities on cenote diving, it is easy, and deadly, to
get lost. Unfortunately, that's exactly what happened to Georgia
Eubanks-Garrison. Again, this station offers our deepest
condolences to the family.*

Tara turned off the television and sat in the darkness waiting for
the first light of morning. Matthias was probably nearing Nashville
by now.

Lord, keep him safe.

She thought again of Chet Garrison. She hoped that her instincts
were wrong, and that perhaps he and Georgia did accidentally lose
their way, but she couldn't help feeling that he was responsible for
her death. She wondered exactly what he would have had to gain
from her death, but then again, Matthias had insisted that Chet
cared about his new bride. Hopefully, Tara's suspicions weren't
true. If that was the case, she was indeed sorry for Chet Garrison,
because he'd obviously experience the mourning that she endured
a year ago. In any case, she wondered, wondered what really
happened, wondered if Chet Garrison was actually a cold-blooded

killer, and wondered how soon it would be until Matthias would actually be talking with Georgia's husband.

Lord, please keep Matthias safe.

Chapter Twenty-nine

Exactly one week after he'd left to conduct Georgia's funeral, Matthias was flown back to Steamboat Springs, courtesy of Grayson Eubanks. He'd called Tara twice during his absence. She could tell that the proceedings were taking their toll on the entire Eubanks family, and Matthias. He had sounded quite tearful and exhausted, mentioning the heartbreaking condition of Grayson Eubanks and the remainder of Georgia's family. Tara couldn't help but notice that Matthias had neglected to mention Chet during either call.

She was at the church helping Sister Maddie with her weekly cleaning when Matthias arrived. Tara had just completed polishing the last pew when the church door creaked open. Matthias looked as if he hadn't slept in days. His blue eyes were bloodshot and swollen, and his clothes extremely wrinkled from the flight.

"I tried to call you after we landed. When I didn't get an answer, I thought you'd left," he said, concern written clearly on his face. "Then, when I passed the church, I saw your car."

"I picked it up from Mike's shop last week. It's running fine, though I've missed the company of having someone to ride with."

"I've missed that too," he admitted, moving toward her and nodding to Sister Maddie.

"I asked if Mara could help me clean up before you came back," Sister Maddie informed, though Matthias was fairly certain that the church had not been in dire need of a detailed cleaning. Sister Maddie always kept the building immaculate, but she had probably wanted the opportunity to visit with Mara, more than likely to find out exactly what was happening between her and their beloved preacher.

Matthias smiled at the elderly lady. She really did care about him. It was almost like having an additional mother to look after him when his biological one wasn't available.

"Mara, can I speak to you in my office for just a moment?" he asked.

Sister Maddie began to hum, as though she weren't lingering on every word.

"Of course," Tara answered, resting the polishing rag on the back of a pew. She followed him into the small office.

"I've missed you," he said, running his hands through his hair. "I've missed you more than I could have thought possible."

"I've missed you, too."

"Listen, I'm truly exhausted. But, I had to tell you— I've been thinking a lot about things between us. I want to know more about you, Mara, if you're willing to tell me. And, well, there's something I want to talk specifically to you about, but not right now. I don't want to say the wrong thing, and right now, I'm too tired to speak very long and maintain my coherence. Can we get together later today to talk?"

Tara observed the urgency in his voice, and although she didn't know what he needed to say, she felt that she needed a little time to be prepared...for anything.

"Why don't you just let yourself rest today? You do look exhausted. I promise that I won't leave. I didn't leave while you were gone; I certainly won't leave now that you're back. We can get together tomorrow and talk, if that's okay."

Matthias hesitated. She didn't say no, but he thought he detected a bit of nervousness in her tone. "Okay," he finally agreed, realizing that, with the small amount of sleep he had achieved in the past week, he could very well go to sleep and not wake up until tomorrow.

Walking with him to the church parking lot, Tara finally gained the courage to ask him what had been gnawing at her for a week. "Matthias," she began.

"Yes?"

"Georgia's husband. You haven't mentioned him. How is Mr. Garrison holding up?"

Matthias stopped walking, seemingly in heavy thought. "I'm not sure, Mara. I mean, he was in mourning, but he was so quiet. He never spoke, never said a word. I suppose that's his way of coping, but I fear that he may blame himself. I don't know exactly what happened in the cave, but I do know that he tried to help her and wasn't successful. It's very sad."

"Is he still in Nashville?" Tara asked, trying to sound as though she were merely concerned for the poor man, instead of wondering about his part in Georgia's death.

"No. He actually rode back on the plane with me," Matthias said, opening the door of his car. "Strangest thing. He just sat there, staring straight ahead. He didn't say a word throughout the entire trip. It reminded me of the way he had looked the first time I met him. I had actually forgotten about it until all of this."

"When was that?"

"I guess it was last year, last spring. He came here, to the church building, really upset. He said he needed to talk to me about something. Then, he abruptly changed his mind, saying he didn't need to talk at all. I truly had forgotten it until now, but his face— well, his face is so tense now and his eyes are so distressed. I guess that's what reminded me of the day he came into the church. He looked exactly the same," Matthias finished, climbing into the car. "We need to pray for him, Mara. We need to pray for him and all of the Eubanks family. It's so very sad to lose someone so young."

Matthias sat at the steering wheel, now realizing the impact of what he had just stated. "I'm sorry, Mara. I know you lost your husband and your baby. Of course you know what it feels like to lose someone so dear and so young. Please forgive me. I'm so very tired. It was thoughtless."

"There's nothing to forgive." She leaned into the car, kissed him softly. "You go get some sleep. Call me tomorrow. And, I will pray. I will pray for all of them."

She stood in the parking lot and watched him drive away, unable to stop thinking about what Matthias had said. Chet's face had looked the same, the same as it did last spring—after he'd helped murder Johnny. Tara silently prayed as she steadily walked toward the building.

God, please be with the Eubanks family. Help them to be strong during this difficult time. And Lord, I pray that Chet Garrison didn't murder his wife, that he has truly turned his life around, and if that is the case, please be with him as he mourns. And if it be Your will, Lord, Tara hesitated before adding, *Help me find out what actually happened. If it be Your will, help me learn the truth.*

After Tara and Sister Maddie completed cleaning the church building, she drove back to her condominium. She parked the car, and then remembered that Chet Garrison was just a short drive up the mountain. Without taking time to change her mind, she cranked the car and began the drive toward his chalet.

Seeing the wrought iron gate and brick columns, Tara couldn't prevent a foreboding sense of danger making her skin tingle and stomach quake. A red bow, evidently left over from Christmas, hung from one of the black gateposts. The long ribbon whipped through the breeze, as though it were preparing to...strike.

Tara knew she shouldn't have come here. She pulled the Mustang into the paved area in front of the chalet's gated entrance and was backing the car to turn around when a shiny black Mercedes came barreling up the mountain, nearly running right into her. She waved and mouthed an apology to the driver, knowing that in fact the driver of the car had been speeding and would have probably been considered at fault if an accident had occurred.

The glare of the sun reflecting from the snow hid the driver's face from Tara's view through the windshield; however, as the car stopped to let her completely back up and begin her descent down the mountain, Tara had a clear view of the driver through his side window. Her body shook with maddened fear as the crystal clear image of Billy Reynolds stared back at her when she passed.

Chapter Thirty

Annoyed at the fact that he had to wait for the cute little blonde to turn her car around, Billy rapidly punched the code into Chet's keypad entry. *Code Denied* flashed on the digital screen above the square of numbers. Billy snarled, banged on the intercom button at the bottom of the keypad.

"May I help you?"

"He's changed the code! I'm here to see Chet," Billy growled into the microphone, utterly perturbed at the very female voice on the other end.

"Mr. Garrison isn't accepting guests at this time, nor is he talking to the media," she quickly informed.

"He'll see me."

"And who might you be?" she asked again, obviously thinking that she was dealing with a complete nuisance, instead of someone who had the power to have her removed. From this estate, or from the world in general. His choice.

"Billy Reynolds. Now, let me in!" he screamed.

The gates immediately swung open and the Mercedes disappeared inside.

Billy entered the elaborate chalet as though he owned it, storming past the housekeeper who attempted to take his coat and completely unimpressed by the extravagant décor.

"Where is he?" he bellowed, stomping across the marble floor.

Chet exited his second floor bedroom to stand on the balcony above. "Well, Billy, what a surprise," he said sarcastically, puffing on a thick cigar. "I thought we were still keeping our distance. You know, laying low."

Billy snarled as he began the hike up a circular staircase to reach the second floor.

"You could have taken the elevator." Chet smirked when Billy neared.

"What were you thinking?" Billy raged, shoving Chet against the railing of the balcony. "How much attention are you trying to draw to yourself?" he continued, now pushing Chet back into the bedroom and slamming the door.

"Mr. Garrison, are you okay?" the same female voice echoed through the room's intercom. "Should I call for help?"

"Maybe she should," Billy hissed, watching Chet make his way to the intercom.

"We're fine, Elle. It's just an old, dear friend, obviously upset about Georgia. We're just fine. Please do not allow us to be disturbed, unless of course, it is Mr. Eubanks."

"Certainly," the voice responded before Chet released the intercom transmitter.

"Billy, I can explain," Chet began coolly.

"Explain!" Billy ordered.

"The Summit wasn't doing as well as I had expected. I was hurting for cash, you know, and well, let's face it, our other *business* has had a slow year on the west coast, so I needed more funds. Think about it. Who has better cash flow than Eubanks Enterprises?"

"You murdered an heiress. You married her, and then you murdered her. How long do you think it will be until Daddy Eubanks figures it out? And trust me, Grayson Eubanks will not allow anyone to live once they've harmed his family."

"Now, Billy. You don't think that Georgia was actually murdered, do you? I mean, everyone saw how upset I was. I'm still in mourning of course." He grinned wickedly. "And, by all means, I tried to save her, tried earnestly to save her." He puffed on the cigar, paced leisurely toward an expansive window that overlooked the slopes below.

"He'll find out," Billy said, though he wondered if Chet could actually pull this off. And then he added, "Why did you do it, Chet? You could have had the Eubanks money and Georgia Eubanks too. You didn't have to kill her to get the money."

"Do you really think her old man would have put up with a husband who wasn't truly faithful to his little princess? You know me, Billy. How am I supposed to stick myself with one woman? Forever? I mean, sure, I'll take the *for better* but not the *for worse*."

"How do you expect to hold onto any of Eubanks now? You murdered your main source of cash flow."

"Now, now, Billy. Don't think for one moment that Grayson Eubanks is going to let the man who his daughter chose to marry, the man who tried faithfully to save her life, even risking his own life to do so, ever hurt for money. No, indeed. As a matter of fact, 'Daddy' has already mentioned as much to me. He'll be finalizing everything by the end of the month. Says that's what his baby would have wanted."

Billy stared in disbelief. Chet had come a long way from the stammering wreck he had been last year when they murdered those two in New Orleans.

"He doesn't suspect anything?" Billy asked, still skeptical.

"Not a thing, friend. Now, will you calm down? How about a cigar?"

"No. No, I've got to get back to Tampa. Shouldn't have come here, but I thought you'd really blown it. I have to admit, Chet, you've surprised me this time. I didn't think you had it in you."

"Trust me. I do," Chet affirmed as he watched Billy head for the door. "Oh, Billy," Chet called.

"Yeah?"

"If you see Elle, ask her to come to my room. She's helping me to get through my mourning period, you know," he said with a wink, and he loosened the belt on his robe.

"No problem," Billy said, shaking his head as he closed the bedroom door.

*****

Tara stared at her reflection in the bathroom mirror.

"He didn't recognize me. Surely he didn't recognize me. God, please don't let him realize who I am."

She started the shower water and turned it as hot as it would go. Then she methodically removed her clothes and stepped into the scalding water, standing motionless as it pelted against her, turning her skin a brilliant scarlet. Finally determining that she was indeed safe from the horrible man, she adjusted the thermostat and continued her shower, unable to stop the visualization of the monster who had killed Johnny.

He's here. Billy Reynolds is here. Why? What is he doing with Chet? Does that prove that Chet murdered Georgia, or is Billy here for something else entirely? How can I stay here if Billy Reynolds is near? What am I going to do?

Tara climbed out of the shower and dried off, her thoughts still reeling from the awareness that Billy Reynolds was so close. She wanted to call Matthias, but didn't know what to say.

"He doesn't know what they did," she told herself. "I don't want to put him in danger. I can't risk losing him too."

God, please help me.

Tara picked up the latest issue of The Steamboat Pilot from the bedside table. She read the article about Georgia's accident once again.

"Mrs. Eubanks-Garrison and her husband were inadvertently separated from the remainder of the group..."

Tara remembered the beauty of cenote diving, jutting stalagmites, suspended stalactites and crystal clear water providing the perfect dive. She remembered the group that they had been with. Two guides helped them, one leading the group and one following.

How did you get separated from the group, Chet? You killed her, didn't you? You murdered your wife.

Tara opened the vertical blinds and stared into the stark whiteness of the mountain.

God help me.

She walked back to the couch and watched the sun dip beneath the mountain, and this horrible day drew to a close. Her eyes burned with tears and she continued to sit, thinking about Johnny. And Georgia.

She was about to close her eyes and attempt to sleep when she saw him, skiing down the slope that ran beside her condo. Knowing it was well past the time that the ski lifts stopped operating, she immediately realized that the skier had to be staying in one of the condominiums further up the mountain, or...a chalet.

Tara stood and watched him make his way down the mountain, gracefully gliding right and left, apparently taking in the scenery as he skied. Even though his head was covered, even though he wore large goggles, even though his entire body was encased in a complete ski gear tomb, she knew.

She quickly donned her ski clothes, grabbed the key to her ski locker downstairs and headed out. She didn't want to give herself time to think. God was helping her to find out the truth, and she just had to know. She pulled the ski boots out of the locker and put them on with a vengeance, threw the skis over her right shoulder, wrapped her left hand around the poles and made her way to the ramp exiting the condo.

She stepped outside and quickly noticed the snow had started once again. Amazingly, she could still see his shadow, slowly making its way down toward the base of the mountain. She hurriedly skied down the ramp and entered the slope, fiercely pumping the snow behind her with her poles. The snow fell harder as she neared the bottom of the slopes. Her goggles were frosted over, and she could no longer see the man that she thought…

"Watch out!" she heard him scream as she plummeted into him in a fury of skis and poles.

Stay with me, God. Stay with me.

"Are you okay?" he asked with a grunt, trying to stand and steady himself once again. "Obviously, I didn't see you coming."

"Sorry," she managed. Standing, Tara made sure that the goggles and ski cap clearly hid her face. She dusted herself off and looked up, peering instantly into the ruddy face of Chet Garrison.

"It's getting a bit dark to be skiing that quickly down the mountain, don't you think?" he asked.

"Lost a bit of control, I guess."

"I should say so," he said with a chuckle. He eyed her as she tried to get the lodged snow out of her boot. She balanced on one foot while aggressively beating the side of her opposite boot, attempting to force the packed snow to release. Unfortunately, all she managed to do was lose her balance and tumble back into the white mass.

Chet laughed at her, leaned over to help her up. He continued to help her dislodge the packed snow and reconnect the boot to the ski.

"Sorry," she repeated after both skis were back in place.

"Not at all. Obviously, I was in your way. Where were you headed, by the way? It's nearing dark, you know, and all of the lifts are closed," Chet acknowledged. He now noticed that despite the mounds of clothes she was wore, she appeared very petite. And the blond strands of hair that peaked from beneath her ski cap definitely held promise. He desperately wanted a better look at the face behind the mask though. No doubt, a woman managing that kind of speed down the mountain without a care to those obstructing her path would be a woman of adventure, and perhaps a woman for whom he would like to adventure.

"I didn't have a definite destination in mind when I started. Mainly, I just wanted another good run down the mountain," Tara answered.

"Well, I would say you ended this one with a bang. How about joining me for another?"

"The lifts are closed."

"I know," he said, grabbing her hand and pulling her down the remainder of the slope to the gondola. "But, where there's a will…"

Chet Garrison removed his skis outside the gondola station then motioned for Tara to do the same. They walked inside and he quickly located one of the lift attendants finishing the daily clean up. Tara watched him walk over to the man, obviously allowing the attendant to recognize him. The employee started talking rapidly, and although she couldn't hear everything that was said, she knew that he was telling Chet how sorry he was about Georgia's death. Chet accepted the words of thoughtfulness, then continued talking, occasionally pointing toward Tara.

The attendant left Chet and approached Tara, while Chet loaded the two sets of skis into the nearest silver gondola.

"It's so nice of you to try to help your brother cope right now," he whispered. "And I think you were right— skiing does help you feel peaceful, doesn't it?"

"Yes," Tara managed. She walked toward the gondola.

He said I was his sister? He said I wanted him to go skiing after he had lost his wife? Skiing? Oh dear God, please. I need to know. Did he? Did he actually murder her?

"Come on in," Chet instructed when Tara approached the gondola. He waved to the attendant and the silver bullet began its quick ascent up the mountain.

"I'm afraid when you barreled into me, I forgot to ask your name," Chet said.

"Mara."

"Mara. Very nice. I don't believe I've ever heard it."

She didn't respond.

"Quiet, aren't you?" he asked when the gondola pulled into the mid-mountain station. The doors slowly opened and he stepped out, quickly tossing both sets of skis over his shoulder.

"I guess I'm just surprised we could get a ride up here after the lifts had closed. You must have quite a bit of clout with the staff."

"I have my ways," he said with a wink. He'd hoped she would have removed the large goggles during the gondola ride. Somehow, he knew that she was hiding exquisite eyes, among other equally exquisite parts. And he'd bet that if he played his cards right, he would know all of those wonderful parts intimately before the night was over. He smiled at the thought.

"What's your pleasure? Green, blue or black?" Chet asked, nodding toward the slopes that branched out like spider legs in every direction.

"Black," she said without hesitation.

"My kind of woman," he said, watching her take the lead.

Tara quickly zigzagged her way down the darkened slope with Chet following closely. She squinted, forcing her eyes to see more clearly, since darkness completely enveloped the lower half of the slope.

When the run ended at one of the smaller chair lifts, Tara paused to catch her breath. Chet sprayed her with snow as he stopped within feet of her, then laughed while she struggled to shake the excess snow from her ski suit.

"Ready to go again?" he asked, nodding toward the motionless chair lift.

"It's closed." She didn't know how she would find out the truth, and she was quickly realizing the danger of being on the slope alone with Chet Garrison. If something were to happen, no one would even know that she were here.

God, why am I so foolish? Help me.

"It's only closed to those who don't have a key," Chet claimed gloatingly. He skied closer to the lift. "Luckily, I just 'borrowed' one from the guy down below."

Tara squinted into the darkness, not believing that he was about to head to the top again. Snow swirled wickedly around the top of the mountain, like spirals of smoke above boiling water. Even in the darkness, Tara knew the weather was worsening. They shouldn't head back to the top, and yet, if she wanted to know the truth, she could only find out from one person. Chet.

The chairlift motor whirred to life and snow-covered chairs started circling the lower maintenance building for the lift.

"Come on!" he yelled.

She skied to stand beside the swirling chairs, waiting for Chet to tell her when they should approach.

"Okay. Not this chair, the next one. Now," he directed, moving quickly behind the preceding chair.

Chet shuffled the blanket of snow from the seat and they quickly sat down. She reached to pull the safety bar down in front of them, but Chet stopped her attempt.

"No need. It's safe," he said with a smile. "Besides, it will save us some time at the end when we get off. Chances are, we won't be able to see the end coming in this darkness anyway. So you better help me pay attention," he added, edging closer to her in the seat.

Unlike the gondola, this chairlift crept up the mountain at a snail's pace. Metal chairs creaked and groaned, occasionally swaying on the steel cable with the increasing wind. The snow that had felt soft and delicate against their skin when they were at the base of the mountain now pelted violently, stinging every inch of exposed skin. Tara had tucked her mouth into the top of her ski coat to keep warm. Because of this, her voice was muffled, and Chet wasn't sure when she finally spoke if he had heard her correctly.

"Did you kill her?" the distorted voice shakily asked.

Thinking he must have imagined it, Chet turned to face the woman beside him on the lift. Knowing that he *couldn't* have heard what he thought, he reasoned that his mind was playing tricks on him. He was paranoid; she said something else, something different entirely.

"What did you say?" he yelled against the wind howling against the mountain.

"Did you kill her?" Tara screamed, enunciating every word. "Did you kill her the way you helped to kill Johnny?"

Realization hit Chet harder than the cold icy snow. "You! You're—dead!" he screamed, yanking off her goggles and knowing exactly who sat beside him. How was she still alive? How was she here? And then, without hesitation, he knew, knew exactly what he had to do.

He grasped the metal railing on the back of the chair with his left hand, fisted his right hand and pounded it into her face. Tara's body slumped against the side rail before she started slipping from the wet seat.

Chet didn't stop. He continued hitting her, pushing her, while Tara struggled to hold on.

Brutally, he kicked her, hit her, pushed her, trying everything he could to throw her from the chair. Tara could see the darkened shadows of sharp rocks looming underneath. She felt her skin become heated, covered in the stickiness of blood. She was hanging now, dangling like a Christmas ornament from a weak branch, with merely her fingertips holding death at bay. The chair creaked louder and rocked fiercely as she clung to the metal bar.

God, let me die. Just let me die.

She wanted to let go, wanted to end the yearlong nightmare, but He wouldn't let her. Her fingers were clenched around the hard metal, and although she wanted to release them, she couldn't. She couldn't let go. Then she knew. God wasn't letting her die. Not now. Not yet.

Please. Let me die!

Chet struggled to pry her fingers away from the chair, but she continued to hang on, the weight of her body and skis pulling against her.

"Let go!" he yelled, shaking the chair to make her release. "Let go!" he repeated, aggressively lunging to push her free.

Tara wasn't even sure what actually happened. She was praying, willing God to let her die, when Chet tried viciously to push her from the lift. The chair began to swing harder, wind ripped aggressively around them, and then, weight slammed against her body.

And yet she held on, unable to let go.

She heard him gasping, screaming as he plummeted.

And yet she held on.

Until finally, the large shadow of Chet Garrison disappeared into the sharp jagged fortress below.

Tara cried into the frigid cold wind. "What have I done? Dear God, what have I done?" Her throat ached from gasping the freezing cold air. Her screams were so hidden by the screeching wind that even she couldn't hear the sound.

The weight of her body and skis more than she could bear, Tara strained to pull herself back onto the chair, but she was too weak, too exhausted from the fight. She just wanted to let go, to fall to the ground below, but she couldn't.

Spiraling pillars of snow stretched out like elongated fingers from the mountain below, pushing upward with the furious wind and beckoning her body downward. Icy snow whipped bitterly around her, freezing the sticky blood that covered her face. Suspended limply from the freezing chair, she blinked her now unprotected eyes madly in the pulsating snow. Seeing the end of the lift, she watched the chairs ahead swing madly as they circled to begin their descent. There wasn't any way to pull her body up.

God forgive me. Forgive me. Let me go to Heaven. Let me be with Johnny.

She let go.

Chapter Thirty-one

Billy Reynolds stared incredulously at the flat television screen that conspicuously adorned virtually an entire wall of his home office. What had happened after he left Chet yesterday afternoon?

He had been glaring intently at the screen ever since he had received the call from Elle. Newscast after newscast tried vehemently to air the story first, or to get more of the story, before the other channels could intercept the news. Billy watched as yet another attractive blonde tried to master the art of smiling beautifully while appearing sincere with sympathy. And like all of the previous ditzes who'd kept the news stations hopping today, this one aired the story that the head of his west coast operations was gone.

"For those of you just tuning in, today's top story is the apparent suicide of Mr. Chet Garrison, husband of Mrs. Georgia Eubanks-Garrison, who died New Year's Eve.

Evidently still mourning over the passing of his beloved bride, Mr. Garrison apparently chose to end his life last evening by jumping from a ski lift on one of the slopes surrounding his northern Colorado home. An employee of the elite ski resort spotted the body of Mr. Garrison while performing a routine morning check of ski lifts on the mountain.

Grayson Eubanks, of Eubanks Enterprises and father-in-law to Mr. Garrison, issued the following statement regarding the death of his son-in-law: 'The entire Eubanks family has experienced a tremendous loss in the untimely deaths of our beloved Georgia and her adoring husband, Chet. Our lives will never be the same.'"

"All right, Grayson Eubanks. You've messed with the wrong man this time," Billy hissed into the screen. "So, you figured out he killed her and you had him murdered. I saw him yesterday. He was no more planning on killing himself than I was. And, it doesn't matter how much money you've got; I can play your game. You're messing with my business, my money, my power now, and no one plays Billy Reynolds for a fool!" he bellowed, grasping the remote and flinging it at the screen.

He was still fuming when he heard a knock at his office door.

"What is it!" he yelled, daring anyone to step inside.

"Mr. Reynolds, there is a Mr. Hathaway on line two. He says you had to speak to him, and that it is urgent."

"Yes, Carla, put him through."

Hawk Hathaway was the best at what he did. What he did, essentially, was anything Billy commanded. If anyone threatened to cause a problem for the business, Billy merely mentioned the name to Hawk, and the problem was resolved, without question. Billy paid handsomely for the man's services, but he was worth every dime. Of all of Billy's employees, Hawk was the most vital key to the business running efficiently.

Billy anxiously stormed to his desk and picked up the receiver. "What have you got, Hawk?"

"Maybe nothing, maybe something. Chet have any siblings?" the raspy voice queried.

"No. Why?" Billy asked, obviously thrown by the question.

"Well, according to one of the employees at the Steamboat Gondola, Chet had the guy start one of the lifts so he and his 'sister' could try to forget his troubles by skiing down the mountain."

"He definitely doesn't have a sister. I've known him since grade school. He's an only child, and his parents are deceased. He has no family, Hawk."

"I'm on it," Hawk affirmed.

"Check with Elle, his housekeeper. He was spending quite a bit of time with her, I believe. See if she was with him, or knows who was."

"Already checked with her. She wasn't there, wasn't even at the house when it happened. Said she went to a little coffee shop/bookstore kind of thing. Let's see. A place called *Off the Beaten Path*. I checked there this afternoon. Her story checks. So, whatever female accompanied him, it wasn't his faithful housekeeper."

"Let me know if you find anything else. I'll let you know if I learn anything on this end."

"Will do," the thick voice said before disconnecting.

"A sister," Billy muttered. "Would Grayson Eubanks have hired a woman to do a man's job?"

* * * * *

Tara moaned in agony as she rolled over on the cheap hotel mattress. Her body had screamed in pain throughout the painful journey down the mountain, but the convulsive pulsating that poured through her veins now only enumerated the fact that the worst was yet to come. Finding her way back to the condominium in the ebony of night would have been hard enough, without the fact that her eyes had been encrusted with frozen blood.

She'd abandoned her skis in the snow bank that saved her and had trodden aimlessly down the mountain falling continually in the brutal snowstorm until somehow she had ended the perilous journey at the condominium. It had been nearly dawn by the time she entered the building, but she knew she couldn't stop. She staggered into her room, struggling to pack her things as quickly as possible, then attempted to clean the blood from her face before slowly journeying to the car. Fortunately, it was close enough to daybreak that the streets had been freshly cleared by the morning snowplows and salt trucks, allowing her to make the four-hour journey to Denver.

The cheap motel room smelled of soured milk and whiskey, making Tara's head spin even more as she lay on the flimsy mattress, but she had needed something fast, before anyone began looking for her. And she had needed someone who wouldn't notice or care that she still showed evidence of a brutal battle, with cuts and blood abounding on every inch of exposed skin.

The broken mirror in the tiny room had affirmed that she hadn't done a very good job at all of cleaning her face this morning. Even on the places where the blood had been washed away, the faint streaks of red against her white skin warranted evidence of what had been. Luckily, the motel didn't have a true office, but merely the first room had a paper sign taped to the window identifying it as such. And the battered woman who answered the door had only been concerned with the fact that Tara paid in cash, plenty of cash.

Tara could feel the fever ravaging her body as she shivered on the filthy sheets. "I'm going to die here," she whispered. "Let me die here, God. You know what I did. I didn't learn. I didn't stop. I murdered him too. Dear God, just let me die. I don't deserve to live. God, forgive me. Johnny, forgive me. Matthias, forgive me," she mumbled incoherently as her body surrendered to the pain.

*****

Billy Reynolds couldn't sleep. Something wasn't right. It wasn't just Chet's murder. It was more. Something didn't connect. He paced the room trying to think. Hawk said that Chet had taken his sister on the lift. So this "sister" had been with him, at the very least had been the last person to see him, before he died. Chet died with, and perhaps at the hand of, a female. It had seemed odd that Eubanks would have hired a female to make the hit, but Billy hadn't refuted the idea. However, something else kept factoring into the entire scenario.

Then, Billy had it. Why hadn't he thought of it before? Dave. Dave's murder was still a mystery, and even though Billy had now pulled Hawk to work on Chet's, perhaps the answers to both murders were one in the same. Dave died with, or at the hand of, a female, the sexy redhead he'd left the bar with. Now Chet was dead, and was last seen with a female. What if it was the same female? What if it was someone they both knew? What if this was someone who know about Billy's operations and was trying to destroy him? Billy's head ached from the theory.

"Think! Think!" he ordered himself as he quickened his pace around his room. "Dave had been doing business as usual in Mexico, but he had been very active with the ladies. Perhaps one felt that she had been burned one too many times, but—no. That wouldn't figure into her wanting to see Chet dead."

Billy sat at his desk, running through the tremendous stacks of newspapers, notes and photos he had kept regarding Dave, Georgia and now Chet.

"Okay. I know what happened to Georgia," he said, discarding the stack of information about her death. "But what is the correlation between Dave and Chet's murders? There has to be something. It has to be this woman. It's the same girl. I can feel it," he said, still combing his brain for answers. "What female would want them both dead? What woman would know that they were even affiliated?"

Billy thought of his last conversation with Chet. Chet had been more smug than Billy had ever seen him. Billy had even been amazed at the fact that the secure individual he was speaking with could have been the same whimpering coward from just a year before in—

"New Orleans!" He hurriedly picked up the phone and punched Hawk's number.

"Yeah," Hawk answered, obviously asleep.

"Hawk. There was a double murder. Or actually," he said, reconsidering, "there was a murder in New Orleans, last Mardi Gras. It was a man, Johnny—" Billy struggled to remember the name. "Boudreaux," he recalled. "Johnny Boudreaux. I need you to take a look at it. I think this may be our lead for both Dave and

Chet. This Johnny Boudreaux was found in Lake Pontchartrain on the day after Mardi Gras. His wife was thought to be the prime murder suspect, or to have been murdered herself. Let me know if they ever found her body and," he hesitated, "let me know if she *is* still missing."

"Will do," the hoarse voice responded.

"Oh, and Hawk."

"Yeah."

If she is still missing, get me the most recent photographs you can find of her. I'm thinking perhaps we may need to help the cops locate a fugitive."

"Will do."

*****

A week after Billy had made his request to Hawk, the photograph of Tara Boudreaux and her late husband came in an email, along with the information that she was indeed still missing. Billy studied the picture of the gorgeous couple. He recognized the man immediately, Johnny Boudreaux, big and bulky, with his arm around a striking brunette with high cheekbones and a killer smile.

"Why, hello, Tara," he whispered while he critically viewed the picture on the screen. Somehow, her face seemed more familiar to him than he would have imagined. It was dark that night, and he remembered the woman's body vividly. Petite, but shapely. However, he hadn't been able to visualize the face in his memory.

But now, the face…he knew it. He felt that he had seen it recently. But when? Where?

Billy sat at his desk and tried to concentrate. Leaning back in the chair, he closed his eyes and pictured the face. Tara Boudreaux's face…mouthing an apology.

"She was there! I saw her!" Billy screamed, picking up his cell and dialing.

"You got the picture, I take it?" Hawk answered.

"Yes. Listen. Show that photo around Steamboat. Take it everywhere. The town's not that big. She was there, and I'm betting she's Chet's non-existent *sister*. I want to know everything, anything you can find out. Also, I think she may have been in Playa del Carmen with Dave. Find out everything and let me know immediately!"

"Will do."

"Oh, and Hawk," Billy started.

"Yeah."

"She's driving a Mustang, green, at least she was driving one last week."

"Got it."

Billy hung up the phone and stared again at the gorgeous female who had no idea that her days were undoubtedly now numbered.

Chapter Thirty-two

With teeth chattering and gloved hands shoved into his flannel-lined parka, Matthias stood patiently at the church mailbox.

Mr. Lankford, Steamboat's sole mailman, frowned as he neared the freezing preacher. "It's been three weeks, Matthias. Every day you stand, waiting in the cold for this mail. Why don't you just tell me what you're looking for, and if it comes, I'll walk it in. You're gonna catch pneumonia, and you have to keep yourself well for your congregation, if not for yourself," the postman informed, dutifully handing over the stack of envelopes.

Ed Lankford looked at the once vibrant preacher, standing in the cold, eyes swollen, face drawn, clothes wrinkled as though he'd slept in them. The postman knew something horrible had happened to the man. He wondered if preaching that Eubanks girl's funeral had upset him this much, or if it had something to do with the suicide of her husband. He'd heard they both had attended the young preacher's church. But still, he didn't know why being upset over those kids could make him so obsessive about the mail. In either case, he hoped that the gentle preacher found what he was looking for in today's stack; a thunderous snowstorm was said to be on its way, and he sure didn't want Matthias standing out all morning in a snowstorm tomorrow while he waited on Ed.

Matthias tried to smile at the concerned fellow. He thumbed through the stack, as he had done every day since she left. Church bulletins and bills loaded the top, but then a single postcard rested on the bottom. Matthias knew he had found what he was waiting for. He thanked Ed and turned, eagerly making his way back into the building to read her card in private.

"Thank the Lord," the postman muttered as he saw the way the preacher embraced the tiny card.

Closing the church doors against the gusty wind, Matthias walked into his office, quickly noticing the postmark.

"Denver," he said, turning the card over to read the message.

Matthias, I never planned to leave you the way I did—but I had to. I've done something horrible. I've sinned, and I know God can't forgive me again. I know you wanted me to tell you everything, what I was hiding, and why. I'm sorry. I can't. I can't put you in danger too. You deserve someone who can stay true to you, and to God. I've turned from Him again. I won't let myself do it to you. Please forgive me. Mara

Matthias sat the card down. His head dropped, shoulders trembled. He wasn't prone to tears, never cried, even at the funerals that pierced his heart. But now, his chest pulled with agony and his eyes filled.

He knew she'd been in Denver when she mailed the card, but he knew just as well that she wouldn't be there now. She would have kept moving, running from whatever ghosts haunted her past and had now invaded their future. Matthias prayed to God that she would come back to him, that she would understand the true depths of God's forgiveness and the true depths of his own love.

*****

Astounded by Hawk's thoroughness, Billy took in the mountain of information piled on his desk. In two weeks, Hawk had found out practically everything about Tara Boudreaux's whereabouts for the past eleven months. Billy was, once again, impressed by the man's commitment.

He read the material carefully, not wanting to miss a single detail. Hawk had located a man in Playa del Carmen who said he'd rented her a nice hacienda, merely five doors down from Dave's villa, and that she'd paid cash every month, using the name Ann James. An "Ann James" had been booked on an American Airlines flight from Dallas/Fort Worth to Cancun merely three weeks after Johnny Boudreaux was murdered and had returned to Dallas/Fort Worth. He saw that she didn't return immediately following Dave's murder; a lapse of approximately ten weeks gaped between the two dates. Hawk had not been able to determine her location during that period, but was still looking into it.

"I wonder where you went after your first kill," Billy said, while continuing to read Hawk's notes.

She arrived in Steamboat during the third week of November, rented a condo located a half-mile from Chet's chalet and, once again, paid cash. This time, predictably, she'd used the name "Ann James," but Hawk noted that she was known as "Mara" around town. He'd also learned that she had become very active in a local church, the community church of Steamboat Springs. Hawk included information about her social life.

"So, you had your eye on the preacher," Billy said with an evil grin. "How sweet."

Hawk concluded by saying that the landlady hadn't seen her in the past few weeks, but that the woman didn't feel Ms. James had vacated, since she had paid in advance for the condo through the end of February.

"Interesting," Billy said, sitting the papers on his desk. "You paid through February because you didn't intend on leaving anytime soon, but something happened to force your hand with Chet, didn't it? What was it, I wonder? Georgia? Yes, you couldn't stand it that he had murdered again, could you dear? How quaint, a murderer with a conscience. And, now that you've gotten rid of Dave and Chet, well, it doesn't take a genius to know where you are heading next, does it? Except this time, my dear, you will be expected."

*****

Tara loaded her bag into the back seat of the Mustang, taking one last look at the pitiful excuse for a motel that had been her sanctuary for the past three weeks. Her body had finally healed, with only faint bruises identifying the reality of what had happened that fateful night. She had originally strained her thoughts, trying to make herself forget every gory detail, but in the past few weeks, while lying on the flattened mattress and reflecting on the year behind her, Tara determined that in order to stay strong, she needed to remember, not forget. Remember what happened nearly a year ago, in the darkness following Mardi Gras.

She committed to memory every detail from leaving the parade route to screaming Johnny's name to realizing that Johnny, and their baby, were gone. She recalled every element of her encounter with Dave Danielson, stalking him for months, finding him intoxicated on the darkened veranda and murdering him.

And finally, she remembered the snowy night on the chair lift with Chet, asking him if he killed his wife, struggling with him, then watching as he plummeted to his death. Tara remembered everything, and she knew exactly what she had to do now. There was one left. One horrible face remaining to laugh at her in her dreams.

But not for long.

Chapter Thirty-three

Carla stood apprehensively outside Billy's bedroom. She had been his housekeeper for over ten years now, but she never knew what mood awaited her on the other side of that door. She knocked again, a little more loudly.

"Come on in, Carla," he said calmly.

Sweet God in Heaven, thank you. He's in a good mood.

"I made your reservations, Mr. Reynolds," she said, watching as he meticulously placed a starched black shirt in his garment bag. His leather suitcase lay open on the bed, and Carla could view an elaborate onyx carnival mask atop the stack of folded clothes.

"Thank you, Carla. I made a few copies of my itinerary for New Orleans. Will you come take a look at this with me?"

"Certainly, sir." She timidly approached.

Billy handed her several copies of his schedule, keeping one to review.

"Okay, Carla. This will tell you anything you need to know about my plans for the next week, until Mardi Gras is over. My hotel is listed here, followed by room number and phone information. Scheduled dinner plans are also annotated, in addition to my plans to attend the Endymion Ball."

Carla stared at the detailed list. Mr. Reynolds had never given her more than a telephone number to reach him for emergencies. She wondered why this trip was different than all of the rest.

"Carla—"

"Yes, sir?"

"I'm expecting some guests to visit me while I am attending the Mardi Gras festivities this year. Should they call here, please tell them my exact plans. Every detail. Tell them anything they need to know to locate me. I certainly don't want to miss seeing them."

"Yes, sir. And, who should I expect to call?"

"Just give the information to anyone who requests it, Carla. It will be fine," Billy assured.

"Yes, sir."

"That's all, Carla."

"Thank you, sir."

*****

Getting paid monthly, Jade Roberts usually let her mail accumulate before going through the endless assortment of bills and junk mail at the beginning of the month, trashing whatever wasn't needed and paying whatever was necessary. Midway through the pile, she saw it. Instantly recognizing the handwriting, she reprimanded herself for not checking the stack daily. There was no telling how long the postcard had lain hidden in the pile. She recognized the photograph immediately, the extremely futuristic, stark white structure that looked like something out of Star Wars and composed the Denver Airport.

"She's in Denver."

Quickly flipping the card over, Jade read Tara's message.

Jade, I'm sorry it has been so long since I last wrote. I've missed you. Missed our friendship. I've done horrible things. I've changed. Telling you, or anyone else, would risk putting you in danger too. I can't go on this way, but it will all be over soon. Please understand how much your friendship has meant to me. Love, Tara

Jade flipped the postcard again, trying to make out the date, but it was completely blurred.

"Tara, why won't you let me help!" she screamed. Jade ran to the bedroom, pulled her suitcase from the closet and madly began packing. "If Denver is where you are, then I'll find you. I gave up too easily in Dallas. I won't give up this time."

Within a half-hour, Jade had packed, called to request time off from work and made a flight reservation from Atlanta to Denver. The only seat available on the plane was in first-class, but she had recited her credit card number without delay. She would worry about how to pay for it when the bill came due. Tara was more important.

"I won't lose you this time," she said, speeding to the airport.

She boarded the plane two hours later with just her laptop and one small carry-on. Accepting a copy of *The Atlanta Journal-Constitution* from the flight attendant, she flipped through the pages, scanning the articles in an effort to decide which section to read first. One particular article caught her eye immediately, the name in the headline grabbing her attention.

Chet Garrison's Death—Suicide, or Murder?

Authorities in Steamboat Springs, Colorado, an elite ski town located in the northern part of the state, have verified that new information suggests that perhaps Chet Garrison, husband of deceased heiress Georgia Eubanks-Garrison, did not actually commit suicide on the slopes of Steamboat January 8th. Although they have yet to release exact information regarding suspects, sources close to the investigation have suggested that Mr. Garrison was in the company of an attractive female when he boarded the fateful ski lift. Steamboat authorities are expected to release additional information regarding the investigation later today.

Jade couldn't believe it. She had heard all of the news regarding Georgia Eubanks' death and the suicide of her husband, but she hadn't made the connection before. Chet Garrison. Chet. Now, she knew exactly who that was. She recalled the nervous man she had met on the stairwell that day in Reynolds' Sea and Ski. He had married Georgia Eubanks? The heiress? The girl had died on her honeymoon and then her husband had committed suicide. Or had he? Jade's head hurt as she read the article again. One of the flight attendants noticed her frown and offered a hot towel, for which

Jade was indeed grateful. She looked again at the information provided in the article. He'd lived in Steamboat Springs, Colorado. He was dead, but perhaps not by suicide; he could have been murdered, and an attractive female involved. Jade laid the paper down and anxiously opened her computer bag to withdraw Tara's postcard.

"I've done some horrible things. I've changed. Telling you, or anyone else, would risk putting you in danger too. I can't go on this way, but it will all be over soon. Please understand how much your friendship has meant to me."

Jade shook her head at the thought. Could Tara be the "attractive female" they saw with Chet the night he died? She flipped the postcard over again, straining her eyes to see the date, but she just couldn't make it out. When had Tara mailed this? Maybe she mailed this while en route to Steamboat Springs. If she is the woman mentioned here, then searching Denver would be a waste of time, Jade decided. She was going directly to Steamboat.

Jade leaned her head against the large pillow that first class seating had enabled for the journey. She was so anxious to get there, and the flight had barely started. She vividly remembered the last time she had seen Tara at the hotel in Hattiesburg. Jade had no doubt that at least one of the boxes she'd brought to Tara had been filled with cash, since Tara left the large bag of money on the bedside table. If she had only known that Tara was planning to leave when she brought her those boxes and the addresses…

"The addresses," Jade said aloud, removing the towel from her forehead. She'd given Tara all of their addresses. Obviously, she had located Chet, but now Jade wondered…had she found Billy and Dave too?

She pulled her computer bag back into her lap, opened it and turned on the laptop. She motioned for the flight attendant, standing just a few feet away.

"Can I access the Internet here?"

"Certainly," the attendant smiled, indicating the simple instructions on the seat.

"Thank you," Jade said, easily connecting and beginning her search.

By the time the airplane began its descent into Denver, she had every bit of information she needed. Newspaper archives from Mexico had confirmed that Dave Danielson was dead. *Dead.* And now, Chet Garrison was dead too. She pulled the postcard out once again.

"I've done some horrible things..."

Could Tara have killed them both? They *had* murdered Johnny, and Tara had seen them do it. But could she commit murder? And why hadn't she gone after Billy? He was the one that she said actually shot Johnny, and yet, Jade had searched previous issues of the *Tampa Tribune* and found that Billy Reynolds had personally opened three new Sea and Ski stores as recently as last week. Jade looked again at Tara's words.

"But it will all be over soon. Please understand how much your friendship has meant to me."

"Dear God, no," Jade whispered as she studied the words. That's it. Tara did murder them, but she can't live with it anymore. She says it will all be over soon.

She's going to kill herself!

Jade felt a tear slip its way down her cheek.

Stop it. I will not cry. I will not let her die. God, help me. Help me get to her in time.

Jade exited the plane and hurried to the first car rental agent she spotted. Within ten minutes, she was loading her laptop and carry-on into the back seat of an Explorer with directions to Steamboat Springs in her hand.

"Wait for me, Tara. Give me a chance to help you," she cried, driving quickly out of Denver.

*****

"Reynolds residence," Carla said as she answered the phone. She waited, but only heard silence. "Hello? Reynolds residence," she repeated. "Hola!"

"Hello. Is Mr. Reynolds in?" Tara said in a whisper.

"No, I am afraid Mr. Reynolds is traveling. Can I help you?"

Traveling. Traveling where?

"Would you happen to have the number where he is staying?" Tara tentatively asked.

"Oh, yes. You must be one of the guests he mentioned. Just one moment, and I'll get the information you need."

Tara listened as the receiver clunked on a hard surface. She could hear the lady's heels clicking across a hard floor, probably slate or marble. She tried to remain calm.

He's not there, but there is nothing to worry about. Just find out where he is.

She'd bought a temporary cell phone specifically to make this call, to ensure that Billy Reynolds was in Tampa or to learn exactly where to find the murderer.

Finally, she heard the woman pick up the receiver on the other end.

"Miss? You still there?" Carla asked.

"Still here," Tara replied.

"Okay. I have quite a bit of information. Do you need it all?"

Tara quickly fumbled to get her pen and paper ready.

"Yes, please." She furiously jotted down every detail that the woman so easily furnished, then thanked the lady and disconnected.

"Mardi Gras. How fitting," Tara said, placing her notes on the passenger seat of the car. "And the ball is in two days." She swallowed, took a deep breath. "I've always wanted to go to a ball."

Chapter Thirty-four

Jade entered Steamboat Springs and was immediately struck by the beauty of the exquisite ski town. She was pleased that the town was relatively small, village-like, and she hoped it wouldn't take her long to locate Tara.

She pulled into a local service station, purchased a city map outlining the main street, side streets and roads up the mountain. That was it, the entire town. Jade reasoned that in a place this size, everybody probably knew just about everybody. She opened her purse, found a picture of herself with Tara and brought the picture to the station's cashier. The friendly woman said that the girl in the picture did look familiar, but she couldn't be sure when she had last seen the lady. Jade thanked the woman and returned to her search.

Deciding that the best way to cover ground quickly would be to simply start at one end of town and work her way to the other, Jade drove the Explorer up Mount Werner road toward the condominiums and chalets. Tara would probably have selected a condominium over a hotel, if she planned on staying for a while. And a chalet would have been a bit large for one woman to rent without appearing conspicuous, so Jade started with the condominiums that were furthest up the mountain and resolved to work her way down.

The office managers at the first two sets of condos had no recollection of ever seeing anyone that remotely resembled Tara; however, the woman at the third set turned out to be the precise person Jade needed.

"Hello," Jade said, approaching the elderly lady behind the counter.

"Hello!" the woman yelled gleefully. She slapped a thick novel upside down on the counter. "Are you looking for a place to stay in Steamboat? We have a couple of units available," she informed. "Beautiful this time of year, you know."

"No, I don't believe I need anywhere to stay right now. I'm looking for a friend of mine," Jade said, displaying the photo.

"That's odd," the lady said.

"Odd?"

"Yes, that's the same color of hair Mara had in the picture that the man showed me a few days ago. Goodness, everyone is looking for the girl. I think she must have taken a vacation from her vacation, so to speak. I haven't seen her in a few weeks, but she's paid up through the end of February, so she'll be back. Want me to give her a message?"

Jade's heart felt as though it would burst through her chest. Tara had lived here, but she was gone.

"She's paid through the end of February?" Jade asked. She'd known in her heart that Tara had been here, but to hear it verified…

"Oh, yes. Such a sweet girl. She'll be back though. She really likes it here," the woman said, still looking at the picture. "You know I rather like her hair that color too."

"Her hair?" Jade tried to comprehend everything the lady rattled. "It isn't that color now?"

"Oh, no, she's a true blonde, or at least I thought she was. Really light, nearly white hair. It's quite beautiful, but this auburn color looks nice on Mara too."

"Mara," Jade repeated.

"Yes, that is who you're asking about, right? The girl in the picture? Ann James, I guess is what you're used to. That's how she registered. But she asked us to call her Mara. Catchy name, huh?"

"Yes," Jade said, still struggling to clear her head. So, Tara had a condo here. Jade suddenly remembered something else the woman had said.

"Did you say that there was a man looking for her too?"

"He sure was. But, you know, I thought it kind of odd. He just didn't seem the type that Mara would hang around with, you know? Kind of shady looking."

Who? Who would it be? Billy? Has he found her? Is that why she isn't here? Oh, dear God, please be with her. Keep her safe. Don't let it be Billy!

Jade didn't know whether to wait until Tara came back, or to try and figure out where she had gone. What if Billy had already figured out what she had done and he'd found her first? Panic shot through Jade's veins.

"Did you want to rent a condo, ma'am? The one next to your friend is available. You could stay there while you wait on her to get back," the sweet lady asked.

"Oh," Jade thought. "Yes. Yes, I think I will."

Still smiling, the woman took the key labeled B-22 from the desk and quickly moved to mark the unit B-22 as *Occupied*.

Jade paid for the room, retrieved her bag from the car and entered the condo next-door to Tara's.

*****

Tara entered the plush dress shop in Metairie, merely fifteen minutes from New Orleans. And Billy Reynolds. She browsed the elaborate evening gowns with matching ball masks. The prices were outrageous, but she knew she wouldn't need her cash supply much longer, so she could drop a small fortune on turning some heads, primarily the head of Mr. Billy Reynolds.

"May I help you?" an ebony haired woman inquired as she watched Tara shifting the dresses on a circular rack. The beautifully thick Cajun accent reminded Tara of Johnny, and she stood mesmerized by the sound.

"Miss, can I help you? I would be happy to help you choose a few selections and try them on, or we can have one of our models show them to you."

"I need a dress for a ball," Tara stammered.

"Which ball?" the woman asked, noting the dress Tara held.

"Endymion."

"Oh, my dear, that's tomorrow night!" the woman exclaimed. "Well, we'll need to get busy, won't we? Is there a price range we're looking at?" she asked, suddenly in high gear at the thought of outfitting a woman for a ball at the very last minute.

"I want to look better than I've ever looked. I need it to be breathtaking, no matter the cost," Tara said, watching the woman's eyes gleam with excitement.

"I have the perfect dress then," she said smugly. Her shoulders rose triumphantly and her pointed nose lifted a notch as she ushered Tara to the back room of the prestigious shop.

Tara gasped when she saw it. It was incredible. Red. Very red. Deep and rich, with a beaded bodice that cut nearly to the navel and was held up by the tiniest of straps.

"Your figure should do wonders for this dress," the woman acknowledged. "Petite, but curvy, a stunning combination. You're what, a size 4?"

Tara nodded. "May I?" she asked, reaching for the hanger.

"Oh, certainly," she said, handing the exquisite creation to Tara. "I can't wait to see you try it on. We have the shoes and handbag to match, and of course," she started as she reached behind the dress to withdraw an elegant carnival mask, beaded with black onyx and accented with red feathers, "we can't forget the mask."

Tara entered the dressing room. It smelled of rose petals and pralines. She turned to view a silver tray of the New Orleans treats and a large vase filled with red roses.

She stepped into the dress, immediately noticing the perfect length and perfect fit; it accented every inch of her. Exiting the dressing room, the friendly attendant gasped then called several other women in to see the masterpiece.

Tara stood upon the mini-runway positioned in front of a multi-mirrored wall to examine the view. This was it, the perfect dress to grab any man's attention. She turned and peered admiringly at the main feature of the dress, and the one that she had previously overlooked. The entire back of the dress was an intricate weaving of thread-like red satin straps that wove themselves elegantly into a severe point, exposing just enough that Tara knew she wouldn't be able to wear undergarments.

The curvy straps reminded her instantly of that day long ago, when she'd first witnessed the image. Twining deep red, nearly obscuring the white hidden beneath.

A sharp plunge at the bottom of the back gently curved outward, exposing enough skin to be considered deadly. There wasn't anything else to be said. Every woman in the room was in fact...speechless.

Tara finally broke the silence. "I'll take it," she managed, stepping from the runway toward the dressing room.

"If you didn't, I'd have had to shoot you," another woman said, peeling her eyes from the vision of Tara so she could continue shopping. "I sure hope that my husband doesn't ever see anything like that, or maybe...he could see her, and then come on home to me." Fits of giggles exploded through the shop, causing her to add, "Hey, I don't care what gets him going, as long as he keeps it going at home."

Satisfied that she would capture Billy's attention tomorrow night, Tara paid for the gown and set out to find a hotel, preferably close, but not too close, to the man who'd killed her husband.

Chapter Thirty-five

Although Jade's condo was extremely nice, clean and elegantly positioned next to the slope outside, she couldn't enjoy any of it. Patience was never something she had been very good at; now proved to be no exception. She hadn't slept at all, straining her ears throughout the night to hear any noise next door, hoping against hope that Tara would return. However, her call to the front desk this morning had confirmed that Tara hadn't been seen.

She sat at the small breakfast nook, thumbing through the Steamboat Springs brochures and wondering what to do. Tara had been staying next door. Jade had requested to merely go into Tara's room and see if she had left any trace of where she was going, but the woman had said she couldn't open a guest's room, even for a friend.

Now Jade's mind continued to return to the shady character who had been here just a few days ago, asking about Tara. Surely, he was searching for her too. What if he found her first? What if it was Billy?

Jade decided that she had to do something. Sitting around and waiting wasn't getting anything done. She stared around the room wondering if Tara's room was laid out the same. She peered at the balcony, watched the skiers pass by, undeterred by the cold wind that stirred the snow against the slope. Walking out to the balcony, Jade eyed the narrow brick divider between her own balcony and Tara's.

It didn't take a moment's hesitation; she climbed the iron railing. Snow gently fell around her. "Don't look down," she whispered, stretching her hand to Tara's rail. Grasping the cold, wet metal as tightly as possible, she extended her leg until her foot slid between the vertical poles on Tara's side. Then, ever so carefully, she edged her way across.

Breathing a deep sigh of relief, Jade climbed over the top of the railing to stand firmly on Tara's side.

Thank you, God.

She moved toward the sliding door, hoping that perhaps Tara left it open.

Please, let me in. Let me in, for her sake. Help me find her.

Jade pulled the handle, and the door squeakily slid open. She rushed inside. Identical to her condo, complete with southwestern décor, Tara's place was immaculate. It didn't even look as though she'd been here at all.

"How long have you been gone, Tara? And, are you really coming back?"

Jade went into the small bathroom and found no sign of toiletries or make-up. The bed was made and the kitchen clean. Spotless.

"You aren't coming back, are you?" Jade said, tears burning their way out of her already bloodshot eyes.

What am I not seeing here?

Jade scanned everything, every paper, every brochure, and every piece of furniture, and yet she saw nothing to indicate anything about Tara's location. She sat down on the couch and cried.

Okay, Jade. Concentrate. There's got to be something here. Something that will help me...

She saw it. It stood out because it wasn't decorated in the traditional coral and turquoise southwestern colors. A thin book, brightly colored, turned at an angle on the breakfast table. It looked friendly, almost inviting, as though beckoning Jade to pick it up. So she did.

She opened the guest book. Surely Tara wouldn't have signed a guest book if she didn't want anyone to know she was here, or would she? Jade flipped to the last entry in the book. It was written anonymously, but she recognized her friend's handwriting with ease.

The view from your condo is lovely. I am truly enjoying my stay here. Steamboat Springs is better than I could have ever anticipated. I have fallen in love with the land, the town and the people. What a wonderful place to visit, and perhaps live one day. I am actually thinking about the latter as a possibility. My stay has been heightened with an intense study of the Bible at the Community Church of Steamboat Springs. I would hope that anyone who reads this would desire to attend. The fellowship is outstanding and the preacher, Matthias McClain, is—in a word—wonderful.

Tara had written a scripture at the bottom of the page.

"You ought to forgive and comfort him, so that he will not be overwhelmed by excessive sorrow." 2 Corinthians 2:7

Jade took the book with her, leaving the condominium in search of the Community Church and the preacher, Matthias McClain.

*****

Tara located a stylish hotel, merely one block from the one where Billy Reynolds had registered. Entering through elongated revolving doors, she quickly scanned the ornate lobby, crowded and loud, with many guests obviously on a steadfast path to complete intoxication, if they hadn't obtained that goal already. Mardi Gras beads adorned the necks of practically everyone present, and tall hurricane glasses were visible everywhere. She lost her nervousness and began to feel confident that she would complete her plans today.

The lobby glistened with elaborate ivory marble columns and a slate emerald floor. Massive floral arrangements and picturesque fountains were placed sporadically, offering several focal points throughout the adjoining bars and hotel restaurants, all accessible via the lobby. Tara casually entered the red-roped entrance to the check-in counter.

Two men stood ahead of her, one dressed as though he just stepped off of his yacht and the other clad in perfect Mardi Gras attire—casual shirt, jeans and a ton of beads. Tara listened intently as the first man was told there were no vacancies until after Mardi Gras. The woman kindly informed the irritated gentleman that he could perhaps find a room in Slidell and drive into New Orleans for the festivities, explaining that rooms were generally booked for Mardi Gras a year in advance.

Tara's mind worked vigorously as the rich man stormed out of the hotel and the Mardi Gras man managed to slur the information that he had forgotten his room number. Grinning, the woman wrote the number on a small piece of hotel stationery, along with verbally giving him instructions for reaching his destination. Tara doubted that he would find it, regardless of her help. He had obviously had one too many hurricanes, even if it wasn't yet afternoon.

Acknowledging the fact that Mardi Gras is the most difficult time to get a room in New Orleans, Tara was prepared to pay whatever was necessary to obtain a room, particularly in close proximity to Billy Reynolds.

"Do you have a room available?" Tara asked with a smile.

"I'm sorry. We do not have any vacancies presently, and probably won't have any rooms until after Mardi Gras—" the woman began, her speech quite rehearsed.

Tara interrupted her before she continued, "I only need it for one night."

"I'm sorry. We are very busy during—"

"I truly need a room here, tonight, just one night," Tara interrupted again. "Please check to see if you have had any cancellations today. Please," she pleaded, trying to maintain her calmness.

"I'll check, but it is extremely rare for someone to cancel at this late notice. They would lose their deposit and fifty percent of the—"

Come on. Just one room. Please!

"Wait a minute. Just one second," the woman said, punching keys on the computer screen in front of her. "I guess you're in luck, but I must inform you, our rooms are quite expensive now during the holiday."

"That's fine. How much?" Tara said, obviously relieved.

"Six hundred," the woman replied.

Tara fished out the bills and thanked her as she received the key.

*****

Jade found the church without any problems. She ran inside the tiny building, quickly locating the preacher, sitting on a pew, his head bowed reverently in prayer. Jade stood silently until he raised his head and wiped his face.

Matthias had heard the church doors open, but didn't bother to turn around. He knew it wouldn't be her, and he really didn't want to see anyone else right now. But he was a servant of God, so it was his responsibility to help. He wiped the tears away, stood and turned to see the woman staring at him, looking frantic. She clutched a book to her chest, but Matthias quickly surmised it was too thin to be a Bible. Her hair was short, blond and combed in several different directions, or perhaps not combed at all; however, she still looked stylish in a very individualistic, unique sense. Matthias tried to momentarily break from his thoughts of Tara and help the stranger, since that's exactly what God would want him to do. And, hopefully, if he continued to do what God wanted, perhaps God would bless him by bringing her back. "Can I help you?"

Jade immediately noticed the swollen eyes and damp lashes from his tears.

Let him know. Let him help me find her.

"Are you Matthias McClain?" Jade asked breathlessly.

"Yes."

"I am looking for my friend, my best friend. She mentioned you in this book, so I was hoping that you might know where she is now," Jade sputtered. "Here's her picture."

Matthias took the picture, staring in disbelief. "Mara."

"You do know her! Thank God! Do you know where she is? I need to find her. I'm afraid she could be in danger," Jade spurted, trying to make him understand.

"She left. Four weeks ago now. Gone. I wish I knew where she went. I've prayed to God, asking for his help, but I still do not know where she is now. I know that she was in Denver last week, but I'm sure she has left by now."

"Denver," Jade said, frantically trying to put it all together. She remembered the postcard from Tara. She had thought that Tara had mailed it on her way to Steamboat Springs, but perhaps she mailed it after—after she had killed both Dave and Chet. If she mailed it after, then...

"Wait!" Jade yelled, more to herself than to Matthias. She ran outside the church building to the Explorer, searching through her computer bag until she found it. She ran back inside, holding the postcard.

"She must have mailed this to me last week," Jade told Matthias, handing him the postcard. He immediately stepped into his office, picked up the matching postcard from his desk and compared it to Jade's.

"This is the one she sent me," he said, handing his own card to Jade while he scanned hers.

"Her real name. Tara," he said.

"Yes."

Jade read the card Tara had sent to Matthias, instantly realizing why the preacher had been so upset. "She cares about you," Jade affirmed. "She didn't want to leave you. I think she was actually planning on staying here. Read this," Jade said, opening the guest book to Tara's entry. She watched Matthias read the note, tears slipping down his cheeks and his jaw visibly tightening.

"Then, why did she leave?"

"She said she didn't want to put you in danger. I'm afraid something happened the last night she was here. Something she couldn't get over. She felt she had no choice but to leave, but now I'm afraid—" Jade stopped, unsure of how much to tell him as to her suspicions of what Tara had done.

"Please. Tell me. I love her," Matthias said. "Let me help you find her. Please."

Jade looked at the man, instantly realizing that he was truly in love with Tara.

"Did you know her husband was murdered last year?" Jade asked.

"She told me that she lost a husband and baby, but I didn't know they were murdered," Matthias answered. "Tell me."

"I didn't know about the baby," Jade said, suddenly feeling more aware than ever of how awful last Mardi Gras had been for her friend.

"She saw the men that murdered him. She watched it happen. They even beat her and left her to die, but she didn't. A homeless couple came to her aid, caring for her until I could get there. And then I helped her learn exactly who the three men were who had killed Johnny. We were planning to give the names to the police in New Orleans, or at least that was what I thought. But, Tara left. She couldn't go through with it and she left. I searched for her, but I couldn't find any trace of her anywhere. But, you see, I thought she was in hiding, from the police, and from those men."

"And she wasn't?" Matthias asked.

"No. I think that the 'horrible things' that she mentions in my postcard..." she hesitated.

"Tell me. Please."

"Two of the men have been murdered. One is still alive. I think Tara is trying to avenge Johnny's death. And, I'm afraid that if she actually was in Denver last week, then 'It will all be over soon' is talking about the third man, who is the most dangerous of the three, and who, I suspect, knows exactly what she's doing. I'm afraid she's really in danger now."

Matthias tried to comprehend the reality of it. "Mara couldn't hurt anyone, not intentionally."

"I don't think so either, but I don't know what happened when she confronted Dave, or Chet."

"Chet? Garrison?" Matthias asked, knowing the answer. He remembered all of her questions about the newlyweds, the wedding and Georgia's funeral. He also remembered that the day she left was the day he received another call from Grayson Eubanks, this time to preach at his son-in-law's funeral. "Dear God."

"We have to get to her," Jade said. "The woman at her condominium said a shady looking guy was there a few days ago with a picture of Tara, asking questions and looking for her. If it wasn't Billy, I will guarantee that it's an acquaintance. And, I'd also bet that Tara probably doesn't even realize he's onto her. We've got to find her before he does."

"We'll find her. With God's help, we will. Where is this 'Billy'?"

"His name is Billy Reynolds," Jade said, moving into Matthias' office. "He lives in Tampa," she said, withdrawing her cell.

"Who are you calling?" Matthias said.

"You'll see," Jade said, waving her hand. "We *will* find her, even if I have to go straight to Billy Reynolds to get the answers."

Matthias listened to Jade's request.

"Tampa," she paused. "Florida," she paused again. "William Reynolds," she finished, quickly jotting down the number on a piece of paper. She hung up and dialed the number, before she had a chance to change her mind.

"Reynolds residence," Carla answered.

"Yes. I'm trying to locate Mr. Billy Reynolds," Jade said, keeping her voice steady.

"Mr. Reynolds is in New Orleans. He left his schedule for his guests. I can give you the information if you like."

"Yes, thank you," Jade said, reaching for a bigger sheet of paper. She scribbled down Billy's hotel information and daily schedule. "Thank you very much," Jade said, hanging up the phone.

"Well? Where is he?" Matthias asked, trying to read the sketchy notes on the paper.

"New Orleans. At Mardi Gras," Jade whispered, apparently in shock. "I didn't even realize it had been a year since Johnny was murdered."

"And, do you think Mara is there?"

"I'm betting my life on it," Jade said, spotting the laptop on his desk.

"Can I use it?" Jade asked, moving toward the desk.

"Of course."

She hurriedly entered the appropriate web address while Matthias read Tara's entry in the guest book again. "She was thinking about staying," he muttered.

"Maybe she'll come back here. Don't give up, and if you have anything you need to bring with you, throw it in a bag. We're going to New Orleans."

"When?" Matthias asked, amazed at how quickly she had made the arrangements.

"Not as soon as I would have liked, but we'll just have to work with it. We leave the Hayden Airport on United 6444 at 4:45 this afternoon, arriving in Denver at 5:34 p.m. Then, we connect with United 434, which arrives in New Orleans at 10:20 p.m."

"Do you know where to go once we get there?" he asked, checking his watch to see how much time they had.

"I have the address and room number of Billy's hotel, but his plan, according to his housekeeper, is to attend the Endymion Ball this evening. We can start at the hotel, then move to the ball. Hopefully, we'll find Tara before she finds him."

"Or he finds her."

Chapter Thirty-six

Tara had spent the entire day preparing, not only for the ball, but for Billy's murder. She had thought of nothing else since she'd started the long drive from Denver, and she finally believed her plan was complete.

Unfortunately, she was required to spend the majority of the day dealing with the most despised and disreputable individuals on the hidden back streets of the French Quarter in order to obtain everything that she needed, but finally, at long last, it was done. She was ready. She took one last look in the full-length mirror before leaving.

Hawk watched intently as she exited the lobby. A doorman jumped eagerly to help her into the limousine she had reserved earlier. Hawk had easily located the woman, foolishly using the same alias of "Ann James" when she'd registered at the hotel this morning. Although he knew she would never live to see tomorrow, he deeply regretted the fact that he had never had the opportunity to take care of her himself. Now, seeing the stunning woman, he realized exactly why Billy wanted her last night living to be spent with him. She was breathtakingly beautiful in the flaming red dress, with her blonde hair piled high and several mouthwatering strands falling loosely around her shoulder. Hawk thought about how those fallen strands added to the appeal. He couldn't help but think that there was something very sexy about marred perfection.

He dialed Billy.

"She's on her way. Slinky red dress. Blond hair. You won't be able to miss her. No one will," he said, vividly remembering her graceful glide through the hotel lobby.

"That's what I'm counting on. Thanks, Hawk. Head on home. I've got it from here."

"I bet you do," Hawk said, ending the call and feeling a little sorry for the beautiful murderess, totally unaware of the trap she'd entered.

Billy sat at a side table with his eyes fixed on the colossal doors that identified the entrance to the grand ballroom within the New Orleans Superdome. Several red dresses had passed through the entrance since the time of Hawk's call, but Billy was fairly certain that Tara Boudreaux had not been one of them. He had noticed one pretty blonde, but she was taller than the woman he remembered. As Billy watched her though, he began wondering if perhaps high heels could have explained the adjustment in height. He sought the woman once again, trying to make the determination, and had barely returned his gaze to the door when he saw her.

She was the most exquisite creature that had entered thus far and, Billy felt certain, there would be none other to compare to the vision that stole the attention of every male in the room. She gracefully descended the velvety red staircase to officially enter the ball. Billy watched carefully as two handsome men in white tuxedoes didn't waste a moment's time in meeting the elegant lady. With the dancing officially started, she accepted an offer with one of the men. They danced beautifully across the floor, until the second gentleman stepped in. Billy couldn't help but notice the woman's occasional glance around the room, as though she were looking for someone. He held the onyx mask firmly in place while he stalked his prey.

Looking for me, aren't you, my dear? Well, you'll see me soon. And I will definitely be seeing more of you.

Tara tried to locate him in the crowd of tuxedoed men, but she hadn't accounted for the Mardi Gras masks as a brutal obstacle to locating Billy Reynolds. Many of the masks were so elaborately feathered and beaded that the faces beneath were completely shadowed. She therefore decided that she would simply make her way slowly throughout the ballroom, until she met him, face-to-face. She wasn't scared of finding him. On the contrary, she needed to find him. And she would. Billy Reynolds would die, and he would die tonight.

*****

Jade was crying when they finally boarded the plane in Denver. The snowstorm that had surprised the city had delayed their flight an hour. It was exactly 8:00 p.m. when the plane finally began its departure.

"He's at the ball. What if she went there too?" she moaned to Matthias, who had been virtually silent since they had left Steamboat Springs.

"God be with her," Matthias whispered.

"And God be with us," Jade added. "Help us get there in time."

They traveled without speaking, Jade crying and Matthias praying throughout the seemingly long flight to New Orleans.

*****

Tara had danced intermittently during the nearly three hours since she'd arrived at the ball. It was almost eleven o'clock, and she still hadn't seen any sign of Billy Reynolds. She left the ballroom to cool off on the terrace outside. The balcony had a circular staircase, providing access to a small, serene garden which, unlike the crowded ballroom, was completely vacated. Spanish moss cascaded from the trees on either side of the small retreat and cast sooty slithering shadows across the ground.

Just like last year.

Tara ventured down the steps, eager to step away from her failed attempt to confront Billy. Frustrated that she had put so much time and effort into this evening, she was disheartened to conclude that he wasn't even here. Maybe the housekeeper had given her the wrong information. Perhaps Billy was attended a different ball entirely. In either case, Tara was tired. Physically, mentally and emotionally exhausted. She wondered how she could have thought that murdering Billy Reynolds would have been something she could do with ease.

She shivered from the cold, but wasn't ready to go back inside. Her thoughts weren't of Billy anymore. She thought of Matthias, of everything he had tried to tell her about forgiveness and God's love.

Tears filled her eyes when she realized that he truly cared for her, that he truly loved her. What if he found out the truth? How would he forgive her?

Her mind worked its way through the countless verses Matthias had recited to her about forgiveness. She remembered how she had realized that he was right, and that God could forgive her for what she did to Dave. But, then—Chet. How could God forgive her again? He couldn't, she had decided. So she'd resolved to find Billy and complete the entire plan, but now she couldn't find him. Why? She knew he was coming here. She knew how she'd kill him. It was all figured out, down to the last detail, except...

Is it You, God? Are You here with me? Did You keep him from coming tonight? You knew, didn't You? You knew that if I couldn't go through with it tonight, I would have to think about it, wondering if it were You. You, stepping in to intervene once again. You, trying to keep me from sinning, from murdering again. Do You still want me? Can You forgive me again? Oh, God, please forgive me. Why am I here?

Tara clutched her hands around a cold wrought iron gate that bordered a small section of the garden.

"I need to go," she whispered. She turned away, finally deciding that what she needed to do was leave New Orleans completely. She wanted to start over. God would help her. She knew He wanted her. He was trying to save her soul, and this time, she would let Him. She would let Him, and she would let Matthias know. She would tell him everything, and if he still wanted her after learning the truth, then...

Tara wasn't sure at first what had stopped her thoughts so abruptly. Then it was obvious. Cold, hard metal pressed firmly against her back; a gloved hand clamped around her arm.

"You don't want to leave the party so early, do you? At least, not unaccompanied," a hissing voice sounded in her ear.

Why hadn't she seen him? "Billy Reynolds," she acknowledged.

"Tara Boudreaux," he replied, smiling wickedly. "Well, now that we've been formally introduced, we can move on to better things, can't we dear? You did come here looking for someone, didn't you? I dare say you've finally found him."

Billy's tuxedo jacket draped over his arm to conceal the gun.

"Sure is chilly out here, isn't it?" he said, moving her toward the garden's gated passageway to the street. "I think I'll just take you somewhere where I can warm you up properly."

Ushering her through the narrow pathway, Billy let the gun occasionally leave her skin, but she knew, knew that he still pointed it at her and knew she had no choice but to go.

God, be with me.

Billy had already called for his limousine, now parked just outside of the garden's gate. He had been watching her, stalking her the way she'd tried to stalk him. Tara's skinned burned with apprehension. He had been expecting her. The chauffeur saw them coming and immediately opened the door, undoubtedly unaware that Tara had been taken against her will. She didn't try to get his attention. She knew better.

They arrived at Billy's hotel at the same time that Matthias and Jade hailed a cab at the airport. Jade threw a wad of cash at the driver then handed him the hotel address.

"Please! Hurry! I'll give you more when we get there if you'll just hurry!"

The cab driver, noticing she had already paid him more than three times the normal fare, stomped the gas in an effort to pick up the extra cash upon arrival.

Matthias fell silent again, still praying.

*****

Billy shoved Tara inside his room. Closing the door behind him, he held the gun firmly, pointing it at her heart.

"Now, Mrs. Boudreaux, you've been a very busy lady since I last saw you, haven't you?"

Tara stared at the evil face. It had been a long time since last Mardi Gras, but she had seen him since then. She had seen him, laughing, taunting her in her nightmares. She had relived the memory over and over, watching him draw the gun, seeing him shoot Johnny and watching Johnny's body fall. Her eyes burned with contempt, welled with sorrow.

"Oh, don't tell me you're crying over poor Dave and Chet now. No, I don't think you are. You're probably remembering, aren't you? You remember that pitiful husband of yours, standing there, sounding like a fool, asking for his lost wife. Now, I wonder what he would think if he could see me now. If he knew that I had his precious, and quite striking, wife at my complete mercy, to essentially do whatever I desire."

He stepped forward, still pointing the gun at her and reached his hand out to touch the exposed skin beneath her breasts, in the deep cut of the sexy dress.

Tara flinched, immediately raised a fisted hand. But she wasn't quick enough.

Billy grabbed the hand with ease. "Let's don't do anything we'll regret, shall we?"

Tara glared at the man. Her mind raced to the plan she had constructed earlier, her own plan to kill him. Perhaps, there was still a way...

"What's the matter? Did your careful scheming go awry? Oh, yes, I figured it out. You were able to get to Dave and Chet, but did you really think I wouldn't put it together? The sexy redhead Dave left with in Mexico? The blonde 'sister' Chet took on the slope? Yes, I've known. Actually, I've been expecting you, my dear. No doubt you're the woman who called my housekeeper asking about me. Wasn't it mighty helpful for her to tell you how to find me? Didn't think it was peculiar at all, did you? Stupid girl. You thought you were so smart, didn't you? Well, now we'll see. Oh, there will be somebody murdered tonight, so at least that part of your plan is right. It's just that you didn't know exactly who the victim would be, did you?"

Maybe I do. Maybe, just maybe, I still do.

Tara's mind raced as she watched him closely. He wasn't letting the gun falter. She thought she could still do it, but she didn't know what to do about the gun. And she honestly didn't know whether she would be dead before getting the chance.

"Let's see, with Chet, you pushed him from a ski lift I believe. Now, that's original," he said, mockingly. "But, with Dave. If my sources are right," Billy said, stepping toward the dresser and, never taking his eyes from Tara, feeling his way to open the drawer and expel several shiny red scarves, "You blindfolded him and tied him to the bedposts. Not quite so original, but definitely more appealing, don't you think?" Holding the red scarves, he moved toward her. They curled from his grasp like long crimson serpents, while the gun remained pointed at her heart. "If you'll notice, this room has a rather large bed, which happens to have four bedposts. Go on. To the bed, my dear," he ordered. She stood and walked to the bed. "Relax. Sit down," he instructed, pointing toward the headboard. "Now, your wrists." Tara held her right arm out, curious as to what he would do with the gun while he fastened the scarf. "Both wrists." Wondering what he was doing, she brought the other arm up and watched as Billy grabbed them both with his free hand. She stared in disbelief as he laid the gun on the bed beside her and began wrapping one of the red strips of silk around both wrists. Tara tried to twist her wrists to the side as he knotted the shiny fabric. She hadn't given up the hope of escaping yet, and if she was going to do it, she would have to be able to free her arms.

With her wrists tied together, she watched Billy tie the other end of the scarf to one of the posts at the head of the bed. With both arms stretched awkwardly above her head, she simply laid there while he tied a scarf around her head, covering her eyes with the blood-colored fabric.

Now she had no idea where the gun was, or where Billy was for that matter, until she felt another scarf tighten around her right ankle. Likewise, the last scarf pulled around her left ankle then her leg was jerked to the side, supposedly to the opposite post. Tara listened intently, trying to determine where he was, trying to know what was coming. She heard his tuxedo rustle as he began removing his clothes.

Help me. Dear God, help me.

The bed gave with his weight as he climbed beside her. She tried to move away from him, but her body was tied so peculiarly, with her arms angled at one side of the headboard and her legs tied apart, that the movement hurt her, made her groan in pain. He edged his way nearer, obviously trying to scare her. And succeeding.

Stay calm. Stay calm. Think.

Billy ran his hand down the length of her extended arms, causing Tara to instantly shiver in fear and revulsion. She heard his low laugh, amused at her panic. Tara shuddered as her body pressed into the bed from the increasing pressure of Billy's weight, moving closer to her, stretching out against her.

"Now, Tara, let's see what that husband of yours was so intent on protecting," he whispered, his hot breath burning her neck.

Tara turned her face away, clamping her lips together. Billy noticed the action, and was instantly intrigued.

"So, you're afraid I'm going to kiss you," he sneered. "Well, believe me, I'll be doing much more before we're done, perhaps a few times. Then I'll send you to join your adoring husband. But I wouldn't want to leave you disappointed. A kiss is so intimate, anyway, isn't it, Tara?" he crooned.

Taking her face in his hands and determined not to let her resist, he forced his mouth on top of hers. Forcing his tongue inside, he pushed madly, trying to hurt her, trying to humiliate her by touching every part of her.

Tara cringed as his tongue probed and pushed, intensifying the pressure of his mouth violently attacking hers.

And then, he felt it. Something wasn't right. She was kissing him? No. But she was doing something. Was it kissing? Did she like this? Billy wasn't sure what was happening. She started moving her head, moving toward him, actually pushing her tongue into his mouth. She was kissing him! She was enjoying this! Tied up, blindfolded and manhandled by him—she liked it! Billy couldn't stop himself. She was beautiful, brutally beautiful, and she enjoyed what he was doing to her. Billy rolled on top of her, letting her continue. Letting her probe and push her tongue around his mouth. He was actually groaning from the unexpected pleasure of it when…

Tara pushed with every ounce of strength she had, forcing the small pouch of pills into his mouth and hopefully down this throat.

Billy heaved himself off of her and manically grabbed his throat.

"What—" he managed to choke out, while the deadly array of pills severely burned the lining of his throat like battery acid. They moved rapidly through his body, quickly releasing their fatal contents. Billy tried to make his way across the room to the gun that lay on the dresser. His throat was on fire; he could feel it closing around something. And, he couldn't breathe. He— couldn't—breathe. He was going to kill her! He reached the gun and turned toward her, but his vision began to blur. The room spun wickedly, spiraling around him in swirls of white and red.

Tara's head throbbed in slow, thick pulses, like a dying heart. Her mind raced with recollections of the past twelve months. She remembered Jade's description of the European woman with the hidden pouch in her mouth. She vividly recalled her own nervousness when she had purchased the lethal drugs in the secluded alleys of the French Quarter this morning. And then, she remembered securing the pouch in her mouth, marveling at the way it had adhered, just like Jade had described. She listened to the sounds that surrounded her, straining to hear Billy as he fought the attack, as he tried to complete his own plan. Still blindfolded, Tara heard him as he staggered across the floor. She knew his destination. She listened as the gun scraped across the top of the dresser, heard the click as he released the safety. She braced herself and heard—his body fall.

Tara worked hysterically to free her arms. She twisted her wrists intensely until she felt the slightest give in the silky fabric and slid one arm free. Quickly removing the blindfold, she saw him. Naked, sprawled out across the floor with the gun beside him. She gasped as she saw his mouth, already a deep blue from the deadly toxins of the pills she had stuffed into the pouch. She hurried to release her other arm and legs before quickly leaving the room...and Billy Reynolds.

*****

Jade tried to control her outrage when the cab driver once again drove away from the wrong hotel. He had inadvertently taken them to three hotels, with apparently similar names to the one where Billy was actually staying.

"The address! Take us to this address!" she screamed while he maneuvered the cab down the crowded streets.

"The parade route. You don't understand. Streets blocked, streets crowded. Parade just ended, ma'am. You must be patient," he explained, still hoping for a healthy tip.

Jade continued to fume.

Matthias continued to pray.

They finally stopped in front of Billy's hotel, amid a colorful array of flashing red and blue lights. Police cars and officers were everywhere, scouring the scene.

"What happened?" Jade asked a man standing near the building.

"It's a murder," the man slurred, his breath thick with alcohol. "Found some guy in a room upstairs, naked, drugged and dead. That's what they're saying, anyway," the man continued, taking another slurp of his drink, as though he were merely watching a live episode of Jerry Springer.

"Dear God," Matthias said. "Where is she?"

Chapter Thirty-seven

Jeremiah followed the dark shadow as it steadily moved down the street ahead. He had known that she would return. He had been fairly certain that it would happen during Mardi Gras, one year from when they'd first met. Her suffering groans from the bridge above him had jolted him from sleep. He had expected her to return to the spot where her husband had been slain. Now, quietly walking down the street behind her thin shadow, Jeremiah wiped his tear-stained cheeks with the back of his hand. What had happened to the young woman since he had cared for her twelve months ago? Not one day had passed that he hadn't thought of her, prayed for her, cried for her. Such pain should have never come to a woman like her. She was good. He could feel it when he had cared for her. She was good and she had been hurt, deeply hurt, by the forces of evil that can tear at a person's soul until they're lost forever.

Daily he had prayed for that precious soul. As he watched the shadow stumble down the street ahead, he knew she had a goal, a purpose. She was tormented by something, either by the death of her husband and loss of her babe, or by even more, something that had further wounded her soul. Surely nothing had happened to surpass the horror of a year ago.

Or had it?

Tara struggled to keep her pace as she staggered down the murky back streets of New Orleans. The hotel had been so far away from the overpass, and she hadn't dared take a cab. But she had to go back one last time, to see where Johnny had been taken from her and to remember. She saw it all, the three men that took her husband and child. Then she remembered each of them, the way they had looked, when *they* had died.

Her body aching with each agonizing step, Tara continued toward her goal. It was finished. The three laughing faces that had taunted her nights were gone, each of them dying at her hand. Tara whimpered into the darkness. Her head throbbed in agony as she pictured each of them. Dave. Chet. Billy. Three men. Murdered. Only a year ago, she would have never dreamed she was capable of hurting anything, or anyone. Then, she had lost Johnny, she had lost their baby, and she had lost herself. Lost her soul. She had committed murder, taken lives that were not hers to take.

Her thoughts urgently centered on Matthias. He'd convinced her that she could be forgiven, that perhaps she could still make it one day, to Johnny and their baby girl. And he was right. God could have forgiven her. She had begged for His forgiveness. She had prayed to Him, pleaded to Him to listen, to be with her, to forgive her for what she had done. And He had listened. She had started to feel peace again with God, with church, with Matthias.

But Mardi Gras returned to New Orleans, and so did she.

She had not only returned to the city that started her terror; she had searched out the one man who had destroyed her life, hunted him down and killed him. No. That wasn't true. She had planned on killing him, but she couldn't. She wasn't able to continue her plan.

Something in her made her stop, made her want to simply remove herself from the evil of Billy Reynolds.

He had attacked *her* in the end.

Tara reached for the ground and fell to the curb. She wrapped her arms around her legs and rocked, whimpering as the tears stung her face. It didn't matter. God wouldn't want her anymore. She was a murderer, a cold-blooded murderer. She was no better than those awful men. No better at all.

Tara moaned unbearably as she pushed herself up and stood beside the curb.

Jeremiah wiped away more tears as he watched the crippled spirit obviously in turmoil with her God. "Don't give up, child," he whispered. "Please don't let her give up, Lord."

Tara began to toddle once again down the gloomy street while Jeremiah followed a safe distance behind. After a few initial steps, she quickened her pace, walking purposely, intent on reaching her goal.

Chapter Thirty-eight

The cab driver did everything humanly possible to edge the taxi through the parade-aftermath that filled every street surrounding the French Quarter. Jade was certain by the sight and sounds of the police frenzy that they had witnessed at Billy Reynolds' hotel that Tara had been gone for quite a while—long enough for the police to have learned of the body and for a good portion of the NOPD to have arrived at the scene.

"She could be anywhere," Jade wailed to Matthias as their cab trudged down the busy street.

Matthias did his best to remain calm, while Jade, in contrast, yelled profusely at the pedestrians that now encircled their vehicle.

"Think, Jade. Try to think of where she may have gone. We've got to stay composed enough to think, or we'll never find her. Dear God, please help us find her," Matthias prayed, remembering the beautiful girl he had come to know so well, and love so deeply.

It doesn't matter what she has done, Lord. I can help her to make it right. You can forgive her. Help me to show her the wonders of

Your love. Help me to teach her to live, to love life, to love You and perhaps to love me.

Jade pounded her head against the headrest in frustration at the motionless cars ahead. She struggled to remember anything that Tara had said about her plans, but couldn't. "She couldn't be that far away, but I don't have any idea of where to look!"

"What if she chose to hide in the crowd?" Matthias questioned, searching the hordes of people on either side of the street.

"No. I don't think she would have wanted to stay here at all. I think she would have wanted to leave—get away from Mardi Gras and the horrible memories of it."

"Think, Jade. What would she do?"

Jade thought of everything Tara had written on her postcard. She struggled to remember every conversation that they had in Hattiesburg.

"I was thinking that there would be no way that someone would survive a fall from that bridge. I wanted to jump, Jade. I wanted to jump so bad that I could feel myself climbing on the railing. All I had to do was take one step..."

"Oh, dear God, no! I know where she is! Please, God, keep her safe till we get there!" Jade threw another fistful of cash at the driver. "Take us to the high-rise bridge! Now! Please! Hurry! Get there any way you can!" She screamed as he jerked the car onto a side street, knocking down a barricade and continuing the quest. "She's going to the high-rise bridge, Matthias! She doesn't want to live anymore! She's going to kill herself! God, please let us get there in time!"

Tara continued down the darkened back streets that had been barricaded and vacated for the parade routes. Although she knew it was well past midnight, she could still hear the low rumble of screams and squeals of drunken tourists as they partied into the night. Merely one year ago, she was a participant in the ritual; she had actually participated with those who partied themselves into a stupor to somehow prepare themselves to give up the sinful thing they loved the most for the forty days of Lent. Now, she was trying to escape the anguish that began here one year ago, in the early morning hours of Ash Wednesday.

Looming imminently ahead of her, the dark mountainous shadow that was undoubtedly the high-rise bridge beckoned. She was less than a mile from the tremendous structure that would help her take her life. With one last bit of energy, she quickened her pace to reach her final destiny—the true death of her soul. "You don't want me anymore, God," she muttered. "I'm not supposed to put my God to the test. Well, I'm not testing You anymore. I'm done. It's finished. I've lost my soul. Now, I'll lose my life as well."

*****

The taxi wheeled violently through the empty streets. Matthias stared determinedly into the darkened gap in the sky that visibly marked the lack of street lighting below. He knew in his heart that they were near the large canal—and Tara.

"The darkness ahead, is it the canal?" he asked as they continued to gather speed.

"Yes," the cab driver responded.

As they approached the high rise, Jade could see occasional taillights from cars that had made it out of the barricaded boundaries as well and were now venturing over the monstrous bridge. On the opposite side of the bridge—the side for traffic heading into New Orleans—there was no traffic. Certainly, no one would be driving into New Orleans at this time of night following Mardi Gras; all traffic was attempting an exit from the mad scene. But the other side wasn't completely empty. Two shadows pitched themselves against the dull night sky casting a horrifying image.

"She's there! On the bridge!" Jade yelled as she flung the cab door open, forcing the driver to swerve to a sudden stop.

"You're crazy!" the driver yelled while Jade jumped out. Matthias flung himself from the car as well and dodged an eighteen-wheeler to reach the other side of the road.

Tara stood at the highest point of the bridge looking beaten and defeated. She wobbled atop the railing and gripped a metal post anchoring a warning sign above. She heard a woman screaming in the distance. It vaguely sounded like her name, but it couldn't be. Then she heard him, Matthias, yelling "Mara! Mara!" and then finally, "Tara!" She turned to look at him, but instead she saw another figure leaning against the side of the bridge, not ten feet away. Her eyes focused in recognition as Jeremiah took a step forward.

"I remember you," she whispered, instantly recalling the salty taste of soup that the older man had faithfully delivered daily in his mission to keep her alive.

"Please come down. God doesn't want you to go this way," Jeremiah pleaded.

"God doesn't want me anymore. He doesn't need me. You don't know what I've done," Tara answered, peering into the murky water below.

"He—He does need you," Matthias panted as he ran to stand in front of Jeremiah. "I need you too. I love you, Mara—Tara. I love you."

Jade hurried to stand beside the dark man who had been speaking to her best friend. "Don't do it, Tara. Please, let us help you," she begged.

"Leave me alone. I don't deserve to live. I murdered them! I murdered them all! God will never forgive me now!" Tara wailed into the night as she leaned out and tried to let go. She saw Matthias as he moved forward. "Don't come any closer, Matthias!"

"God can forgive you, Tara," he said, taking another step. "God can forgive you for murder. God can forgive you for anything. He forgave David when he had Uriah murdered. Do you remember?"

Tara blankly nodded her head, but she continued to contemplate the distance to the water below.

"And David was even called a 'Man after God's own heart', remember?" Matthias went on as he took another step.

She nodded again.

"He can forgive you, Tara, if you want His forgiveness. What He would not be able to forgive is *this* murder—the one you are about to commit. Taking your own life would allow you no chance at forgiveness. You know that, don't you? You wouldn't have the chance to ask forgiveness, wouldn't be forgiven, wouldn't have the blessed opportunity to go to Heaven, to see God, to see Johnny, or to see your baby," Matthias continued as he stepped again. He was an arm's length away now. Just another step.

Jade held her breath as Matthias neared Tara's teetering body, now barely clinging to the metal post that separated her life from death. She barely recognized the slowing of cars that had stopped to view the display from the other side of the bridge, not that anyone had stopped to help. "God, please help her," Jade whispered.

"God is here, child," Jeremiah answered. "He's watching. He's here."

Jade blinked at the man, who stared at Tara and Matthias with quiet apprehension.

It happened so quickly that Jade wasn't sure she had seen correctly. Tara turned her head from the vision of water below to the man now standing beside her on the bridge.

"No, Matthias, No!" Tara screamed when Matthias lunged forward to grab her. For a moment that seemed an eternity, they quivered together, shaking methodically on the metal railing. Tara instinctively grabbed tighter to the arms now surrounding her and Matthias was caught off-guard. His balance wavered and they plummeted—frantically trying to grasp each other—Tara's will to live rejuvenated by the love of the man willing to risk his life for her—Matthias' will to save her forcing him to cover her, protect her, as they plunged into the hostile water together.

Epilogue

Jade Roberts lay crumpled against the side of the New Orleans high-rise as the red and blue beams of police cars flashed violent streams of reality. Jeremiah crouched beside her, holding a brown, woolen blanket steady around her shoulders.

"Tara—and Matthias—both of them," she stuttered.

"Yes," Jeremiah acknowledged with a tear gliding down his ebony cheek.

"They were good. She was good. Why did He do this to them? Why did God do this to them?" she spat bitterly, crying into the scratchy blanket the policeman had provided.

"He had to save her," Jeremiah answered truthfully.

"Matthias was trying to save her, but he—he—"

"No, child. I mean God. God had to save her," Jeremiah added.

Jade looked bewildered as she stared at this stranger. What did he mean, 'God had to save her'?

Jeremiah saw the look, and knew what she was thinking. "The child was trying to kill herself, and she would have succeeded. She would have committed a murder for which no forgiveness could have been obtained—her own murder. She would have had no chance of seeing the eternal wonderment of God's creation—of Heaven above. She would have never seen her beloved Johnny, or her beautiful babe again. God couldn't let that happen. So He sent Matthias to help her, to save her. You see, the child had asked for forgiveness—sincerely asked for forgiveness for the others—and she didn't commit this murder, did she? No. Matthias stopped her. She would have jumped, but when he climbed that railing too, she had made the decision not to die—she had clung to him—she hadn't killed herself. She didn't want to hurt Matthias, thus she couldn't hurt herself—at that moment, the two were one."

"But they died," Jade whimpered.

"They did. But we all do. And she will never suffer again, my child. Matthias is a good example to us all. He did his job well."

"You—you knew Brother Matthias?" Jade asked, looking up from wiping a tear on the rough blanket.

But he was gone. Instead, a large Styrofoam cup sat beside her on the pavement. Jade peered into the darkness for some sign of where the man had gone, but he wasn't there. She reached for the white cup, surprised that it was steaming. The aroma of saltiness tinged her nostrils and she lifted the cup to drink the thick, healing liquid that the angel had provided.

"Be not forgetful to entertain strangers: for thereby some have entertained angels unawares." Hebrews 13:2

ABOUT THE AUTHOR

K.A. ZAiNE has called New Orleans, Atlanta, Huntsville, Tuscaloosa and many Southern cities in between "home." A former NASA Subcontractor Senior Writer turned author, ZAiNE enjoys traveling, reading…and all things Cajun. www.**KAZAiNE**.com